Pyramidia

Stephanie Sanders-Jacob

SLASHIC HORROR
PRESS

Other titles by Stephanie Sanders-Jacob

Singing All the Way Up

The characters and events in this book are fictitious. Any similarity to real persons, living or dead, is coincidental and not intended by the author.

SLASHIC HORROR
PRESS

Originally published in Australia by Slashic Horror Press in 2024.

ISBN-13: 978-0-6457638-7-4
Cover design by Christy Aldridge at Grim Poppy Designs
Interior design by David-Jack Fletcher
Edited by David-Jack Fletcher

For Naomi, an independent girl.

Chapter One

Harriet was hiding in the pantry. Or, she was hiding in the little closet she was calling a pantry because it was dank and dark and full of weird things in jars. Ancient things. She pulled them off the shelves as she hid, rolling them between her hands, watching the contents—gelatinous peaches and beans—swirl in their jewel-tone juices.

She was hiding because someone was knocking on the door, and had been knocking on the door for a full five minutes—an inconceivable amount of time, an improper amount of time. It was absurd to stand there that long, knocking, waiting.

Peering through the crack in the closet door, all she-could see were her unpacked moving boxes strewn throughout the kitchen. The front door, vibrating now on its hinges, could not be seen from her hiding spot, which was the very reason she'd chosen it.

"Open up," a voice called.

Harriet clutched a jar of unidentifiable mush to her chest. The voice—it sounded cop-like, authoritarian. She tried to remember if she'd done anything illegal lately and couldn't come up with anything warranting a home visit.

The door rattled. She wished they would go away, leave her alone. All she wanted to do was unpack in peace.

"It's your Mary Jane dealer," the voice shouted.

Mary Jane? Was that legal here? Harriet slipped out of the pantry. She was halfway to the front door when she realized that "It's your Mary Jane dealer" was just the type of thing the police would say to lure her out. She would not go easily, no sir.

"Slide your badge beneath the door," Harriet called, trying to sound as imposing as possible.

There was a shuffling sound, the knocking paused. "I have my business license but it's on my phone," the voice said.

Harriet was impressed. Not only did drug dealers come door to door in this town, but they were accredited too.

"I'm going to open the door," Harriet said. "Nice and slow. No funny business."

"Okay," the person on the other side said.

Harriet eased the door open a slit, revealing a small woman buried in garish, patterned fabric. Layers and layers of it.

"Hi!" the woman gasped, her beaded, plastic necklaces clacking together.

"Um…"

"I'm Lucy," she said with an eager smile. "I'm Bentwood's number one Mary Jane distributor!"

She didn't look like the town's top dealer, with her neon makeup and toppling bun of hair, but maybe that's why she was so successful. She was able to evade detection.

"Harriet."

"It's so nice to meet you, Harriet," Lucy said. "I've wanted to come over here and say hello ever since I heard you moved in. But I've been so busy, you know." She patted at her messy hair bun to tidy it, even though it was beyond saving. "I'm so glad you answered the door."

"Um…"

"If you ever need any Mary Jane, please let me know. I'm so close, you don't even have to pay shipping. I could drive it over, no big deal."

"Oh, uh, thanks," Harriet said.

"Here." Lucy produced a stack of brochures from her many-layered ensemble, and pushed them toward Harriet. "Here's all my info and some of the newest product line. We're doing Fancy Fiesta! It's so fun."

Harriet, realizing she was still hugging the jar of—whatever it was sloshing around in there—fumbled with the brochures. Handed the jar to Lucy.

"Oh," Lucy cooed. "Thank you."

Harriet winced. The brochures were a rainbow of fabric and fonts. There was a group of smiling ladies, all white and throwing their arms around each other, wearing the same sorts of nightmarish outfits Lucy was wearing—all draped in clashing patterns, knotted shirts atop flowing dresses upon printed leggings. It was dizzying. "So it's not drugs?"

Lucy's smile faltered. "Drugs? What? Well, it can be kind of addictive. Some of my girls have replaced their entire closets with Mary Jane."

"Oh," Harriet said through a wry smile.

"Oh my gosh, you'd look so *cute* in the new line. Look." Lucy nodded at the brochures and Harriet flipped through them until Lucy cried, "There!"

More women, this time in clothing printed with cacti, sombreros, and limes, gazed up at her with depraved longing. "Wow," Harriet said, meaning it.

"That's the new line—Fancy Fiesta!" Lucy said, her voice a few octaves too high. "I'll be getting some in soon. Maybe Tuesday."

"Oh, um, that's great," Harriet said.

"Oh my gosh, I just thought of something. With your physique, you could totally sell this stuff. You look *just* like the models." Lucy nodded down at the blank-eyed women with their toothy grins.

Harriet, who was a little pudgy and whose back curved like an S, leaving one shoulder higher than the other, had never been complimented on her physique, or even had the word used in her presence. She blushed, despite herself.

"Here, hold on." Lucy was bounding back down the little path toward her small, rusted Toyota, jar of something swishing wildly and her beads smacking. She bent, dug through her car, which, Harriet realized with horror, was filled to the roof with clothing. She wondered how Lucy could even see to drive.

"Here!" Lucy ran back toward her, layers of fabric blowing behind her like a cape. "This is for you," she gasped between breaths.

"Oh," Harriet said, reaching out for the lump of material.

"They're leggings." Lucy smiled. "One size fits most."

Harriet unfurled them, let the bottoms brush her feet. They were navy blue and spangled with some type of bug—fluorescent-green mosquitos? "Wow," Harriet said, trying not to laugh. "Thank you?"

"You're *so* welcome!" Lucy said. "And once you wear those, you're gonna want more. You get a discount if you're a distributor, you know. My info is all on the back. You can call, text, or message me on Facebook anytime. Oh em gee, you should add me on Facebook! We're practically besties already."

"Oh, uh, sure?" Harriet nodded, knowing full well she would never add this creature on anything.

Lucy smiled, her mouth wide and filled with square teeth. "I'm so glad you're here," she said. "You're a teacher, right?"

Harriet's S-shaped back straightened a little. She hadn't spoken to anyone but the landlord when she'd moved to Bentwood not even a week earlier, and he didn't seem like the gossiping type. "Yes," she said.

"All the teachers love Mary Jane," Lucy said, attending to her hair bun again.

"I bet," Harriet said.

"Well, you enjoy those," Lucy said. "And thank you so much for the canned"—she searched for words with an awkward smile—"um, goods. I love homemade!"

Harriet thought about warning her, explaining that the jars had been there long before she arrived, maybe since the dawn of time itself, but decided not to. The jar was lost to the mounds of clothing in her car anyway, wouldn't be seen for another season or two.

"Yes," Harriet said. "Thank you."

She watched Lucy prance away before she slammed the door and threw the brochures in the trash.

Chapter Two

The house was more of a hunting cabin than anything. There was no bedroom, only a fold-out couch in the living room, which stunk of mold and the deep tang of woodsmoke. The previous tenant, the landlord's mother, had lived there some fifty odd years before passing away, and it showed. There were the jars in the pantry, like she'd been hording for the apocalypse, but there were other things too—frayed and flowered towels folded into cabinets, pictures of old men framed on the wall, yellowing and water stained, the front half of a dead deer hanging over the door.

The cabin was nestled in the middle of a thick wood in the town center—the so-called "Bent Woods" of Bentwood. The trees were stooped and shed yellow leaves, even in the summer, and scraped against each other with horrible, unharmonious wails. Harriet thought they might be sick with something, some sort of rot. A blight.

Though it was a disgusting, ugly place, and it was always damp from the shade from the trees, Harriet had rented it because she thought it might afford her some privacy. But there had already been Lucy. And there were always people cutting through the woods, trying to get from one side of town to the other, traipsing across her mossy, root-humped yard. They wouldn't let her forget she was forever in the midst of town and not somewhere remote, quiet; somewhere she could think.

She sighed, ripped open another box.

While she had absolutely nothing else to do, unpacking was taking forever. She kept setting down the forks, the unneeded bed linens, and wandering from window to window, peering into the black spaces between the trees.

Once, she thought she saw a woman staring back in at her only to realize it was her own reflection, haggard and pale.

She'd ask the landlord to install some blinds next time he came. That would be good. That would help. And she'd ask him if he'd been talking to Lucy, had divulged her career. It seemed unlikely, though, as he was an odd, solemn man. She couldn't imagine him buying Mary Jane—of any variety.

But this was a small town—people talk. It might have even been someone at the school. It wouldn't be far-fetched to imagine a group of them discussing the new Gifted Ed teacher in town. Lucy said the teachers loved Mary Jane—perhaps her tendrils reached that far, leached the gossip from the folds of their violent, bedazzled clothes.

She lifted a stack of books from a box—all literature of the highest quality, none of that *Fifty Shades* smut for Harriet—and, expecting to see the dingy cardboard at the bottom, jolted to find the Mary Jane pamphlets sitting there, bright and pristine as ever. She swore she'd thrown them away. Hadn't she thrown them away?

She marched to the trash can, dove a hand in deep, and thrashed it about. There was something sticky, something wet, but no papers. No brochures.

Harriet wiped the goo from her hand with one of the dead lady's towels, tossed it onto the counter in a crumpled ball. She had thrown the brochures away—she was sure of it. And even if she hadn't, how had they gotten to the bottom of one of her moving boxes? She stalked back and forth, from the kitchen to the living room, glancing at her pacing reflection in the window. It made no sense.

She plucked the pamphlets from the bottom of the box, avoided the psychotic gaze of the women on the front, and threw them into the trash once more. She did it with purpose. She did it with intent. She watched them fall into the remains of last night's spaghetti. There was sauce on all those ladies' faces now, like blood, like vomit. She vowed to remember this moment for a very long time.

Chapter Three

Harriet believed in ghosts, but only as peripheral, ineffectual things—a creaking in the wood flooring, the lingering smell of perfume. They were objects of curiosity, too weak to be feared, too evanescent to matter. But now she sat in the dark, the trashcan a pale smudge in the corner of the kitchen, and waited.

Something had taken the brochures out of the trash. Something real, something solid. At first, she'd been indifferent about it, annoyed but unaffected. She had unpacked a box of toiletries, brushed her teeth. But as she flossed, the thought tightened around her mind like a lasso and she dropped the string into the dirty sink.

Something had moved the brochures.

So now she clutched a butcher knife, hands trembling, and listened to the house sigh and settle around her. She wasn't sure what the knife was for, but it made her feel big so she kept it.

The minutes slipped by and nothing happened. On occasion, she'd creep forward, throw open the trashcan lid, and light the interior with her phone screen. The women's teeth glowed bright against the brochure. They were still there.

Harriet retreated to the little table in the corner, put her head in her hands. She couldn't sleep, not in this state, but being awake—waiting and listening in the humid dark—was maddening. The lights were off. She could flip them on, pretend at some semblance of a normal night spent in her new house, but her reflection in the window was worse than the shadows, she twitched each time she saw it.

Illuminating the place would also make it too easy for those outside to see in. Why did she think there were people outside? It was the middle of the night. She was in a forest. But she felt eyes on her, didn't she? She felt examined, studied.

She shivered.

Blinds were her top priority. Maybe in the morning she'd go and buy some herself—to hell with the landlord. She wouldn't wait. Couldn't.

She was half crazy with it all and she felt ashamed. She had wanted more than anything to move away, to have her own place. But now she missed the grating laugh of her roommate, the perpetual smell of fried onions. She'd never been scared there.

There were pictures on the wall, old ones all stained sepia, and crooked in their frames. She could just make out the light spots against the wood paneling. Perhaps it was one of the gruff-looking men, glassy-eyed babies, who tormented her now. Her arms tingled as her hairs stood on end. Should she go look at them? Study their faces? Or maybe it was the woman who lived here last—the landlord's mother—angered by Harriet's blasé treatment of her towels, the meager things she'd left behind. There didn't seem to be any pictures of her, but her presence was stifling, oppressive. She lurked in every drawer, every corner. Harriet closed her eyes against the dark and rubbed her temples. She was letting her mind slip down this treacherous, endless slope, and she had to make it stop.

Leaving the trashcan vigil, Harriet curled up on the sagging couch, heard the springs groan in protest. She tried to bury her head beneath a pillow, but it stank like smoke and she pushed it away.

There would be no sleep for her tonight.

She sighed and felt for her phone on the end table.

She watched an old sitcom—one her parents liked. It made her sad in an embarrassed, nostalgic way. The writing was bad, the acting worse, but their voices felt like home and she was able to forget about ghosts and windows and the women in her trashcan. She relaxed, stretched her legs until her toes touched the armrest, but she didn't sleep.

Chapter Four

Morning came at last, and the house was hot. The heat intensified the stewing smells wafting from dusty curtains, the dark maw of the fireplace. It was hard to breathe all that thickness. Harriet needed air that wasn't pungent with another person's life. She needed to take a walk.

She dropped her wallet into a simple canvas tote bag and pulled her hair back in a sloppy ponytail. She'd have a look for those blinds in town today. It was a relief to pull open the door, tumble out of the fetid little cabin. Hoping to taste something other than rot, Harriet breathed in deep, but the house was still heavy on her tongue.

She'd prowled around the muddy land around the

house a few times already, but she hadn't gone any farther than her car on the driveway. Now, she walked past it with great ceremony, taking slow, solemn steps. She liked to make an occasion of things. It helped one remember.

Harriet walked down the rutted path, tripping now and then on stones not yet ground into the earth by tires. The trees seemed to bend away from the path, opposite to the pretty, leafy tunnels one sometimes sees on postcards and one-thousand-piece puzzles. The sky above was open and gray, like static. It left Harriet feeling uneasy, exposed. But it was better than the house, she reminded herself. It was better to be outside.

When she emerged from the woods—they ended all at once, abruptly, which did not please Harriet's sense of ceremony—she was thrust into town, onto a thoroughfare lined with little shops and cars and prim, straight trees growing out of metal collars. Harriet wondered if the town resented her landlord's family for holding onto that precious land, right at the center of town, or if they took a strange pride in it. It was rather unique. Like Central Park gone haywire, overgrown and wrong.

She crossed the street, trying to get as far from the crooked trees as she could, and walked along the sidewalk, past an empty coffee shop, and a barber that smelled like dog shampoo. She used to have a little dog and its eyes were always gunky, running red rivulets onto its soft, white face. And she'd scrub at them, only making the dog's eyes weep more, and—

"Harriet!"

Her heart slammed to the front of her chest as she stopped. She felt sick, feverish with the prickling of her skin.

"Yoo hoo! Harriiiieeeeet!" The voice came from behind her, was singsong sweet.

She thought of running, of bolting across the street and diving deep into those knotted woods, sealing herself away in the stinking, claustrophobic house. Instead, she swung around, dreading what she would see there.

A car, so full that daylight couldn't be seen from one end to the other, and an enrobed form clambering out, waving a hand. "Harriet!"

"Lucy," she whispered.

Lucy, today wearing at least seven pieces of an intricate, layered and knotted rayon, waddled toward her, still yelling, "Harriet!"

Harriet forced her lips to move, to part into a smile. "Hello, Lucy."

"Isn't this lucky? I was in town doing some errands and look who I run into!" Sweat poured down Lucy's brow into her eyes and she swiped at them with a ring-encrusted hand.

"Aren't you hot in all that?" Harriet asked, gesturing at the layers, the great pink and purple mass of it.

"No, not at all," Lucy said, who was quite red in the

face. "It breathes, you see."

Harriet recoiled, imagining the clothing coming to life, wrapping around her and pulling her into Lucy's folds.

"It's perfect for all seasons." Lucy recited.

"I see," Harriet said, still lost in her dark reverie.

"Harriet, I meant to ask you, what's your last name?"

"What?" Harriet asked.

"Well, I went to add you on Facebook and realized I didn't know your last name. Silly me." She dabbed at her sweat with the sleeve of her duster.

Harriet's face twitched in disgust. Should she lie? In the fall, when school started, everyone would know her last name—Miss Pendleton, she'd be called, known only by her last name. It was no use hiding it. She sighed. "Pendleton."

"Oh, that's a lovely name. Harriet Pendleton. It has a very scholarly sound to it, doesn't it? Perfect for a teacher." Lucy clapped her hands together—a motion that put Harriet in mind of a toddler.

"Listen, I have to get home. It was, uh, nice seeing you." She moved to push past Lucy, toward the opening in the trees that marked her driveway.

"Wait!" cried Lucy, gripping her arm.

Harriet stared at the fingers digging into her fat. Why was this woman touching her? She tried to pull away.

Lucy stepped closer. Her breath mingled with Harriet's and her eyes were big, deep saucers. "I have to tell you something."

"What?" Harriet gasped, looking down at Lucy in disbelief.

"It's a secret. Can you keep a secret?" Lucy was whispering now, leaning so close their noses almost touched.

"About Bentwood?" Harriet asked. "About the house?" She thought of her limpid reflection in the windows, the brochures moving on their own, the dead woman and her many, many towels. She shivered despite the heat.

"I wanted to let you know that we're having a sale. Buy two get one free, all weekend."

The fingers loosened around Harriet's bicep and she fell back. "What?" she asked. "What?"

"It's supposed to be for VIPs only, but I knew you would appreciate it. Don't tell anyone I told you, okay?"

"What?"

"Mary Jane," Lucy whispered.

"No," Harriet moaned.

"I know! It's hard to believe."

Harriet struggled, thrashed against Lucy, felt all that fabric press and bulge against her. And then she was running.

"Yes!" Lucy cried. "Don't miss out! Get home and put your order in! Run, girl!"

Back down the street, back down the stone path through the bent wood, and into the sanctuary of the fusty little cabin in the middle of it all. She didn't stop once.

Chapter Five

There was another month before school started, and Harriet thought about getting a summer job. It'd help distract her from the ghosts, from herself. It'd be something insubstantial like at the little ice cream stand on the edge of town or bagging groceries. She even picked up an application from the ice cream place, but the teenage girls there in their polo shirts raised their eyebrows at her, handed the paper over with a snideness of the wrist—Harriet could detect those kinds of things, those subtle movements hidden in otherwise bland gestures. She would obsess over it, replaying again and again how the girl had flicked the paper at her; an aggressive, sharp movement.

So, she didn't apply to anything. Instead, she sorted through her boxes and roamed, aimless, through the house, opening and closing the same bare cupboards again and again, expecting to find something changed. Nothing ever changed. There was never anything more than dust, rusted utensils and tools. But this repetition did not soothe Harriet; it only made her more suspicious, more restless.

She opened Facebook and closed it again, distressed by the red, throbbing icon indicating a new friend request. She knew who it was. She didn't need to look. She could block Lucy, but that was a short-term solution, she knew. She was sure to run into the woman and have to answer for it. She needed time to think, time to prepare. She'd let the friend request hang there for as long as she could.

In the depth of her anxiety, she had even tried on the mosquito pants. She didn't have a full-length mirror, but she didn't need one to see there was a bright-green bug positioned on her crotch—as if anyone needed more of a reason to stay clear of that region. It was just too much for Harriet, overwhelmed by the ostentatious print and hazy feel of them against her legs. She balled up the leggings and stuffed them in a bag. She'd take them to Goodwill. Someone else could deal with them.

She needed them out of her house so bad that she decided to go right then. It was a humid Saturday morning, the kind of weather that would make the house unbearable by midday. She still hadn't bought those blinds, hadn't been back to town at all since her run in with Lucy. Perhaps she'd try again. And she could look for a window air conditioner while she was at it. She smiled. It felt good to have a list. At least it was something to do, something to think about.

She traded her dumpy pajamas for a dumpy outfit—jeans, saggy in the butt, and a threadbare t-shirt—and left the house. She'd walk again, though she knew if she did happen to find an air conditioner, she'd have to come back with the car to get it. She didn't mind, though; the more time she wasted was less time trapped in the soot and dust of the house.

So, once more she ventured out of the bent woods into the town proper. This time she walked uninterrupted all the way past the flat-faced buildings that marked downtown, and into a parking lot next to a bank. It was filled with people, with stalls festooned with banners and buntings. She had no idea what it was, but she wandered into the midst of it, swinging the bag of bug pants wide so no one would bump into her.

There were old men selling tomatoes, a lady sitting behind a table of wilted potted flowers, and a booth piled high with—*Oh god, no*—bright, stretchy clothes. Harriet turned to flee, but she'd already been spotted.

"Harriet!" Lucy cried. "Harriet!"

She sighed, turned back to face the too-bright, neon-pink booth.

"Hello, Lucy," she said, hiding her contempt behind

a thin smile.

"I'm so glad you're here! Are you enjoying the farmers market?" Lucy asked. She wore a garish outfit composed only of shades of blue—cerulean, navy, dusky baby blue—all jumbled together and dotted with various things—waves, butterflies, clouds. The effect was searing.

"Oh yes," Harriet said. "Immensely."

"It's one of my favorite places to sell. I'm here *every* Saturday," Lucy said, straightening a tilting pile of shirts.

She saw people were giving Lucy's booth a wide berth, were staring at her out of the corner of their eyes, agog that someone would approach the forbidden stall. "That's good to know. And how are sales?" she asked, feeling vindictive.

Lucy's smile faltered, but her voice was cheery, sweet. "Oh, you know."

"I don't," Harriet said. "I don't know at all."

"It's just getting harder, is all," Lucy said. "You see, the clothes are so good everyone wants to sell them."

"I do see," Harriet said, pleased with her needling. "Bentwood's got something of a Mary Jane market saturation situation."

Lucy nodded. "It does."

Harriet pondered this. She hadn't seen another living soul in Bentwood wearing the stuff. A quick look around the farmers market revealed nothing but muted denim and casual shirts, nothing throbbing with patterns, prints, color. "Is this your only job?"

"Yes," Lucy said. "I quit my job at the bank so I could sell full time." Her voice was high-pitched again, saccharine.

"That's commitment."

"It is." Lucy agreed. "And I dipped into my 401k to buy my starter kit."

"Oh?" Harriet asked. She was luxuriating in the stupidity of this woman, basking in the warm glow of it.

"You have to spend money to make money, right? It was a small price to pay to start my own business though."

"But you only get a cut, don't you?"

"Well, with every sale I'm paying myself back for the merchandise I bought—and then some." Lucy puffed her chest with pride. "And I get bonuses if I recruit so many people, meet certain sales goals."

"Hmm." Harriet was not seeing how this equated to owning one's own business. Her father had been a repair man, driving all over the city in his boxy white van. He never got any bonuses, never had to pay for opportunities.

"In fact, you can join today for five thousand, if you're interested," Lucy said.

Harriet took a literal step back, putting space between herself and Lucy's booth. "What?" The price shocked her, as did the offer.

"You can put it on a credit card," Lucy said. "You'll earn it back in no time."

"But you were just— You were *just* telling me the market is saturated."

Lucy ran her hand over the piles of clothes before her. "You could get a discount, though. On all this." She caressed a shirt. "And besides, you just got here. You could sell to your friends back home, people at your old job."

Harriet thought about the data entry job she had left— the flickering lights, the lonesome hours spent pecking away at a keyboard in a cold, gray office that stunk like steamed broccoli. She had been thrilled when the Gifted Education position had finally appeared in her never-ending searches— she'd been trying to find a job in her field for years. The data entry thing had drained her, made her a sullen, angry person, but she'd still managed to charm the school board, principal, and superintendent. It took everything she had left.

"I don't think so," she said.

"Oh." Lucy hung her head, crestfallen. "Well...maybe some other time."

"Maybe," Harriet said. "Would you ever go back to the bank?"

Lucy pulled a cardigan to her chest, held it like a baby. She shrugged. "They didn't really like me there."

Harriet was surprised at the pang in her gut when Lucy admitted that. Even more surprised to realize she felt sorry for the woman. She'd only asked so she could laugh at her for losing a good job, but now she just felt flat and sad.

"I'm sorry to hear that," she said.

"Can I tell you something, Harriet?"

"If it's about another sale, I'm afraid not."

"No, no." Lucy stepped closer, her breath warm on Harriet's cheek. "It's *them*." She tilted her head toward a table to her right. "They're taking all my girls. I'm not making my bonuses anymore because my downline, well, they switched companies."

Harriet turned, saw a table draped in an astonishing, bright white. Three tall, beautiful women stood behind it, also dressed in virginal white sundresses. Their hair was long and straight and shone in the sun. They were timeless, like marble statues. "Who are they?" Harriet asked.

"Serenitea." Lucy spat. "Some kind of healthy tea company."

One of the women, the one with sleek black hair, stirred a powder into a clear, glass mug, and Harriet watched the water turn crimson, dazzling.

"It's a pyramid scheme." Lucy continued. "A scam."

Harriet furrowed her brow. "But Mary Jane—I don't—"

"Mary Jane is NOT a pyramid scheme." Lucy interrupted. "Pyramid schemes are illegal."

"Oh, uh, okay," Harriet said.

The dark-haired woman offered a passerby the cup of ruby liquid and they drank, smiled, and nodded.

"Never drink that stuff," Lucy said. "It's not regulated by the FDA."

Harriet had no interest in encountering another hungry "independent distributor", whatever their wares may be. She nodded. "Listen, Lucy. I have to go. I have some errands to run."

"Oh!" Lucy chirped. "Will you add me on Facebook? I sent you a request."

"I haven't been on," Harriet said.

"Oh," Lucy said. "Well, I really want to be your friend."

Harriet winced. "Of course," she said. "I have to go now. Buh bye."

"Bye," Lucy said, and Harriet noted a rare despondency in her voice.

Harriet sighed a breath of relief as she walked away from Lucy's lonely booth. The further she went, the lighter she felt. Lucy might be bedazzled, but she was a leaden anchor, pulling anyone in her orbit down into her polyester sadness, and it was good to be free of her.

Harriet walked slow, looking at the booths situated about the parking lot, taking her time now that she was out of danger. She met the eyes of a smiling, ruddy faced woman seated behind a table.

"Hi," the woman said.

"Hi," Harriet said.

Golden jars of honey and neat little packages of comb sat piled on the woman's table. Harriet's mouth watered.

"I have samples. Try anything you like." The woman tapped a jar. "This one here is clover. This one, wildflower."

"You like bugs?" The question tumbled out of her before she had time to stop it.

"What?" the woman asked, her eyes crinkling in amusement. "I guess so. I guess I have to."

"Here," Harriet said, passing the bag of mosquito leggings to the bee lady. "You can have these."

The woman glanced inside the bag, furrowed her brow. "Oh, um, thanks…"

"They have bugs on them." Harriet explained. "I'm Harriet."

"Kelsey," she said. Her hand was warm and rough, work hardened.

Chapter Six

She took home a small container of honey—an old baby food jar scraped clean and filled with the glorious stuff. She ate it with a spoon, all in one go. It was mellow and sweet with the faint taste of flowers—she'd never had honey so delicious.

It tainted her dreams, made them sticky and swarm with bees. She was walking through the sweltering hot cabin, trying to find the source of a deep, thrumming buzzing. She opened cabinets and doors, pried boards from the floor. The buzzing grew louder, more intense, but all she ever found were jars of black, rotten preserves, stained avocado-green towels.

She dreamed of the bee lady, sturdy and real in her

stiff, duck canvas clothing. She was shedding her baggy work pants, wiggling her way into the tight mosquito leggings. Her legs looked ridiculous—too feminine, too curvy—beneath her shapeless Carhartt jacket. Harriet knew it was wrong to see this, these tender layers of the bee lady, so she forced herself awake, away from the confusing sight.

Dawn was breaking.

Harriet felt worn and gray, a little sore. She'd had a fitful sleep, and the day before had been exhausting—the farmers market was the most interaction she'd had in months. It felt like she'd never been well rested, not really. She rubbed her eyes, wished she could fall back to sleep, but the bare windows let in too much light.

With a groan, she hoisted herself off the lumpy couch and shuffled into the kitchen. Everything was as she'd left it—a complete mess, half unpacked. She made a pot of bitter coffee, even though caffeine never did much for her. It was more of a ritual than anything, something to do.

Settling back on the couch, she balanced her mug on the armrest and tapped her phone to life. Bentwood Farmers Market, she googled. There was only one applicable hit—everything else was for a faraway place called Brentwood. She tapped the link at the top and found herself on an archaic-looking page, boxy green text on a beige background. It hurt her eyes. "Saturdays May–September, 9 a.m.–noon, Federal First Bank parking lot," it read. Below that, a pixelated clipart flower. It was a bad website. Harriet liked it a lot. This was the kind of small-town stuff she'd been hoping for.

Though the farmers market was beset by pyramid schemes, it was, so far, Harriet's favorite thing about Bentwood. She could still taste the honey on her lips, sticky and sweet.

Poor Lucy, she thought, surprising herself. The woman was no doubt an idiot, but she'd looked so sad behind her pile of ugly, stretchy clothes. Harriet wondered how long she had stood in the sun, watching people swing wide of her booth, avoid meeting her eyes. "*I really want to be your friend,*" she had said. They were the words of a child, naive and pure.

She opened Facebook and accepted Lucy's request. At least she could look at her profile this way, critique her further.

Lucy's profile picture was a full body shot. She was standing in the middle of a sun-dappled wooded lane—definitely not the bent woods, as the trees were lush and straight—posing as if in mid-laugh. She had a hand on her leg and her mouth was open wide, her eyes almost shut. It was a professional photograph, meaning Lucy either had a photographer in the family or had hired someone to take pictures of her modeling the motley Mary Jane she wore in the photo. This time it was a tropical mix of clothing—oranges, blues, and pinks. She was trying so hard to look like those women from the brochures, carefree and happy in their horrid clothes that were far too expensive.

She clicked "like" on the photograph—there weren't many reactions. No sooner had she done that, she received a notification from Lucy—an invitation to an event. Harriet sighed, tapped the notification.

"You're invited to the BIGGEST and BEST Mary Jane party of the year!" it said. "Come enjoy some wine and SHOP TIL YOU DROP!" Harriet found the capitalization threatening, unsettling. There were fifteen or so people marked as "Going", with a hundred and fifty left to reply.

Harriet closed the app without responding. She'd accepted the woman's friend request—was that not enough?

It was so exhausting, fending off this woman. She placed the phone and the coffee mug on the end table, and let herself slump into a semi-reclined position. She shut her eyes, attempting once more to fall back to sleep. But her phone chirped and vibrated, rattled against the mug and the base of a brass lamp. She sighed, pulled the phone back toward her face.

There was a message from Lucy. *Harriet! I'm so glad we're friends! I sent you an invite to a party. I hope you can come! It's at my house :)*

Harriet didn't want to reply, but she'd clicked the message, marking it as "Read." Lucy would know she'd seen it. *I don't know if I can make it, but I'll try.* She typed.

Please? It'll be so fun. The Mary Jane is just an excuse to get together and drink.

31

Harriet frowned, tapped on the event once more. This time she clicked the "Going" button.

Yay! Lucy replied. A parade of dancing emojis followed.

I don't know if I can make it. Harriet reiterated. *I have to get my lessons together for school.*

You deserve a break! And some teachers will be there! Omg!! You can network before you start. How fun! :)

Harriet considered this. It might indeed be good to meet some of her coworkers before the start of school, but she did not classify that as "fun". And did she really want to meet the type of teachers who went to a Mary Jane party? *I'll try.* Harriet typed.

Thank you so much! We'll have a great time. See you next week if I don't run into you before then! :)

Harriet sighed—it'd be a miracle if she didn't run into Lucy in the coming days. The woman had a talent of making herself everywhere, hiding behind every post and tree, it seemed.

She closed her eyes again and let her phone rest on her chest. It'd be a long week.

Chapter Seven

Harriet tried to work on her lesson plans, attempting to list out what books and essays to which she'd subject her students, but she was distracted, had resumed her nervous pacing. She didn't want to go to the party, but she didn't want to stay in the cabin, either. She wanted to be alone. That was the problem. She never felt alone enough. Something was there with her, bumping and creaking in the night, going through her trash. Sometimes she'd enter a room and a sudden chill would descend upon her and her arm hairs would stand on end—the feeling of being watched, of being examined. It was stifling, all consuming. Going outside, sitting on the little concrete stoop, was the only time she felt at peace.

So when Friday night came, she thought about driving far out of town, to a city with a mall or movie theater, and hiding out for a while. She thought about inventing a cold, a family emergency, and spending an evening on the stoop, watching the forest deepen into darkness. But as 7 p.m. neared, she found herself dabbing makeup on her face, pulling on a shimmery black shirt. She told herself she was curious in a mean, cautious way—after seeing Lucy's car, she couldn't help but wonder what her house was like—but she knew there was more to it than that. She needed Lucy, in a strange way; she was her only distraction from hauntings and tiredness and the looming threat of school.

Lucy's house was on the edge of town in a subdivision that might have been nice in the sixties, but now looked worn and tired. Little ranches, all identical, and surrounded by sparse, yellow yards, dotted the roadside. Harriet struggled to find the right one; none of them had a driveway full of cars, people parked on the curb. She checked the address—maybe she was on the wrong street. She opened the Facebook event page thinking she had gotten the date wrong.

But, alas, she was at the right place, at the right time.

She parked in the drive and waited a few minutes before climbing out, hoping someone else would arrive. She considered pulling back out, going home, but Lucy had already spotted her and was hanging out the door, her hand flopping about in a wild wave.

Harriet sighed, gave a weak wave in response. She'd brought a bottle of wine, and almost dropped it getting out of the car.

"Hi!" Lucy called. "You're the first one here!"

"Wow," Harriet said. "Early bird gets the worm." She wasn't sure why she said that, or to what worm she was referring.

"Come on in," Lucy said. "I just got the snacks all spread out."

Harriet set the wine down on the sideboard as she entered the house. She couldn't concentrate on both holding wine and examining Lucy's house. She wiped her hands on her pant legs, ready to get to work.

It was a small, cramped place, full of strange ottomans and "Live, Laugh, Love" signs, some sloppy with smeared paint—maybe handmade. *Seems like something Lucy would make,* Harriet thought. There was a large glass jug full of wine corks. Harriet shuddered. She couldn't handle trash as decoration. She had a hard enough time staying organized, making sure everything was thrown away. How was she supposed to deal with this?

"Are you cold? I can turn the AC down," Lucy said.

"No," Harriet shouted. Being hot in this place would be a nightmare, worse than the cloying heat of the cabin. She imagined sweating into the cheeses laid out on a folding table in the middle of the living room, passing out, and hitting her head on a metal cutout of Ohio—there were three of those hanging from the wall.

"You really like Ohio, huh?" she asked.

"Well, we live there," Lucy said.

"I suppose so," Harriet said, who didn't understand the need to be reminded with tchotchkes.

"I was going to wait for the others to get started, but *oh my gosh*, you should *totally* get first look at the new stock. Pick something out before the others get here."

Lucy ushered her down a hall into a spare bedroom. Racks of clothing lined the walls, and another ottoman—this time white pleather—sat in the middle of it all. "You can try things on in here. There's a mirror on the back of the door," Lucy said.

Harriet had no intention of getting naked in this woman's house. "Oh," she said.

"Here," Lucy said, plunging her hand into a rack of cardigans. "These are all new. So are the leggings in the dresser there. Just pull out a drawer!"

"Thanks," Harriet said from the hallway, refusing to enter the rainbow-hued room. "Maybe I'll look later."

"Look now!" Lucy begged. "Please?"

"Lucy, I'm not sure I can afford this right now. I haven't worked in a while."

"Oh," Lucy said, crestfallen. "I understand. I'm a little strapped for cash too. I haven't met my quota for the month."

Harriet frowned. This was the most depressing party she'd ever been to.

"Let's have some food while we wait!" Lucy flashed a smile—a sad, toothy thing. "Come on."

Harriet followed her back into the living room and seated herself on one of the plush ottomans. Her eyes were drawn to a family portrait on the wall—Lucy, in her Mary Jane as ever, with a tall man, a little boy. "Do you live here alone?"

"Oh no," she said. "I have a husband and son but I made them leave. Girls night, you know."

"And what does he do?"

"He's an engineer," Lucy said, making her way to the spread of snacks and wine. "Can I get you a plate of cheeses? Maybe some wine?"

Harriet shrugged. "Wine would be nice."

Lucy poured her an overfull glass. The wine was pink and sweet, something bottom shelf from the grocery store, Harriet was sure. "Thank you," she said through a tentative sip.

Lucy glanced at her watch, pulled out her phone. "I just don't know where everyone is."

Harriet's stomach clenched. She should have known she'd be the only one there, just as she was the only one at Lucy's booth at the farmers market. No one wanted to sit in this place, sipping cheap wine, sifting through piles of unimaginably revolting clothes. It was like getting drunk and stumbling to the thrift store. Actually, that sounded kind of fun. Harriet drained her glass.

"I'm sorry," Lucy said. "I thought more people would come." Her face was red, sweaty.

"It's okay, I don't mind." Harriet was being honest, too. She didn't mind not being seen here. She took it upon herself to pour more wine.

Lucy pulled her back straight, pushed up her chin. Her eyes went glassy. "It's time for the presentation."

"What?" Harriet asked, a little afraid.

Lucy marched to fireplace and began pulling poster boards and brochures from behind a couch.

"Oh, Lucy, I don't think—"

"It's time for the presentation." She repeated, her voice a little too robotic for Harriet's liking. She lined up the posters behind her, put a stack of brochures in the middle of the cheeses. Big, white teeth, and Mary Jane everywhere. "Ahem," she said.

"No," Harriet said, and sipped more wine.

"Welcome to my Mary Jane party," Lucy said, looking over Harriet's shoulder. "Thank you so much for your purchases thus far. I hope you've enjoyed some delicious cheeses and wine." She waved her hand over the food table, a mechanical gesture.

"Lucy, please," Harriet said, growing uncomfortable.

Lucy didn't stop, didn't even look at Harriet. "Did you know you could throw a Mary Jane party just like this one? Full of friendship, food, and fashion?"

Harriet looked over her shoulder, making sure Lucy really was indeed speaking to no one.

"There are two ways you can throw your own party. One: become a host. Two: become a distributor. It's so easy—"

"Lucy!" Harriet called. She clapped her hands, and was relieved to see Lucy blink with the percussive sound. "Stop it. You don't have to do this."

"Becoming a distributor is as easy as taking out your credit card. What's that? You're worried about what your husband will say? Well, you'll make it up to him." Lucy leaned across the table and blinked her eye—a messy, exaggerated wink.

"Oh my god." Harriet stood. Drained her glass again and stepped backward.

"I make"—Lucy's voice warbled—"three thousand dollars a month off my Mary Jane. Not bad for a side hustle!" Cue forced laughter.

Harriet crept backward toward the door, scared to take her eyes off Lucy.

"It has given me the financial freedom to pay off our house and our car. Isn't that fabulous?" her voice was strange, distorted.

Harriet was at the door now, pushing it open with her

elbow.

"For every person who joins under you, you receive a—"

Harriet ran, sprinting through Lucy's dry, crunchy yard to her car. She could still hear the murmur of Lucy's voice, still giving the presentation.

Chapter Eight

Harriet locked the cabin door, happy to seal herself in with the ghosts and stink and disarray. It felt good to put a barrier between her and Lucy. It wasn't that she was scared—though the woman's faraway eyes and droning voice were disturbing—but that she was sad. She wanted to compartmentalize that sadness and push it as far away as possible.

Looking at Lucy was like looking at a three-legged dog—a lot of pity, a little disgust, some strange wonder. Harriet didn't want to feel these things. She wanted to watch movies, work on her lesson plans, and unpack. She didn't want to feel the odd guilt of her internal mocking of Lucy, the sinking despair of realizing she was the only one at the party, the sticky way she had to extricate herself from buying the stretchy clothes every time they met. It was heavy and she didn't want it.

She sliced open a box of shoes, shook them out across the floor. There were glittering heels in among the worn slippers and sandals, and she frowned. She couldn't imagine wearing these anywhere in Bentwood. Where would she go? The farmers market? More of Lucy's soirées? She used to go to fancy restaurants with her parents, to her work's holiday parties. She used to get dressed up and look at herself in the long mirror in the hallway. There was only one mirror here—a round, splotchy thing above the sink. She tossed the heels aside, destined for Goodwill.

The next box held sweaters, other seasonal clothing. She folded the top back up and shoved the box out of the way. It felt silly to unpack those things in the infernal heat. She needed to find the rest of her summer clothes.

She found them beneath a box of newspaper-wrapped glasses. She hadn't folded them before stuffing them in the box, so they were wrinkled and scrunched. With careful precision, she laid out a white blouse and shorts. She placed a pair of brown leather sandals about where her feet would be. She stood above the disembodied outfit, cocked her head. It looked alright. Much better than what she'd been wearing the first time she went to the farmers market.

She'd decided she was going without really realizing

it, and the thought both disturbed and pleased her. She could get more honey—she'd buy a proper jar this time—and maybe see about some of the other stalls. But she'd also be faced with seeing Lucy again. Her throat felt tight. It was just so awkward.

Her phone buzzed once and she pulled it out of her pocket, held it up so the screen lit up. *Hey girl! :) Thank you so much for coming! I had a BLAST!*

Harriet shivered. She wouldn't reply. Sometimes it's best just to go to bed. She turned off the light before stripping, cognizant of the leering woods, and pulled on baggy cotton shorts, a tank top.

She laid on the couch without a blanket, flipping and turning, trying to find what side best facilitated air flow. All positions were uncomfortable, some hurt. She sighed and shut her eyes.

She must have drifted off because there was a noise— she heard it first in her dream, underwater and vague. But it happened again, and she was sitting up, propped up by one arm.

BANG.

She jumped. Something was exploding, tearing apart the air.

BANG.

She stumbled up, blind in the dark, and felt for the lamp switch.

BANG.

The room flickered into being, illuminated. The door was swinging open, a great breath inhaling and then blowing it shut.

BANG.

Her teeth rattled.

The door swung open once more and she caught the handle, pulled it shut again. Harriet locked the cabin door, reluctant to seal herself in the with the ghosts and stink and disarray.

Morning couldn't come soon enough.

Chapter Nine

This time she got there at 9 a.m., right as the vendors finished setting up. She wore her cute, white top and short shorts, and she looked put together, even though her nerves were a jangled mess, and she was tired—so tired. She carried the canvas bag on her arm.

She smiled at the people behind the tables, nodded at the ladies in the long, white dresses. She went to Lucy's booth first, eager to get the interaction over with. Maybe when it was over, out of the way, her heart would slow and even out, and she could peruse the rest of the market in peace.

"Harriet!" Lucy squealed. "You're becoming a regular here!"

Harriet took in Lucy's bright-pink, sleeveless dress. It was so extreme she assumed it would glow under blacklight, a bodiless form shining and moving in the dark. Harriet shuddered. There was a little tattoo on Lucy's shoulder—a heart. It surprised her, and the sadness trickled in, a leak somewhere in her chest. The more she learned about Lucy, the sadder she became.

She shrugged. "Not much else to do on a Saturday morning."

"That's true." Lucy nodded.

"Any sales yet?" Harriet asked, cursing herself for asking something so blatant, so depressing.

Lucy looked down at the folded clothing before her. "Well, I was able to pass out some brochures," she said.

"Already? That's good." She attempted a smile for the sad clown.

"It is."

Harriet wondered if Lucy was going to bring up the strange party, the trance, the uneaten cheeses and corked wines, but she was busying herself, straightening a stack of t-shirts. Her lack of eye contact was telling, Harriet decided. She wanted to know what—exactly—had happened. "Last night…"

Lucy perked up, smiled. "I had a great time," she said. "Didn't you?"

Harriet opened her mouth. Closed it again.

"It was a total success."

"It was?" Harriet looked over her shoulder. No one was close enough to hear. "Lucy, I—"

"I'm so glad you could come! I'm hosting another one soon. Maybe right after school starts."

"I was a little freaked out, to tell you the truth."

Lucy screwed up her face. "Freaked out?" Her voice was small, quiet.

"Yeah," Harriet said. "The presentation. It kind of freaked me out."

"Oh."

"You don't have to do this stuff, you know." Harriet laid a hand on a pile of leggings. "You're better than this, than giving presentations to empty rooms." She was tearing Mary Jane down while raising Lucy up—it was the perfect thing to say, she'd thought. Harriet straightened her shoulders as best she could.

Lucy's eyebrows raised. "But…"

"No buts," Harriet said. "It's true."

"But I'm happy," Lucy said.

The words short-circuited something in Harriet's brain. "Happy?" she asked.

"Yes!" Lucy nodded. "I make three thousand dollars a month with Mary Jane."

"Do you really?" Harriet scoffed.

"Sure," Lucy said.

Harriet eyed her, suspicious. "It's just… There was no one at your party, is all."

"That's not true." Lucy was smiling so wide it looked like it hurt.

"Lucy, it is."

"I'm triple diamond," Lucy said.

Harriet shook her head. "What's that mean?"

Lucy held out her wrist. A bangle with three silver-backed rhinestones dangled there. Beneath it, a green streak across her skin.

"What's that?" Harriet asked.

"Triple diamond," Lucy said, shaking her wrist so the bracelet flopped and swung.

"Okay, but what did you have to do to get that?"

"I'm the area's top distributor." She explained. "I have at least fifteen girls straight under me, with even more under them."

"A pyramid," Harriet said.

"A wealth triangle."

"What? No."

"Doesn't your boss have a lot of people under him? A few people above?"

Harriet wiped away the sweat from her brow. "That's not the same."

Lucy smiled.

"Listen, speaking of bosses, I have to get going. I have

a lot to prepare for school and—"

"You could be your own boss," Lucy said. She held out a brochure.

"No," Harriet said. "Lucy, no."

Lucy's face fell with a hushed sigh. "Maybe next time."

"No," she said. She left and she didn't look back.

She walked past the angelic looking tea ladies and they reached for her, smiled their white, gleaming smiles, but she didn't slow. She was headed straight toward Kelsey's honey booth. A crowd had formed in front of her stall, and Harriet hung back, waiting for them to clear.

At last, an opening formed, and Harriet slipped through. Seeing Kelsey's muted attire, her thoughtful face, was comforting. *Like seeing an old friend*, she thought with some surprise.

"Hello again," Kelsey said.

"Last weeks' was incredible," Harriet said. "I have to have more."

Kelsey slid a small jar across the table.

"No," Harriet said. "Bigger."

"Absolutely." She produced a larger container.

Harriet's mouth watered. "Why is it so good?" she asked. "I've had honey before, but this is something else."

An old man bumped into her but she stood firm.

Kelsey shrugged. "I guess I just have happy bees."

"Happy bees." Harriet repeated.

"You know, if you're interested in this stuff, I teach a class. It's a hundred and fifty, but you get some supplies, get to take home any honey we harvest. It's a lot of fun." Kelsey handed her a linen business card. It felt good in her hand. "I'd really like to see you there."

Harriet blushed. "To be honest…I'm a little afraid of bees."

"I won't let anything happen to you."

Harriet slid the card into her front pocket. "I'm a teacher too," she said.

"Whatcha teach?"

Harriet wasn't sure why she'd said it, but Kelsey's interest seemed genuine. She folded her hands before her and waited for Harriet to reply, eyes smiling. "Gifted Education," she said. "Mostly literature."

"Oh, I'm a *huge* reader," Kelsey said. "I thought you looked bookish."

Harriet tucked a strand of hair behind her ear. "Thank you," she said. Bookish was a high compliment, and she was sure Kelsey meant it as one. Harriet handed her a ten dollar bill.

Kelsey slipped the money into a zippered pouch and before she could pull the change from its depths, Harriet said, "Keep it."

"You sure?"

"Yes," she said. "Keep those bees happy."

Kelsey tucked the pouch away. "Well, thank you. I really appreciate it. Think on that class," she said.

"I will," Harriet said, and she would.

"See you next week?" Kelsey asked.

"Next week." Harriet nodded. She wouldn't miss it.

Chapter Ten

S he was sitting in the teacher's lounge, pretending to write in her planner. She scribbled in the margins, chewed on her pen cap like a rat. Harriet was bored, hopelessly so. There were—*No surprise*—few gifted students at Bentwood Intermediate, and she only taught two classes a day: one in the morning and one again in the afternoon. She was between them, attempting to look busy in the lounge, when the gym teacher walked in.

He was a large, beefy man wearing red shorts and a gray sweater stretched tight across his broad shoulders. Harriet rolled her eyes—he looked so typical, like he smelled of sweat and dodge balls. He sat across from her at the table, pulled a protein bar from his pocket.

"Hi," he said.

Harriet glanced up at him, nodded. She may have been bored, but she wasn't desperate.

"You're new here?" he asked.

"Yes," she said, writing some gibberish across the month of August.

"I'm Harold," he said. "Physical Education."

"Okay," she said. "Harriet."

"What are you teaching?" he asked, scratching his chest with his free hand.

"Gifted Ed," she said, meeting his gaze.

He said, "Wow," and leaned back in his chair so that it moaned in protest. "Gifted, huh? I can see that." He waggled his eyebrows at her, smiled wide.

Harriet made a show of looking at the clock, and began stuffing her belongings back into her bag. "I gotta go, class soon."

"I'll be seeing you," he said. "If you ever want some Phys Ed, you just—"

"It was nice meeting you." She lied, hurrying out the door.

What is wrong with everyone in this town? she thought.

She hadn't heard from Lucy since the strange encounter at the farmers market, but she felt the maudlin threat of her hanging over everything she did. And now there was this gym teacher… The last thing she needed was another solicitor to avoid.

Her final class of the day was slow, boring. The kids were dazed and tired, having been unconditioned during the lazy summer. She went over the syllabus while they sat in silence, yawning and twitching. She couldn't blame them; she was yawning too.

When she at last released them and they bolted away, one boy stayed behind. He was fair, with blond hair and piercing blue eyes. Kind of creepy looking, in an elfish way. He stood next to her seat, shifting from foot to foot, eyes flitting left and right, and his Adam's apple bouncing in his throat. "Can I help you?" she asked.

"My name's Calvin," he said.

"Can I help you, Calvin?"

"Well, my mom gave me something and said to give it to you. It's like a 'Welcome to Bentwood' present, she says."

"Oh?"

Calvin dug through his backpack, rustling through papers and binders and books. She expected him to pull an overripe apple or a Starbucks gift card from the folds, but instead he pulled out a white organza bag tied with a neat ribbon. "Here," he said.

"Oh," Harriet said, unsure of what she held in her hands. "Thank you so much. Tell your mother I am very appreciative."

"You're welcome," Calvin said.

He stood there.

"Yes?" Harriet asked.

"Aren't you going to open it?"

Harriet was never one to open gifts in front of people. It was too hard to hide her emotions, the flicker of disappointment when the paper fell away to reveal something that was always less than whatever she was hoping for. She pulled the ribbon on the bag and it yawned open.

Inside, a packet of tea, and a white and gold business card.

"It's tea," the boy said. "My mom sells it."

"Thank you so much," Harriet said, a little panicked. "I love it."

"She doesn't let me drink it," he said.

"I understand that," she said.

The tea's packaging was elegant and minimal—white with touches of gilded text. "Revitalize," it said. "Rejuvenate. Serenitea." She thought of those long-haired women in their white gowns, pure and holy. Calvin's mother was like that, she realized, and she examined the boy more. His polo shirt was pressed and neat, his hair was combed in perfect, straight lines. She should have known.

"Thanks again, Calvin," she said, trying to usher him along.

He stared at her with those bright, piercing eyes. "So

you like it?"

"Yes, of course I like it. I love tea."

"Great," he said. "Excellent."

When he was gone, she held the tea bag in her hands, tried to smell it through the paper. It was spicy, woody. It smelled good. She slipped the sachet into her purse and threw away the fabric bag, the business card. She didn't intend to drink the tea, but it felt wrong to throw it away so soon, in the room little Calvin had just left. Like hiding a body, she'd dispose of it elsewhere.

Chapter Eleven

She still hadn't finished unpacking. She had tried, had put a few things on the end table, on the bathroom counter, but the rest stayed in boxes. They were spilling over now, having been rifled through a dozen times, and the cabin seemed smaller than ever. Harriet shut her eyes against it and curled onto the couch. She was tired—too tired to move.

Her first week at school hadn't been what she expected. The kids were lifeless, didn't participate in conversation. They just sat there, staring at the clock, desperate to be rid of her. She had thought being a Gifted Education teacher would be engaging and challenging, but so far it proved to be dull. She heard the kids while on her solitary walks through the halls, whooping and laughing in gym class—proof they did come to life at some point throughout the day.

Maybe they need time to warm up to me.

She remembered Harold, the gym teacher, and shivered. She could almost smell his musk, there in the cabin, the metallic bite of him. It was overwhelming. She hadn't met too many other teachers—just the librarian and the English teacher. They were nice enough—at least they didn't leer at her. But she couldn't imagine herself being friends with any of them. They already had tiny worlds unto themselves, worlds without room. She could tell by the way they gossiped, the way they held their heads together in the teacher's lounge, conspiring. They didn't have any use for her.

And then there was Lucy, texting her, even now, about sales and get togethers and offers for new recruits. Harriet had tried being nice to her, had tried to save her, even, but the girl was impervious. Hopeless. A lost cause. She wasn't sure what to do about Lucy. Every time her phone chimed, her stomach squeezed and roiled. She had extended a hand and all she got in return were sales pitches. It hurt more than she cared to admit.

Harriet knew herself well. She knew her wants, her greatest desires, and she knew she was slipping into a subtle depression. She was feeling sorry for herself, her loneliness, her supposed dream job. There was a cloudy darkness around the edges of everything, tainting it. Soon she'd only be showering when her hair turned stringy with grease. She'd eat nothing but microwaved dinners, if she ate at all. She was prone to these episodes—had experienced them many times before—but still they came upon her with grief and shock; always thinking she'd conquered it the last time, had overcome.

She sat up, examined the room she'd slept and lived in for the last month. Why had she come to this pitiful town? This pitiful cabin? Perhaps the data entry job hadn't been so bad after all—at least it was in the city where she at least stood a chance of meeting somebody.

Slumping out of bed, she shuffled into the kitchen. She'd eat her feelings, she decided. It was something to do.

She pulled a Lean Cuisine out of the freezer—something she didn't even remember buying—and placed it on the counter. The instructions said to vent the plastic on the top, so she took a knife and stabbed at the frozen hunk of chicken alfredo until the plastic covering was shredded. It took her remaining energy, but it felt good to stab.

While the tray of noodles spun in the microwave, she opened the refrigerator and looked for something to drink. She could have water, of course, but that wasn't self-destructive enough for her tastes. She wanted something sugary, something sticky, something unregulated by the FDA.

She shut the refrigerator door and walked to the little table on which she'd thrown her purse. It lay there like a poached animal, a deflated sack of leather. From its depths, she pulled the white-and-gold tea packet. It shone in the dim light of the kitchen.

She didn't have a kettle, so when the noodles were done and had stunk up the kitchen with the smell of freezer-burned garlic, she slipped a mug of water inside the microwave and set it to boil.

She stared at the noodles while she waited, unimpressed by the gelatinous sauce, the few chunks of pale chicken. She slid the whole mess of it into the trash.

At last, the microwave dinged and she cautiously pulled the hot mug out of the stained interior. She ripped open the tea packet, careful not to damage the sachet itself, and dropped the fragrant bag into the water. It bled a red swirl into the liquid, tinting it pink, and then a ruby red.

She had planned to spoon a dollop of honey into the drink, but decided at the last moment to try it on its own. If it didn't meet her expectations, it could always be sweetened up afterward.

Harriet raised the mug to her lips and the smell was overwhelming—an articulate blend of deep woods, fruited sugar, and flowers. Her mouth flooded. It smelled so good.

She took a tentative sip and was pleased to find it wasn't unbearable—there was a bitter undercurrent buoying up the other flavors; the complexity was unexpected. Delicious. She carried the mug to the sagging couch. She still didn't have a television and she was tired of listening to shows on the tinny speakers of her phone and laptop, so she stared out the window, watching the light fade away into dusk. The trees swayed and bucked with a growing wind. There'd be a storm tonight.

Her phone chirped, and she balanced the mug on the arm of the couch. She slid the phone from her pocket and found a new pulsing notification—a friend request. She tapped on it and the pristine, unbearably symmetrical face of a woman filled her screen. She had long, perfect hair, parted down the middle, and she stared into the camera. It could have been a passport photo if not for the foliage behind her. She wore white. It was a tea lady.

Harriet frowned. What a coincidence it was that the moment she tried the tea, she received a request from one of the ladies. Were they watching her, standing straight and silent among the bent trees? She scanned the forest once more, seeing nothing but warped limbs and droopy leaves.

Her name was Angela Monroe, a name as smooth and luscious as her skin. She was a beautiful, serious-looking woman. Would it be so bad to have a woman like that stalking you?

She drained the cup and hit "Accept".

Chapter Twelve

She meant to sit staring at the wall. She meant to fill her heart with dread at every bump, every scraping branch upon the window pane. She meant to be miserable. Sleepless. But a lapping calm enveloped her and she found herself washing her face and brushing her teeth. She changed into clean pajamas. She slathered her face in the expensive cream she only used when she was feeling optimistic. The tea had washed over her, had flattened the world out to something so smooth and sleek that she was skipping over it, barely thinking. It was all so easy, getting ready for bed. It was no longer a dreaded chore, but a luxury.

Yawning, she curled up on the couch. Her eyelids felt

so heavy. In fact, all of her felt heavy, as if a weighted blanket settled upon her. It felt good. She slept a long time.

The sun rose bright and clean, and Harriet felt the same. She didn't linger in bed. She didn't even check her phone. She'd emptied two moving boxes before realizing what was happening. She was supposed to be depressed. She was supposed to be moping. She was supposed to be haggard and tired and full of contempt. Something was amiss.

She moved through the cabin with such lightness she wondered if she was a ghost herself, frictionless and hollow. Maybe she was dying, was experiencing some strange euphoric last hurrah before bursting. She held a hand to her chest, felt the deep thumps grow stronger, louder. She was alive and she was awake.

She got ready for work in record time. She could do this. She'd teach those kids whether they liked it or not.

That tea was good shit.

Chapter Thirteen

Her morning class was as smooth as Serenitea. She managed to get a debate going about the symbolism in *Lord of the Flies*. She enjoyed it more than she'd anticipated. But as the day ground on, she felt herself twitching, picking at the skin on her hand. There was a prickling anxiousness rattling in the back of her skull, her chest felt tight. She stared at her reflection in the dirty bathroom mirror, peering between the fingerprints and scratched graffiti. She looked used up, empty. She searched for poltergeists in the reflection behind her, holding her breath in case something moved. She needed more tea.

Avoiding the teacher's lounge, and Harold's lecherous

gaze, Harriet instead sat in her car for a majority of the afternoon, biding her time in the suffocating heat until she could pull Calvin aside and ask him if there was any more tea in that big backpack of his. Her mouth watered.

At last, she found herself in the small classroom once more, seated at the head of the ovular table they used in lieu of desks. It was meant to facilitate discussion, but she wasn't sure if the shape of the table mattered.

The children filed in, flung their backpacks to the floor, and plopped themselves into the plush rolling chairs. "What are we going to do today?" one asked—there was always one asking this, as if it wasn't in the syllabus, and ignoring the fact she had written their agenda on the whiteboard.

"The form and history of the English novel," she said.

Someone moaned.

"It's important stuff," she said. "Impacts everything you read."

She watched Calvin reach into his bag, watched him pull out a binder and a pencil. She felt like a just-plucked guitar string, jittery and loud.

"I'm thirsty." She offered, hoping Calvin would rise to the opportunity.

He didn't look up, just flipped through his papers.

"Me too," said the boy who asked what they'd be doing. "Let's all go to the water fountain. Let's go for a walk."

"No," she said.

"Whatever," he said under his breath.

She taught, half-hearted and parched. Recited her notes verbatim and forgot to ask questions, to ask them if they had any questions. She knew it was a boring class and the knowledge would slide right past them, but she was distracted, afraid.

"Calvin, may I talk to you after class?" she asked a moment before the bell rang.

"Ooh," said the boy who wanted to walk, to drink, to know.

Calvin gave a solemn nod and began packing his bag. When the bell sounded, the children drifted away, leaving Calvin behind.

"Yes, Ms. Pendleton?" He was polite and clean as ever with his collared shirt and trimmed fingernails.

"Calvin, I wanted to thank you again for the tea."

He frowned. "You're welcome, Ms. Pendleton. I'm glad you liked it."

Harriet scooted her chair toward him. "I more than liked it," she said, her eyebrows raised a touch too high. "I *loved* it."

He leaned back, away from her. "That's good to hear. I'll tell my mom."

"Yes, please do. And Calvin?"

"Yes?"

"Do you happen to have any more?"

Calvin's eyes flitted toward the door. "No," he said. "But my mom has lots. She sells it, like I said."

"I lost the business card, Calvin. I need you to tell your mother I need more. I'll give you money."

Calvin looked pale, panicked. "I'm not sure it works that way."

"Sure it does."

"I'm going to be late for science, Ms. Pendleton."

Bile rose in her throat. It was getting away from her. The thought of going through the rest of the day, the entirety of the endless night, feeling this way, this frazzled, desperate way, was killing her. She choked back a sob. "I just really liked it, is all."

"The other ladies, they all talk to my mom on Facebook. Why don't you try that?"

A spark went off in her head, electrifying her. "Angela," she whispered.

"That's her." Calvin shuffled toward the door.

She let him go, didn't stop him from leaving her tealess.

She wasn't sure why she hadn't put it together before. Calvin Monroe—perfect blond child, with the perfect blond mother. *All that neat, immaculately-groomed hair. Of course.* She pulled her phone from her bag.

Hello, Ms. Monroe. She typed. *It's an absolute pleasure to have Calvin in class. I wanted to thank you again for the tea.*

In fact, I was wondering how I could go about getting more. Thank you for your time.

She set her phone face down on the table and exhaled, realizing she had been holding her breath.

"All done in here?" a voice asked from the hall.

Harriet spun around to find a group of children and their teacher bunched around the door, waiting for the room to clear.

"Yes, yes. I'm sorry." She blushed, feeling as if she'd been caught doing something unsavory. It did feel a little rotten, messaging that woman this way. It was undignified. A woman like that, she deserved to be approached as if by a plebeian in a queen's court, all curtseys and groveling and noses to the floor. And then there was Lucy, hovering—jealous and betrayed—in the back of her mind. She shrugged, willing the feelings to go away. She'd done what she needed to do.

She walked back to her car, urging herself not to check her messages, though she had felt the phone vibrate in the pocket of her bag. She wanted to savor this moment.

Meet me at the Grind House. 6 p.m.?

Harriet "Liked" the message. She'd be there.

Chapter Fourteen

Harriet changed into her most bohemian clothing—a long flowy skirt and a macrame vest over a t-shirt. She looked ridiculous, she knew, but she wanted to show Angela that she'd tried, had put herself together just for her. She combed her frizzy hair until it laid as straight and smooth as it would go. It wasn't tea lady levels of perfection, but it would do.

The Grind House was the little coffee shop on the main drag—the one within walking distance of her winding drive. She'd never been inside, but if the wind was right, she could smell the roasting beans and steamed milk. She walked there, sweat dripping into her stinging eyes.

She smoothed her hair one last time before heading in, pressing down on it with her hands. With a deep breath, she pushed her way into the coffee shop.

The smell was devastating—dark and earthy, with hints of baking bread. The espresso machines hissed and spat, someone laughed. It was a dizzying place, assaulting her every sense. She spun, looking for a seat, and found Angela looking straight at her, eyebrow raised.

"Angela." Harriet nodded, attempting to regain her composure.

"Hello, Ms. Pendleton," Angela said. She gestured toward the empty seat opposite her. "Can I get you anything? A latte?"

Harriet plopped into the chair, winced at her own lack of grace. She wished she could stand up and try again, this time sitting with more dignity. "Please, call me Harriet," she said. "I'm alright."

She noticed Angela had a mug of hot water on the saucer before her, tea bag at the ready. *Serenitea.* Angela would never stoop to drinking something other than the sacred nectar. Harriet's mouth was full of spit and she swallowed hard.

"How about a mug of water? Tea's on me."

"Please!" Harriet shouted. "I'd love some."

Angela flashed a knowing smile and floated away toward the counter. When she returned, Harriet was close to bursting. She needed that tea so bad.

Angela placed the full mug in front of Harriet without spilling a drop. "I hear you like the tea," she said, sliding a pack toward Harriet.

"Oh yes," Harriet said. She ripped the packet open with zeal. "It's wonderful."

"I'm so glad to hear that," Angela said. She smiled with just her lips; her face around them was frozen, didn't wrinkle. Harriet suspected Botox. It gave her an icy appearance, as if her emotions weren't real, weren't genuine, as they didn't extend to her cheeks, her eyes. While on others this may look uncanny or botched, on Angela it looked regal, above the realm of human feeling.

Harriet bobbed the tea bag in the water, watched it turn that florid crimson.

"I can sell you some, of course," Angela said.

"That would be great," Harriet said. "I brought cash and my credit card and I also have Venmo." She took a sip of the tea and felt a rush of relief flood her muscles, her organs. She hadn't realized just how tense she'd been before this moment. She felt like she was lying in the sun, warm breeze on her face. "Here," she said, pulling her purse to her lap.

Angela raised a hand. "Not yet," she said.

"Oh."

"I wanted to offer you an opportunity, first."

Harriet's insides roiled. She didn't want an opportunity. She just wanted tea. She wanted a box in her hands, something real she could hold and carry home.

"I can get you thirty percent off." Angela smiled that perfect smile again. "Tea delivered straight to your door. You just have to register as a wellness consultant."

"Wellness consultant?" Harriet wondered what wellness even was—it was a vague buzzword, conjuring images of stretchy athleisure clothes and shining teeth.

Angela shrugged, tossed her long hair over her shoulder. "That's what we call our independent retailers, our business owners."

Harriet frowned. "I'm not sure I'm able to commit to that. I can't sell anything."

"You wouldn't have to sell anything if you didn't want to. You could just buy what you need and relax." Her voice was deep, sonorous. Harriet wanted to curl up inside it.

"Why not just buy it from you?"

Angela shrugged again. "I'd like to help you get a discount," she said. "Besides, if you join, you get to come to our retreats."

"Oh?" Harriet asked. Her mug was almost empty.

"We have these luxurious retreats every month or so. Massages, steaming, champagne. All of it complimentary, *if* you're a consultant." Angela took a dainty sip from her own tea.

Harriet thought about all those straight-haired ladies at the farmers market. How beautiful they looked, how *well*.

If she could look like that, she'd be content. She'd be fulfilled. "You'll be there?" she asked.

"Oh yes," she said. "The next one's at my house."

"I'd love to join," Harriet said. She wanted the tea, yes, but she also wanted to be one of *them*, shining and gorgeous.

"Wonderful." Angela smiled. This time with her teeth. They were a brilliant white, with a slight, sharp point. "I can sign you up right here." She pulled a white tote bag onto the table, slid out her expensive, sleek laptop. "It's only a thousand dollars to get started."

Only? Harriet swallowed. She didn't want to betray to Angela that this was a heinous amount, an unthinkable amount. So she nodded, found her credit card in her bag.

"It'll take a few days to get your starter kit in the mail, but I brought you a welcome gift." She winked, slid a box of tea across the table.

Harriet cradled it in her arms. "What's in this stuff, anyway?" she asked.

Angela blinked. "A proprietary blend of holistic botanicals and spices."

Harriet stared at Angela, blank, and pondered what a botanical was. But then she felt her skin prickle, felt eyes other than Angela's on her.

"Looks like your friend is here," Angela said, nodding toward the register.

Harriet turned slowly, still hugging the box of tea.

There, standing before the muffins and cakes and big tins of beans, was Lucy, clutching a giant frozen drink topped with whipped cream and sprinkles. She stared at Harriet, mouth open. Her eyes were wide, fearful.

"Oh," Harriet said. "That's, uh, not my friend." She turned away, back to Angela.

Angela smiled. "Good."

When Lucy burst from the shop, leaving the door to slam behind her, a shiver ran through Harriet—a blast of cold from somewhere deep.

Chapter Fifteen

Hi Harriet. The message read. *Just wanted to catch up and see if you needed any Mary Jane.*

Harriet deleted the message, rolled over on the couch.

Fall is coming so I know you probably want to update your wardrobe. We have a new line of sweaters, if you're interested.

Harriet deleted that one too. But they just kept coming. Every vibration of her phone sent her sinking further into the cushions.

I can offer you 20% off. It's supposed to be for ruby level distributors and above, but I can hook you up. What were you doing with her, anyway?

Harriet watched the messages roll in. One after another.

Have you seen the new Fall Foliage collection? It's so cute! I'm just wondering why you met with her, is all.

It'd all look so good with your pretty auburn hair. I told you that stuff is dangerous. Why did you drink it?

I have some new leggings, too. Solid colors if that's more your thing. I'm just really hurt. I thought we were friends.

Can we meet?

Harriet sighed. *It's not a big deal.* She typed. *Her kid is in my class and she wanted to talk about his progress.*

:/.

What? Harriet asked.

I saw you with tea.

She gave it to me as a thank you present, for working with her kid.

Don't drink anymore.

Harriet blinked, and scoffed. *Why not?*

It's not regulated by the FDA.

So? Harriet asked. *Neither are vitamins.*

:/.

What? Harriet asked. Her hands were starting to shake from the sheer annoyance. She didn't even know why she was entertaining this back-and-forth exchange.

There was a pause as Lucy typed, deleted her message, and began typing again. *Serenitea is more dangerous than you could ever imagine.*

 What's that supposed to mean?

 I've seen what it does to people.

 Lucy, it's not a big deal. Harriet rolled her eyes, and went to put the phone away. The phone buzzed again.

 Will you meet me? At the park?

 Harriet ground her hand into her eye. *I can't right now. Grading papers.*

 :/.

 Harriet sipped her tea.

Chapter Sixteen

The tea was as good as ever. She drank two cups of it a day: one in the morning to calm her nerves, and another at night to help her sleep. In between, she cleaned the cabin from top to bottom, wrote original lesson plans for class. She taught the children well and rewarded herself with trips to the farmers market. She felt good, renewed, despite craving the stuff from the moment she woke up.

She was absorbed in deleting Lucy's most recent messages when a knock interrupted her thoughts. Someone was at the door. She bristled. *It could be Lucy. What do I do?* She could hide, but that hadn't worked the first time and she doubted it would work now.

The knock came again, sturdy and loud.

"Coming," she called, tip-toeing to the door.

Harriet peered out the window at the side of the door and saw an old man waiting on the stoop. "Who the fuck?" she said, before realizing it was her landlord. She pulled the door open, put on her best smile. "Mr. Morrison."

"I come to see how you're getting on," he said, voice like gravel. "To see if you were needing anything."

"All okey dokey here," Harriet said. Then, remembering the blinds and AC she wanted, said, "Won't you come in?"

The man took off his hunting cap, held it to his stomach. "Thank you," he said, stepping over the threshold. He looked about him, breathed in deep. "I can never forget the smell of this place. Like childhood, it is."

"Um, something like that," Harriet said. "Won't you have a seat?" She piled her pillow and duvet in the corner of the couch and waved a hand at the newly cleared space.

"Oh no," Mr. Morrison said. "I'm not staying long. Just wanted to visit, to see the old place."

"You're really attached, huh?"

"It's where I grew up," he said. "It's where my mother lived and died, bless her soul." He tapped his heart with a gnarled hand, a gesture that reminded Harriet of a lazy sign of the cross.

"I get that," Harriet said.

"She died right there. On the couch."

Harriet blinked, swallowed down something caustic and lumpy. "Oh?"

"In her sleep, they say. Though she did have a knife in her hand. Can't explain that." He shook his head.

Harriet now also felt the urge to sleep with a knife. "Listen, that reminds me," she said. "I was wondering if I could install some blinds. It's awfully exposed here, especially at night and—"

"No," Mr. Morrison said. "Absolutely not. No blinds."

Harriet frowned. "Why not?"

"Mother always kept the windows wide open, clear. To let the outside in."

"I'm not sure I want the outside in," she said.

"Mother wanted them open."

"Okay then," Harriet said. Perhaps she'd tack some blankets on the frames.

The old man cleared his throat.

"Can I interest you in some tea?" Maybe he'd be easier to ply with some hospitality. The sweet, calming tea coursing through his veins also wouldn't do any harm.

"Tea? Pah." He spat. "No. I'm a coffee man."

"I'm afraid I don't have any coffee."

"No coffee? Mother always kept coffee on the stove."

"Well…"

"Anyway, I'm not eating or drinking anything I didn't make with my own two hands. I'm telling you to do the same."

"What?" she asked.

The old man shrugged. "Poison," he said. "All that processed shit is poison."

"I wouldn't have pinned you for a health nut, Mr. Morrison."

His face crumpled. "Nut? I'm not a nut."

"No, of course not. I didn't mean it like that. What about an air conditioner? What would mother say about that?"

Mr. Morrison scanned the room. "It's the end of the season. You don't need anything like that now. Talk to me next year."

Next year? The thought of being in the same place in a year's time was horrifying.

"I am leaving now," Mr. Morrison said as he swung toward the door. "I have to go home."

"Well do come back again soon," she said, hoping he would not. "You're always welcome here."

"Of course I am. I was born here," he said.

The door slammed behind him, making the deer mount above it swing. A shower of dust fell, swirling in the mid-afternoon light.

Harriet plopped onto the couch, rubbed her forehead with a sweaty palm. He'd denied her every want, had made the place more unappealing than ever with his stingy attitude and the information about his mother. She felt the tea's potency waning. She felt frazzled, worn down. She imagined her peace draining away into the deep cushions of the couch, into the dark cracks filled with hair and crumbs and, now, a woman's life.

Someone had died here, in this very spot. She supposed it didn't matter, but it still filled her with a creeping sense of dread, a cold shiver that tingled through her spine. If only there was a real bed in the cabin, somewhere else to lie, to sit.

And what was that about being poisoned? Harriet sighed. Mr. Morrison was an odd man. She wondered if he was born on the couch. She examined it for stains. The whole thing was a mottled brown—it was hard to tell if it was filthy or just ugly. Either way, it was unbearable. She'd ask for a new one, but she knew Mr. Morrison would object. It was a sacred object. A relic.

The trees danced in the windows, taunting her.

Chapter Seventeen

She awoke to a box on her doorstep. It was huge—almost too heavy to carry on her own. She pushed it in through the doorway, denting its corners as she shoved it through the tight opening, and set to ripping it open. Thick, white paper fell away, revealing box after box of Serenitea. Harriet's heart raced. This was a goldmine. This was heaven.

She stacked the tea boxes on the floor beside her. At the bottom of the big box, she found pamphlets and signs and business cards with her name embossed on them in shining gold. She had no intention of selling the stuff, but it felt good to see her name there, official and pretty. She had something in common with the tea ladies now.

Flipping through one of the pamphlets, Harriet couldn't help but notice the vast differences from Mary Jane's. Where Mary Jane was bright and exuberant, Serenitea was understated, elegant. It looked like something you'd pick up off the reception desk of a fancy spa. Inside, there was a woman, walking in a field of lavender, her white dress skimming the buds of the plants. "Reinvent your life," it said. "Reinvigorate your soul." There was no mention of the tea, but Harriet supposed there didn't need to be—they were selling a lifestyle, an image. Harriet wanted to walk unburdened through a field of flowers, smelling the fragrant blooms, or, she wanted people to think she was the sort of woman who'd do that. She wanted to seem one with nature, one with herself. She put the mug of water in the microwave.

Her phone's incessant chime drilled through her with real urgency. Harriet left the water to boil and picked up the device. She had eleven new friend requests. Her heart thundered. *What happened*, she wondered. Had she posted something stupid that had gone viral? Sat on her phone and somehow uploaded a picture of her butt? She hoped not.

She paged through them, almost trembling with nervousness. Long, natural hair, beautiful faces—bright, clear eyes. These were tea ladies, each and every one of them. She looked at her own photo—a blurry candid at a teacher symposium. She felt sloven, accepting the requests, tainting their friend lists with her dark, messy photo. But she didn't want them to think she was ignoring them. She hit "Accept all."

Her phone vibrated in her hand. Two new notifications, arriving at the exact same time. One was a message from Lucy. *What are you doing?* She swiped it away without thinking.

The other was an invitation: "Consultant Retreat," it read. "Relax, Revitalize." Harriet clicked "Going" without even looking at the date or location. She'd be there.

Chapter Eighteen

Harriet carried her big thermos with her through the school hallways. She never set it down, never forgot it in her car. The kids started to joke that there was something a little stronger than coffee in that thing, and she didn't correct them—they were right. Coffee could never make her feel this way, light and carefree. She smiled when they pointed at her, laughed when they laughed.

She even let Harold, the meathead Phys Ed teacher, flirt with her a bit. She didn't flirt back, but she let him talk.

"So, what are you doing this weekend?" he asked. They were alone in the teacher's lounge; there was nowhere to deflect his gaze.

PYRAMIDIA

Her plans consisted of visiting the farmers market, maybe picking up some fresh flowers for the cabin. She'd talk to Kelsey for a while, buy a few things, steer clear of Lucy's burning gaze. It was getting easier to do, avoiding her. She'd tried to save her, she told herself. She had extended a hand, tried to pull her from the polyester depths, but Lucy had lied, insisted she was making money off the schtick. It was easy ignoring her. Harriet's guilt had dissolved in the crimson liquid of Serenitea.

"Not sure," she said. "Maybe drive back home, see my folks."

"Oh," he said, disappointed.

"What about you?"

"My youngest has a meet," he said. "Gonna go to that."

His youngest? The man has kids? She scanned his fingers for a ring.

"I don't wear it," he said.

Harriet's face twitched. *The man can read minds?*

"The ring," he said. "I saw you looking. I don't wear it during the day because I don't want it to get messed up. I'm always spraying down mats with nasty chemicals, getting all sweaty. I don't want to hurt the metal."

"I didn't realize you were married."

He nodded. "Oh, yeah. Been married a long time."

She wasn't sure if this revelation made him all the

87

more gross or neutered him in a way, rendered him harmless. "Interesting," she said.

"Yeah, well, I gotta be going. Was nice talking to you. Enjoy your weekend," he said.

"Uh, you too."

Harold pulled himself up with a groan, swiped a banana from the fruit bowl near the door, and was gone. *How strange*, she thought. Bentwood was opening itself up to her. The more she relaxed, the more secrets she learned, it seemed.

She had one more class to get through before the weekend and she expected it would go well. The kids were listening now, joining in on conversations. The things they said weren't insightful at all—especially for "gifted" students—but it was better than sitting in silence. They called her Miss P. A nickname. She was beginning to belong.

Chapter Nineteen

The retreat was at Angela's house, a big, white soaring thing Harriet couldn't even conceive of living in. She sat outside in her car, staring up at the castle-like building. It was three stories tall and bordered by hedges sculpted by an artist's hand. The well-manicured lawn was a lush, deep green and made the neighbors' yards look brown and scorched in comparison.

Cars were parked in the driveway—nice ones in muted colors: Mercedes, Land Rovers, Porsches. Harriet didn't want to be seen in her red Ford, but she was scared to go in. She had never been anywhere quite so fancy and now her worn clothing seemed archaic, matronesque.

While she had taken wine to Lucy's failed affair, she hesitated to bring anything to this meeting. She had the distinct feeling anything she could offer wouldn't be good enough, would be too blasé.

She at last summoned the courage to approach the door. She rang the camera doorbell, jolting it to life. "Harriet!" It cooed. "Come on in!"

Taking a deep breath, she pushed open the wooden double-doors to find herself in an atrium with a set of marble stairs spilling down to meet her. "Hello?" she called, voice echoing.

There were bowls of white roses on either side of the staircase, and Harriet leaned in to smell them, to feel their soft petals against her nose. Then, the clicking of heels on stone. She pulled away from the flowers, embarrassed.

"I'm so glad you made it!" Angela said, appearing from a corridor to the right of the stairs. "We're all in the morning room, won't you join us?"

"Morning room?" Harriet asked.

Angela waved her hand. "All these old houses have them."

Harriet wanted to tell her that her own ancient house definitely did not have a morning room, or an afternoon or night room for that matter. "Oh," she said.

They walked through hallways lined with vases, paintings in gilded frames until they came to a light-filled room.

Harriet's mouth fell open when she saw the glass walls and vases bursting with more white roses and whispers of greenery. It was a beautiful place, a delicate quartz crystal growing from the back of the house. Stepping inside, Harriet felt a lightness buoy within her; she could breathe easier here, somehow. If she had a room like this, so perfect, so refined and jewel-like and alive, she would never leave. The sun danced through it all—a golden, wavering presence.

The women sat on antique fainting couches and velvet settees. They had been talking in quiet murmurs, like the rustling of leaves, but they fell silent when Harriet entered the room. They turned to look at her, and Harriet's skin prickled. She felt like a gazelle, stared down by lions.

"Hello," she whispered. "I'm Harriet."

"Our newest recruit," Angela said.

The women relaxed, allowed smiles to play across their plump, glossy lips.

"Do sit down," one with red, cascading hair said. "I'm Shannon."

Harriet nodded at her, sat on the ottoman at her feet.

"We're just waiting for Eliza now," Angela said. "Harriet, can I get you anything? Wine, *tea*?"

Harriet glanced around and saw that most everyone was sipping from dainty crystal. "Tea, please," she said, and the women nodded with approval.

Angela poured water from a brass kettle perched on a

cupboard, etched with intricate, ancient carvings. "We brew it extra strong for the retreats. Don't we, girls?"

A murmur of approval.

Angela offered her the delicate cup. "It makes me so happy that you're enjoying the tea, Harriet."

"Oh yes," she said. "It's, uh, immaculate." She tried the elaborate word on, found it didn't fit.

Angela smiled, amused. "I know you weren't thinking of selling, but you'd be a wonderful advocate. You're so passionate about the product."

Harriet shrugged. "I'm not sure I'd be good at it."

The doorbell rang, and Angela glanced at her phone. "It's Eliza," she said. She adjusted her neckline and then left the room in big, easy strides.

The remaining women burst into a frenzy, straightening pillows, smoothing their hair, their dresses. Harriet looked around in panic.

"Eliza is our mother," Shannon whispered. "The originator of our lines."

"What?" Harriet asked.

"We're all her descendants, each and every one of us." Shannon checked her makeup in the reflection of her phone screen.

Angela re-entered the room and the women stilled. She had someone on her arm. Harriet was struck by the long, white-gray hair, the gauzy white dress. Though her hair was

PYRAMIDIA

that of an older woman, her face was smooth, pristine. Harriet gasped. She'd never seen anyone so beautiful.

"Hello," Eliza said. "It's good to see you all again."

"Hello, Eliza," the women said in unison.

Harriet shivered.

Eliza's dark eyes found hers, narrowed a little. "I see we have a new consultant."

"Oh yes," Angela said. "This is Harriet. Harriet, this is Eliza. She's triple ascendant."

Harriet's face burned but she nodded at the woman. "Hello," she said. She had no idea what triple ascendant meant, but it sounded holy.

Guiding Eliza to a settee, Angela helped lower her down to the plush surface.

"Eliza has been triple ascendant for two years—she was the first consultant to reach it," Shannon said.

"Oh," Harriet whispered.

"She's not even a consultant anymore. When you get that high up in the organization, they call you an originator. A wellness originator," a woman with jet black hair said.

"It's amazing," a woman said.

"Phenomenal," another said.

Harriet took a huge swig of tea, choked a little.

Eliza studied a glittering ring on her hand. She seemed bored. "Shall we proceed?" she asked.

"Very well," Angela said, standing straighter, now that

93

Eliza was in the room. "Let's go to the dining room. It's all set up."

The women rose, and Harriet followed. They walked single file down the hallway until they found themselves in a dining room that had been cleared of its tables and chairs. Instead, a massage table dominated the middle of the room. Candles were burning, and the air smelled sweet and clean. Roses spilled from vases and bowls all around them, but Harriet's eyes were drawn to white chairs with holes in the seats. Spilling forth was a thick steam, casting everything in a hazy, cloud-like glow.

"It's beautiful," Harriet said, eyes wide.

"Thank you," Angela said. "I set it up last night."

"You always do such a marvelous job," a woman said, caressing Angela's elbow.

Angela smiled without showing her teeth. "I try."

Someone grabbed Harriet's arm and she jerked away. Shannon, hand still outstretched, frowned. "Angela, why don't you explain to Harriet what we do and why we do it."

"Oh, of course," Angela said. "You're such a natural fit, I keep forgetting this is your first time."

Harriet blushed. All eyes were on her.

"We focus on wellness at these retreats. After all, you can't be a wellness consultant if you're not well. So, we set up a spa area in whoever's house we're in. We've got facials, massage, and yoni steaming today. It changes." Angela waved her hand, nonchalant.

"Yoni steaming?" Harriet asked.

A quiet titter sprang from the women, cheeks flushed.

Angela remained composed. "Yes," she said. "It cleanses the womb."

"Oh," Harriet said, crimson red. "I see."

"I think Harriet should be the first to get a massage," said the dark-haired woman.

"Yes!" another cried.

"Eliza?" Angela asked. "Is this the way?"

Eliza shrugged. "Sure."

"Disrobe," Angela said, and the women began unbuttoning their blouses, pulling at the zippers on their dresses.

Harriet watched in horror as expensive clothing fell away to reveal supple flesh. "I—I don't know," she said.

"We're all sisters here," Angela said. Her body was smooth and toned. "Besides, we put on these gowns." Angela caressed a mound of white silk.

"I didn't shave." Harriet blushed. "I didn't know." Her heart was erratic, violent, and her head was floating up and away, detached from her shoulders.

Eliza stared at her, unwavering, pile of clothes at her feet. Her hip bones, sharp and prominent, threatened to slice Harriet open. Though Harriet guessed Eliza's age was considerable, her body was in much better condition than her own.

"I feel dizzy," Harriet said. "I need to sit down."

There were gentle hands on her elbows, guiding her into one of the yoni steaming chairs. She felt the hot steam dampening her pants. "Am I peeing?" she asked.

"No, not at all," Angela said. "You're alright."

Someone's cool palm caressed her cheek.

The room shimmered and danced. Harriet watched the bodies—clad in flowing silk—warble around through her tear-filled eyes. Her head, floating only minutes before, now felt leaden and heavy—a bowling ball she couldn't keep balanced on the thin stalk of her neck. "I don't feel good," she whispered.

"Should I get her some water?" someone asked.

"Tea," Angela said.

"N-no," Harriet stammered. "No tea."

"No tea?" a woman gasped.

"Too...tired," Harriet said.

Angela's teeth flashed before her—a hypnotic smile free of its fleshy confines. "I'm so daft," she said. Her words reverberated in Harriet's head, ricocheted off the walls of the dark tunnel of her mind. "I forgot she wasn't used to the strength. She's such a natural, it's easy to forget."

"A natural," someone echoed.

"She could be ascendant."

Faraway, a voice. "Ascendant."

Chapter Twenty

Harriet woke atop the massage table, a wreath of women hovering above her. The air was thick, palpable.

"See, she's okay," a voice said.

"Oh, thank goodness," another said.

Angela's blond hair brushed across her face. "Harriet? Can you hear me?"

"I think so." Harriet croaked. Her throat felt raw, full of razors.

A hand felt her forehead. "You passed out," Angela said.

"I was tired," she said. "Real tired." She tried to sit up, but someone held her down.

"Shh," they said. "Try not to move just yet."

"What happened?" Harriet asked.

Angela's face came back into focus. She laid a hand on Harriet's. "I'm so sorry, Harriet. I made the tea too strong. I'm so used to it that way. It's been so long since we've invited a new recruit to a retreat. I forgot."

"Not regulated by the FDA," she whispered.

Angela made a tutting sound. "Now that's got nothing to do with it." Her voice was gentle, but chiding. Motherly.

"The FDA is a scam." The woman with black hair hissed.

"Privately funded." Another added. "Special interest groups."

"Now now," Angela said. "You'll get Harriet worked up. Come, now. Let's try to sit up."

She felt their hands on her back, hoisting her to sitting. She grasped the edges of the table, woozy. "Where are my shoes?" she asked. She wiggled her bare toes, winced at the chipped polish.

The women looked at one another.

"Right here," Angela said. She held Harriet's dirty huaraches.

"My shoes..." She wanted to ask why they were off, but couldn't find the words. Her head was still buzzing.

"I'll help you put them on. Here." Shannon reached for the shoes. Angela let them go, let the red-headed woman strap them to Harriet's soles.

"I have to go," Harriet said, sliding off the table. Her

knees buckled.

Angela grabbed her arm, pulled her up. "I don't know," she said. "You still seem pretty weak. I'd hate for you to leave here and collapse."

"She should have a snack," a woman said.

"Low blood sugar," another said.

Harriet shook her head. "I have to go. I can't be here anymore."

Angela frowned, hurt.

"She should go," Eliza said. All heads turned to look at the matriarch. "She doesn't want to be here. She should go."

"But she's not strong enough," Angela said. "She might pass out again."

Eliza shrugged. "None of our business what she does."

"I'm sorry, Harriet. We'll do better next time, okay? I'm sorry." Angela guided Harriet, who stumbled and wobbled, a newborn fawn.

"It's alright," Harriet said. "I should have eaten first. I don't know." She clutched Angela's arm. Something in her stomach hurt and her clothes felt too small, not right.

"I'm sorry," Angela said. "That's not how I wanted it to go." They stood at the door, across from one another. Angela's forehead was anesthetized, but if it wasn't, it would have been furrowed in concern. "I'm sorry."

"Stop saying you're sorry. I should be the one apologizing. I ruined your party."

99

Angela patted her arm. "You didn't. We still have two hours left. Still lots of time."

"Two hours?" Harriet felt for her phone in her pocket, turned it on to check the time. Her heart thundered. "How long was I out?"

Angela opened the door, let the dark, humid world spill into her marble entryway. "Oh," she said. "I guess I don't know. Goodbye, now. Do message me when you've made it home."

Harriet held the phone to her chest. "Goodbye."

The door shut in her face.

Chapter Twenty-One

Harriet curled onto the couch, mug of tea teetering on the arm. She felt a desperate sadness. Mournful. She didn't want last night to have gone that way. She wanted to leave rejuvenated, reborn, befriended. Instead, she felt shameful. Foolish. If she'd been more prepared, less childish, maybe she wouldn't have fainted. She winced at her own awkwardness, her face burning and her body crumbling with inexplicable pain.

She replayed the strange retreat in her mind again and again—the crystalline room where the women gathered, the way they quietened when Eliza strode into the room. The swiftness with which they removed their clothing, letting it fall to the floor. Her mouth, stained red in the dirty bathroom mirror. She wondered what they thought of her, now that she'd revealed herself to be weak, unworthy, afraid.

Why had Angela made the tea so strong? Why hadn't Angela warned her? Anger boiled, pushing the shame aside for a moment. They didn't have the right to make her feel this way. *It was a hazing ritual—that had to be it.* She was right to be mad.

She made a silent vow to herself. She'd drink less tea. She'd keep her legs shaved.

She pulled her feet beneath her, shut her eyes. While the experience had been strange and demeaning, she still found the tea ladies so beautiful, so dignified—it was tempting to remain part of them, to pass out again and again just to get the chance to sit among them, to bask in their cold glow.

Her phone vibrated against her thigh.

She'd been added to a new group message.

Hi Harriet! Angela wrote. *I went ahead and added you to our consultant chat. Feel free to ask any questions here.*

Welcome, Harriet! Shannon wrote.

Has anyone not hit their goals for the month? Have a buyer interested if anyone needs some numbers. A woman named Georgiana wrote.

All good here. Angela replied. *Thanks though.*

Send her my way. Someone named Katherine. *That is, if no one else needs her.*

Harriet will need a few. Angela wrote.

I'm alright. Harriet wrote. Then, after a few moments of thought, she added: *Thank you for adding me.*

Harriet is a go-getter! She's going to get her numbers without any help! Shannon again.

:) Georgiana typed.

Harriet shut off her phone.

She was staring into nothingness, eyes unfocused and bleary, when there came a knock at the door. It startled her and she made a little yelp. "Who is it?" she called.

The knocking continued, stern, persistent.

The image of a tea lady, swathed in white—or perhaps nothing at all—banging at the other side of her door, sent a shiver through her spine. Had they noticed she'd stopped participating in the group chat and were here to force her to read? They'd always had an uncanny way of knowing just when to pop up, to send a friend request or a message—it was like they were watching, omnipresent.

Harriet squinted out the window, into the forest. There was nothing there. Just crooked limbs and darkness. She felt like an animal caught in a snare, hunkering down while a man approached with a sharp glint in his eye.

"Harriet!" Lucy cried. "Are you in there?"

Harriet breathed a sigh of partial relief. She was free from the tea ladies for now, but then there was Lucy to contend with. She was weak, drained by her tormented musings.

Getting off the couch and approaching the door was a Herculean task; facing Lucy would be even more arduous.

She opened the door, not caring if Lucy—in her technicolor nightmare coat—saw her in her pajamas, hair frizzled and askew, mouth scarlet. "Lucy," she said.

Lucy looked just as unkempt—there were leaves in her hair and mud on her uncharacteristically subdued leggings. "Oh, I'm so glad you're okay," she said between breaths. She fell against Harriet, enveloping her in a smothering hug.

Harriet patted her back, smelled moss and dampness on her hair. "Why wouldn't I be okay?" she asked, extricating herself from Lucy's embrace.

"I don't know," Lucy said. "I just had a feeling you were in trouble."

"A feeling?" Harriet asked. "What?"

"A vision." Lucy confessed.

"A vision!" Harriet said.

Lucy's cheeks reddened. "Maybe I'm a little psychic."

Harriet wanted to laugh, to scoff. A woman possessing any clairvoyance at all would never involve herself in a doomed enterprise like Mary Jane. A psychic woman would be sage, elegant. She'd be dignified. "That's very interesting," she said.

"I knew you were with *them* and I was worried, is all. I know what they do."

"I'm perfectly fine," Harriet said, even though she

wasn't. "In fact, I'm quite reinvigorated and refreshed. Revitalized."

"You—you didn't seem fine when you left, is all. You were stumbling. You were…" Lucy looked down at her feet. She wore, of all things, fabric Mary Janes printed with music notes. They were streaked with mud.

"Lucy," Harriet said. "Why are you covered in twigs and dirt?"

"I'm not sure," Lucy said to her toes.

Harriet closed her eyes for a moment, considering what to say next. "Have you been following me?"

Lucy rubbed her neck. "I've—I've been keeping an eye on you. You don't understand."

"I do understand. You've been stalking me." Harriet burned with rage, with disbelief. She'd been so distracted by her nervousness, her confusion, she hadn't noticed Lucy lurking in the bushes. It wasn't like her to be taken this way, to let something pass her by, unseen. Maybe she had considered herself a little bit psychic, too.

"Not stalking!" Lucy cried. "Watching out for you, is all. Those women—they're not women."

"Lucy, I need you to leave now."

"I'm trying to warn you. You don't see it? You don't see what they do?"

"If you don't leave now, this very moment, I'm calling the cops." Harriet took a step forward, forcing Lucy to back up.

"Listen," Lucy said. "They're not a normal company."

"Yeah, yeah. They're a pyramid scheme. So you've said. Go, Lucy. I'm giving you a chance before I call the police. Take it."

Tears poured down Lucy's face. "I'm just trying to help."

"Go," Harriet said.

And Lucy ran, spilling brochures and business cards from her folds. They tossed in the wind, pages fluttering.

Chapter Twenty-Two

She'd told Lucy she was fine. She told herself she'd drink less tea. Both of those things were lies. She paced, waiting for the water to heat up.

The truth was that Harriet was feeling cored out, hollow. Something had been taken. First, the retreat had gone badly. She made a fool of herself, passing out in front of all those gorgeous, poised women. And she woke up with the sense that something was amiss; her shoes were off, her body felt swollen and heavy and not at all hers. Too much time had passed—almost an hour spent in darkness. Then Lucy had been lurking around the whole time. It had been a violating twenty-four hours. She wished she could lie back down on the couch, take a nap, but her brain was racing and her body felt electrified. She didn't feel safe.

The tea would help. The tea would wrap all the sharp, broken edges of her psyche in woolly batting.

She bobbed the sachet up and down in the water. Ripples of red spread within. It was beautiful. It was soothing. She waited for it to steep, darken into the ruby red she so adored.

Lucy had been so panicked, so adamant that something was wrong. Harriet rubbed the side of her jaw. "*Those women—they're not women.*" What a line spoken from a person whose femininity came swathed in polyester. What had she meant by that? She was jealous—that had to be it. Serenitea had stolen away Lucy's downline, leaving her dry. She couldn't stand Harriet participating in their successful events while her own inelegant parties went ignored.

What a sore loser.

Harriet reached for the teabag string, but stopped herself. Perhaps she could simulate the effect she'd experienced at Angela's house if she let it steep a little more, grow even stronger. While she didn't want to pass out again, she did—in some distant corner of her mind—want to know what happened. If she could replicate it, she could avoid it next time. Easy. She had gotten all A's on all her science fair projects as a kid. She could do a simple experiment like this.

She flicked through her phone while she waited.

A message from Lucy. *I'm so sorry I frightened you.*

Please forgive me :(We really do need to talk, tho. Something's wrong.

Something was wrong, alright, and it was the sender of the message. Harriet pressed "Delete" and then paged to Lucy's profile page and pressed "Block." *There. That was easy.* She felt lighter, a bit less frazzled.

She busied herself, wiping the kitchen counters clean and opening and shutting random cabinets. Since she'd mostly unpacked, the dead lady's objects had faded into the distance, pushed back into the corners of drawers and closets, and it wasn't so bad. There was still the pantry full of jars, too many to hide, but maybe Mr. Morrison would take those away, put them in his own home, wherever that was. She wondered why the landlord hadn't moved back in to his mother's place when she passed if he was so invested in the place. He was a weirdo.

It was getting dark, but Harriet refused to turn on any lights. If she stayed in gloom, no one could see in. She doubted Lucy was still lurking in the underbrush, but wasn't taking any chances.

She picked up the mug, felt the water had turned cold. *Oh well. Nothing wrong with iced tea.* She took a swig, found it a bit more bitter than normal, but otherwise palatable. Next time she'd add some honey. She drained the glass.

Back on the couch, she propped her laptop up on a pillow and put on an old cartoon. The laptop screen illuminated her face, colors flashing and dancing across her skin.

She yawned. The world was evening out, sounds farther away. The darkness beyond the edge of the laptop deepened into a purple bruise. She was tired, sedated, but found herself nowhere near the groggy sickness she'd felt at Angela's. The yoni steaming pots were puffing their hot breaths into the air, she hadn't eaten in anticipation of some sort of charcuterie spread. There wasn't anything to worry about. She shut her eyes.

She woke because it was quiet. Her cartoon had ended, the screen dark. Dead. Closed the laptop lid, set it on the floor.

Harriet checked her phone—two a.m. Had she been sleeping that long? She sat up, stretched. Needed to use the bathroom before settling back in for the rest of the night. She put her phone on the charger and lurched up.

She peed, squinting at the toilet paper roll she'd been too lazy to put in the holder. Her eyes hurt from the lights in the bathroom. She should have never turned them on. She could pee in the dark, it was one of her special talents. But now, inching back through the dark living room, she had trouble seeing, rammed her knee into the end table. "Fuck." She spat.

"Fuck." A voice echoed, small and far away.

Harriet drew her arms to her chest. Her insides were a vacuum, an endless pit. She was screaming.

Light flashed in the window, white skin on black glass. She turned as the figure turned. They faced one another. Her reflection, shaking and scared.

"Jesus," she said, and listened for a reply, for repetition. None came.

She sighed, plopped down on the couch and her reflection did the same. She'd been hearing things, still half asleep. She buried her face in her hands, wasn't watching to see her reflection cock its head and smile.

Chapter Twenty-Three

The kids were paired off, making movie-style posters for *1984*. Markers squeaked against thick cardstock, and Harriet looked at her phone beneath the table.

One missed call from Mr. Morrison and an accompanying voicemail, likely about the overdue rent. She swiped the notifications away, clicked on Facebook Messenger.

Harriet, you haven't met your sales goals.

I never said I wanted to sell. She typed.

You're going to lose your access. Angela wrote.

Access? she replied. She looked up, made sure none of the kids were watching. *You said I didn't have to sell.*

There was a pause while Angela typed. Harriet picked

up her big thermos, two tea strings pinned beneath the lid, and swirled it about.

If you don't meet your goals, you'll lose your access to the website. Not only will you not be able to buy, you'll miss out on the daily wellness tips, leaderboard, and forum. You don't want to lose that! Also, you won't be able to come to any more retreats. Don't you want to come to more?

Harriet didn't respond. She watched Calvin draw a circle on the page before him, perfect and symmetrical. He made it look easy.

Harriet, I'm going to be honest with you. Angela typed. *I'm counting on you. I need every descendant to meet their goals this month—our wellness circle needs to qualify for the cruise and we're nowhere close. Please? I need you.*

Wellness circle—Harriet bristled at the words. Descendant. These MLMs—"Multi-level Marketing" companies— and their stupid, ornamental wording. She took a sip of her tea, took a deep breath. "How's everyone doing?" she asked the room. No one looked up.

I'm ordering my own tea from my page. Doesn't that count? She wrote. She'd spent $300 on tea this month, that had to mean something.

It does a little. Angela wrote. *But we need more. I know you'd be an excellent salesperson. One of the best. Just give it a chance.*

Harriet chewed her bottom lip. She didn't want to sell.

113

It was bad enough she was hooked on the stuff, funneling money into an MLM—a business model she always detested. The retreat, the many, many cups of tea, the membership she purchased to get the discount—the only person hurt by these things was herself. But to sell the stuff, to bring a new person into the fold, was to invite harm upon someone else. She knew it wasn't healthy, wasn't moral, to be drinking the tea, but all of that was a quandary to be stuffed deep within herself to be examined on some distant, sleepless night. Selling was urgent. Selling was now.

She tapped the screen. *I really don't want to. I'm sorry. Besides, I don't know anyone. I'm not exaggerating.* Who would she sell to? Lucy was out of the question. She was against Serenitea to the core—and a stalker. Mr. Morrison only ate food he himself harvested from the earth. She figured Harold as an energy drink only guy. She could leave a sales form in the teacher's lounge, but that was humiliating in a way she didn't want to think about. And that left Kelsey. Kelsey was nice, she'd buy some out of pity, but Harriet didn't want her to know how deep she'd fallen into the pyramid scheme. It made her look stupid, she decided. She wouldn't sell.

I can refer some customers your way. Angela wrote. *People I've been working on for a while. They might be ripe to convert to consultants, which would really give you a boost. Don't you want to make some connections?*

Harriet frowned. She didn't want to make connections. She wanted to curl into herself until there was nothing left. She wanted to be alone. *No.* She typed.

Angela didn't respond right away. Harriet was left to stare at her phone screen in tense agony. Someone sneezed.

At last, her phone vibrated in her hands. *Then I might as well deactivate your account now. Save us some time.*

Harriet felt her face growing hot. *What do you mean? You're cutting me off?*

I didn't want it to come to this, Harriet. But if you're not going to support us, you're on your own.

Her chest hurt, her hands trembled. She was losing control. She took a gulping drink of the tepid tea, choked.

"Ms. Pendleton, are you alright?" a girl asked. The children looked up from their posters.

"I'm fine." Harriet gasped. She dragged a hand over her face. Was she fine? She was losing the only thing that brought some stability to her life. Without the tea, she'd be a frazzled mess, sitting at home in a hot room, surrounded by moving boxes and poltergeists. She wouldn't be able to handle the frustration of class, the annoyance of Harold and Lucy and Mr. Morrison. She'd fall apart. She considered what to say to Angela.

I've been very supportive of the team thus far. I joined your downline and have been buying religiously. I've spent real money on this. I don't know why I'm being treated this way. She wrote, then deleted. She squeezed her hand shut, popped a few joints on her fingers, and tried again. *Go ahead.* She typed. *Delete me.* Her finger hovered above the send button, then moved to the backspace and her message disappeared.

She ground her teeth together until her jaw throbbed. Sleepless nights, the smell of woodsmoke and rot, figures dancing through the woods. She needed something to drown that out, something to numb her raw, aching nerves.

What do you need me to do? She sent.

The reply came in moments. *Man the booth Saturday. Get there early. Wear white.*

She shut her eyes and thought of Lucy's table, alone and abandoned, the sun beating down on all that garish cloth. She thought of Kelsey's warm, worn hands. She didn't want to be seen behind the tea ladies' table, didn't want to be seen at all.

Okay. She wrote. *I'll be there.*

Chapter Twenty-Four

Her face hurt from smiling, and all the talking was making her mouth dry. She needed a bathroom break, but was too nervous to turn to the other women—women she barely knew—and tell them she was leaving their stall. They were meant to work together, to smile and gesture and pour hot water from carafes into crystal clear mugs, then into paper shot glasses. They were sirens, those three, draped in white. And they beckoned the farmers, the mothers, the other stall-keepers to their table, gave them the succulent drink and business cards and set them free again, having ensnared them for a time.

They'd sold a few boxes of the stuff, but they'd passed

out almost all of their brochures and cards.

"Most of our success stories happen online," Elaine said. "It's easier to connect with people on a soul-to-soul level when they're not being rushed." Elaine had voluminous black hair and wore a dress reminiscent of a Grecian goddess. If she were anyone else, she'd look like she was playing dress up, had worn her Halloween costume out of season. But she carried it with poise and grace and it suited her.

"Um," Harriet said, taken aback by the glossy, promotional language. "I see."

"You'll get a bunch of messages tonight. When the buzz wears off and the world creeps back in. Keep an eye on your inbox," Shannon said.

Harriet picked at her own white garment—a simple sundress on which she'd already dripped the red tea. She covered the crimson spot with her hand, embarrassed. "Can I forward them to you two? I don't know if I have time."

Shannon looked at her. "It only takes a few minutes to change someone's life. Besides, Angela asked that we work with you to grow your customer base and descendants."

"I don't want descendants."

"You don't want to be ascendant?"

She thought about Eliza, cold as stone. "No."

"Send them your link, that's all you have to do," Elaine said.

"You can put your link in your profile," Shannon said.

"That way people will see it right away when they look you up."

"Oh that's smart." Elaine nodded.

Harriet sighed. Her current profile read "Educator, bookworm, lifelong learner". Three curated phrases she'd pondered for over an hour. She'd tried different variations, different word orders, but that one had stuck. She didn't want to replace her hard work with a link to buy tea, didn't want the tea to be the first thing people knew her for. She shook her head. "I never wanted to join at all. In fact, I'm here against my own will."

Elaine and Shannon shared a silent look.

"Listen…" Elaine began. "Every small business owner goes through hardships. But you can't quit. You can't give up."

Harriet did a shot of the sample tea.

"That's so true." Shannon nodded her head with enthusiasm.

"Harriet, we welcomed you into our wellness circle so that you might become more well."

"I'm well." She snapped, wiping red liquid from her lips with the back of her hand.

"No, you're not. Until you experience true serenity, you're very *un*well."

"Very unwell." Shannon echoed.

Harriet stared at Lucy's empty booth on the other side of the parking lot. She hadn't shown today. Harriet couldn't decide if that was a good thing or not.

A man approached, and the women dropped their looks of concern. Smiles unfurled across their faces.

"Hello," Shannon said. "Won't you try some of our tea? It's a holistic blend guaranteed to promote wellness. And it tastes great too."

"Sure, why not." The man smiled. Harriet watched his eyes skim over Shannon's body.

Elaine poured him a swallow's worth and he gulped it down with a wink. "That is good," he said. "Do you ladies make this stuff?"

"We're wellness consultants," Shannon said. "Chosen to promote the brand."

"Oh?" The man's brow furrowed.

"You know what? Wouldn't he make a great consultant, girls?"

"Oh yes," Elaine said. "He's got a beautiful glow about him, the epitome of wellness."

"Uh..." Harriet eyed the belly hanging over the man's belt.

"Take this brochure," Shannon said. "My phone number's on the back." She winked.

"Don't mind if I do," he said. "You ladies have a nice day now." He crushed the paper cup in his fist as he walked away.

Harriet turned to Shannon. "Men? Do men sign up

as consultants?" She thought of the naked women in Angela's dining room, their vulnerability, their steamed yonis.

"Sometimes." Shannon shrugged. "We don't discriminate. Most of the time they just support their wives as they embark on their wellness journeys, but if a man wanted to sign up on his own, we wouldn't stop him."

"But the retreats," Harriet said.

"Oh no, we never invite men there," Elaine said, panicked. "The retreats are for a select group of consultants, hand chosen."

"It's very elite," Shannon said.

"But I went," Harriet said. "I was there."

"I know. I was very surprised by that. Angela must have seen something special in you."

"I was surprised too. No offense, but we haven't had a new consultant at a retreat in ages. That's why I'm so confused," Elaine said.

"I'm confused too," Shannon said. "Someone as special as you, and you don't want to be ascendant?"

"Angela is basically handing you the key to success and you won't take it," Elaine said.

"She brought you to Eliza," Shannon said.

"She did," Elaine said.

They stood in silence. Harriet looked at her toes.

"Harriet?"

Her stomach did a flip. She looked up, saw sunshine

and golden hair. "Kelsey."

"I didn't know you, uh, sold this stuff," she said.

"Would you like a sample? It's a holistic blend guaranteed to promote wellness. And it tastes great too," Elaine said.

Kelsey shook her head. "Harriet, are you alright? You look pale."

Harriet choked down a sob. She wanted to jump across the table, pull Kelsey away to safety. She wasn't alright. She was miserable. Standing there in the hot sun while these women cajoled her, demeaned her. She opened her mouth to speak, but Shannon beat her to it.

"It's this heat," Shannon said. "So hot for early fall, don't you think?"

Kelsey shrugged, looked Harriet up and down. "Okay," she said, voice halting and tentative. "I have a cooler with waters in it, if you need something cold to drink."

"She's fine," Elaine said.

"Harriet?" Kelsey asked.

Harriet gave a small nod, looked at the ground again.

"Okay, then. You know where I am," Kelsey said.

A hot tear fell on Harriet's big toe.

Chapter Twenty-Five

Her phone beeped and buzzed, text after text lighting up her screen. Shannon was right—people were contacting her now that the farmers market was over, desperate to get their hands on the stuff.

She took a deep breath and began reading.

Hi. One wrote. *You don't know me but I got your business card at the market today, and I was wondering how I can go about buying some of your tea.*

Three boxes. Another wrote.

How do I order tea?

Hello?

Harriet copied her link from her Serenitea account

and pasted it in response to each message. *Thanks for inquiring,* she replied. *You can get a discount if you apply to be a wellness consultant.* Serenitea offered pre-written responses to share, but they all sounded too stilted, somewhat offensive in their distance. Her hands trembled as she typed. It felt so dirty. It felt so wrong.

Her phone chimed—new emails coming in.

Congratulations! You made your first sale via the online gateway!

Congratulations! You made a sale via the online gateway!

Congratulations! You made a sale via the online gateway!

Congratulations! You have a new descendant.

Harriet threw her phone onto the couch cushion, covered her face with her hands. A descendant? She was ascending. She didn't want to ascend. This was going too fast.

Her phone rang.

"Hello?" she asked, picking up the device.

"Harriet! I'm so happy for you!" It was Angela.

"Um, I made some sales. Can I stop now?"

There was silence on the other end.

"How many do I need?"

"As many as you can get," Angela said. "All of them."

"All of them?"

"We need to make our goals," Angela said.

"Which are?"

Angela sighed. "Well, there are monthly bonuses and

then there's the cruise. Didn't you read this in your onboarding materials?"

"Um, I guess I didn't read those." Harriet admitted.

"Well, never mind that. I was calling to congratulate you. Have you looked at your sales portal?"

"Portal?" Harriet imagined herself falling into the phone screen, swimming in some dark and glassy ether.

"It should say how much you've earned so far."

Harriet opened her laptop, clicked around on the Serenitea homepage. "Oh, I think I found it," she said. "It's on my profile."

"Yes," Angela said.

"Holy shit," Harriet said.

"Right?" Angela said.

Harriet had made $100. It was right there on the screen in big, gold font. "Is this real?" she asked.

"You'll get it next Monday," Angela said.

"What's the catch?" Harriet asked. "Other than moral bankruptcy?"

Angela paused for a moment, then spoke. "There is no catch. Just pay your dues on time and keep at it. The more consultants descendant from you, the more you'll make."

"Dues?"

"Yes. There's a quarterly fee to keep selling. You really should have read the onboarding."

"Well, I didn't. So there's that," Harriet said.

Harriet could hear Angela swallowing. "Anyway, I have a gift for you. Come to our next meeting."

She wrapped her free arm around her midsection, hugging herself tight. The thought of going to another Sereni-tea event made her stomach turn. "I don't really want to come to another retreat just yet," she said. She still wasn't feeling quite right after the last one.

"Oh, no. This isn't a retreat. This is a meeting to discuss marketing and sales. No big deal."

Harriet shut her eyes. A meeting sounded more manageable than a retreat, but she was still hesitant—embarrassed, humiliated. To stand in front of all those women again would be difficult, and she was well aware she was tunneling her way further into the pyramid's core, unforgivable. But there was a present waiting for her there. Despite the agony and shame, she was curious to know what the tea ladies thought she should have. And what was the alternative? Sitting alone, grading papers? "Where is it? When is it?"

"Wednesday at Georgiana's. I'll send you the details."

"Okay," she said.

Her phone vibrated against her ear. She held it away, read the screen. *Congratulations. You have a new descendant!*

Chapter Twenty-Six

Sunday was a blur. She'd turned off notifications on her phone, unwilling to read another congratulatory message. School on Monday was a welcome respite and she woke early, did her hair as best she could.

She was standing at the smart board, drawing a diagram with the stylus, when the bell rang. She'd lost track of time. "Well, I guess we'll come back to this tomorrow," she said, as the students filtered out of the room.

"I didn't get to copy it down all the way," a girl said. She never spoke, never raised her hand.

"That's okay," Harriet said. "I'll do it over tomorrow." Harriet clicked the button to erase the board and began shoving her notebooks, laptop, and pens into her bag.

"Um, Ms. Pendleton," the girl said.

"Yes?"

"My mom met you at the farmers market?" she said, the sentence more of a question than a statement.

Harriet's stomach dropped and she studied the girl. Mousy brown hair, a spattering of freckles across the bridge of her nose, thick pink glasses with scratched lenses. Her mother could have been any one of the countless women she'd encountered on Saturday. "Oh," Harriet said.

"She was really surprised to see you there," she said.

Harriet slung the bag over her shoulder, ready to make her escape. "And why's that?"

The little girl twirled her hair with her finger. "She just thinks you have enough on your plate as a teacher."

"Yeah, well..." Harriet began, defensive. Who was she to question her motives, her use of free time? Had this woman any idea of how monotonous, how boring and lonely being her child's teacher was? She opened her mouth, prepared to strike a low blow, but hesitated. The little girl's eyes were wide, unblinking. "What's your mother's name?"

"Anna," the girl said. "I have to go now." She scampered up, piled her books together.

"I can write you a note." Harriet offered.

"It's okay," she said. She spun around, speed walked through the door.

"No running!" Harriet called, even though the girl wasn't running, wasn't even going that fast. It just felt good to yell.

She followed the girl out of the room and made toward the library. Finding a quiet nook, she slid the laptop back out of her bag and tapped it to life. She looked around, making sure no one could see her screen. No one seemed to pay her any mind. She opened a new tab on her browser and summoned the Serenitea page into being.

Congratulations! It read across the top. She scrolled down, found the sales history she was looking for.

A list of names, contact information, and payments populated the page. It took up half the laptop screen and it surprised Harriet. She'd sold a lot of Serenitea. Enough to cover her own supply for the month. She'd still be in the hole after her dues and the initial cost of signing up, but it was intriguing, nonetheless.

"Stop it," she whispered to herself. A boy looked her way, and she slunk down further in her seat. She didn't want to feel excited about how much she'd earned. She wanted to feel disgusted, above it all. She didn't want to lure people in. She just wanted to drink tea. Still, it was nice to be reimbursed. She shook her head, zoomed in on the list.

"Rachel, Morgan, Sarah." She mouthed as she read. At last she came to it. "Anna. Ha, got you," she said. This time more than the boy turned and stared.

She copied the woman's email address into her notes. She'd have a word with Anna tonight.

Hello, Mrs. Nevins. She typed, fingers breezing over the keyboard. *Thank you so much for your recent purchase.* Harriet smiled, chewed the wooden stick of a long-gone popsicle. *I hope you enjoy the tea. I was wondering, though, since you seem to have time to talk shit about me.* She wrote, then backspaced.

She thought for a moment, then continued. *I was wondering if, since you seem to be curious about my free time, you might be open to learning more about the ways selling Serenitea can enrich your life.*

Harriet almost laughed.

Of course, the extra money is always nice and I couldn't help but notice that your daughter is in need of new glasses. Harriet was proud of this line—hit them where it hurts. *Always available for a little chat! Your wellness consultant, Harriet Pendleton.*

She clicked send and slammed her laptop lid shut. *Fuck that lady.* Harriet was sure the woman would be offended, would never reply, might even send her poor, unsuspecting daughter in with more snide remarks, but that was okay. Harriet could handle them. She ripped open a new box of tea.

Maybe she should have been nicer, tried in earnest to recruit the woman. She could have used her, sucked her dry, reduced her to whatever low state she thought Harriet was in. She shrugged, filled a mug with water.

Checking her email was a compulsion by now, and she did so while the water microwaved, pulling the existing emails down, willing a new one to spawn. One appeared and she felt a moment of delight, a brief rush, before realizing the email was from Anna. She tapped it.

I don't have a daughter. It read. *I'm very confused.*

"Shit," Harriet said. She pressed "Reply," began typing a rambling apology, but the microwave chimed, and she turned off the phone's screen. She had accosted the wrong person. The real Anna, wherever she may be, hadn't bought anything from her. Even Serenitea couldn't bury away her vindictiveness, her jealousy. She wondered how much of herself she'd have to lose in order to be well.

Harriet frowned as she bobbed the tea bag in the steaming water.

Chapter Twenty-Seven

Georgiana's house wasn't as big as Angela's, but it was modern and sleek—all cold metal and glass. Harriet was ushered down into the basement (finished, of course) and found the rest of the tea ladies seated around a large table. The lights were low, dramatic, and each lady's face was lit by their respective phone screens.

"You have a conference table in your house?" Harriet asked.

Georgiana, a petite woman in tailored pants, shrugged. "My husband," she said. "He needs it for his meetings."

Harriet nodded, unsure of what sort of work warranted a room this moody, this big.

"We usually have our meetings here," Shannon said.

"It makes the most sense, with so many of us," Elaine said.

Harriet looked around the room and shivered. Though the ladies were clothed, she couldn't help but remember what they had looked like naked—an apricot mass shimmering through the yoni pot steam. Harriet pulled at the collar of her shirt.

"Here's a seat for you," Georgiana said. She tapped the back of a rolling chair, and Harriet fell into it.

"Where's Eliza?" Harriet asked.

The women looked at one another.

"Eliza doesn't come to these," Angela said. "She's triple ascendant."

Harriet was relieved—something about the older woman frightened her, or perhaps it was just the way the ladies groveled in her presence. She still wasn't sure what "triple ascendant" meant, or why it meant you didn't have to come to meetings, but Harriet was glad for it.

"Can I get you anything, Harriet? Tea?" Georgiana stood near the door, ready to fetch whatever Harriet required.

A few women had translucent cups and saucers before them, some already drained with lipstick marring the rims, but Harriet shook her head. "I'm fine," she said. "Thank you, though."

Georgiana looked to Angela, and Angela nodded.

Harriet studied their faces, annoyed at this unspoken communication.

"Let's get started, then," Angela said.

Georgiana sat next to Harriet and pulled a miniature pad of paper from her pocket. There was a tiny, silver pen attached. It was a ridiculous thing, an antiquated thing, something Harriet would lose straight away. She felt jealous and a little off kilter—she hadn't brought anything to take notes on. Did she want to take notes? What could they possibly talk about that needed note taking? Sell more tea, grow the base of the pyramid. That was the gist of it, right?

"Before we begin, I just wanted to welcome Harriet and introduce her if you missed the last wellness retreat. Harriet?" Angela stared at her, expectant.

What did she want her to do? Harriet forced a smile, nodded at the women.

"Say something about yourself." Georgiana prodded.

"Uhh…" Harriet began. These women had already seen her at her most vulnerable, sweating and fainting and near death. Why did they want fun facts? "I teach Gifted Ed at the middle school. I've just moved to Bentwood over the summer." *My house is haunted, I'm addicted to a pyramid scheme tea, I'm being stalked by a crazed Mary Jane consultant.* Her fake smile hurt her cheeks.

"Calvin is in her class," Angela said, smiling. "He loves it, by the way."

PYRAMIDIA

"Oh. Thank you," Harriet said, caught off guard by the pride she felt. It was touching, in a way, that this dignified woman would trust Harriet with her child. Her fake smile eased, loosened into something more natural.

"That has to be rewarding," a woman across the table said.

Harriet was unsure if she was referring to the job or the compliment. "It is," she said.

"We're lucky to have you," Angela said.

"I'm, um, happy to be here."

"Why don't you start, Harriet? Tell us about your accomplishments this week, sales and recruits, and any challenges you faced."

Harriet looked around the room. Every eye was on her. "Well…" She began, voice shaky. "I guess going to the market really did some good. I got a ton of sales online after, and even some sign ups."

There came a pleased murmur, some scattered applause.

"Harriet's going to be ascendant in no time, isn't she, girls?" Angela asked.

"Record time, if she keeps this up," Elaine said.

"She did great at the market. A real natural," Shannon said.

"Oh, well," Harriet said, face red. She had been petulant and argumentative at the market, but she didn't mind this

135

version of events.

"We have a goal for you, Harriet. Something to strive for." Angela smiled at her from across the table, teeth white and sharp.

"I don't know," Harriet said. "I kind of wanted to do this casually? I like things as they are."

Angela blinked twice. "I understand that. But this goal won't be that hard. We're looking to bring a new consultant into our group."

"A few people signed up under me." Harriet blurted. "I got a few."

Angela waved her hand, wiping her words away mid-air. "And that's great," she said, "but we're looking for a very specific type of person. We don't invite just anyone to our wellness circle, you know. These meetings, the retreat. They're special."

The women around her fidgeted, sighed.

"What are you looking for, then?" Harriet asked, curious to know what qualities brought one into the hallowed halls.

"We need someone young, someone exuberant. Someone to breathe some life into this group. You're the brains, Harriet, but you need to bring us some bubble."

The women tittered.

"Bubble! That's so good, Angela," Shannon said.

"The perfect way to put it," Georgiana said.

Harriet picked at the skin on her arm. She didn't know all that many people, and she didn't associate with anyone who could be described as bubbly, but there was one figure with bizarre clothing, dancing though her mind. "I don't know," she said, sighing.

Angela shrugged. "You can do it. I know you can."

Harriet looked away, studied Georgiana's hands.

"We got you something," Angela said. She ducked, rustled with something beneath the table.

"You're gonna love it," Elaine said.

Angela brought up a box wrapped in white paper with a neat, golden ribbon on top. The women passed it from hand to hand until it sat before Harriet.

"Go ahead, open it," Angela said.

Harriet looked around the room, saw white teeth shining in the dim light. "Uh, thank you," she said as she began to tear at the paper. She struggled to keep the torn wrapping looking neat. She didn't want to just rip it apart like an animal.

After much picking and pulling, she uncovered a sturdy cardboard box. She unfolded the top and reached inside, felt something cool and bulbous.

She raised the kettle out of the box. Someone took a picture, the flash ricocheting off the white enameled surface.

"Well, do you like it?"

Chapter Twenty-Eight

She sat in the quiet dark, playing with her phone. New notifications kept popping up at the top of her screen, but she swiped them away. Between the Serenitea group chat and order reports, there were a lot of them. But scrolling through Facebook was all she wanted to do. She breezed past pictures of her cousins, a photo of her mom in her nurse's scrubs, results from those stupid quizzes that mine your data in return for a comparison to one of the seven dwarfs, and ads. It was mind numbing, but it was addictive too. She refreshed her feed, hoping for something new.

When nothing interesting loaded, she stood, stretched a bit. She was feeling a tad more comfortable in the cabin, now that she'd tacked blankets over the windows. It didn't look great—the blankets were mismatched, some with prints, some fleecy and long enough to puddle on the floor. But it was better than yelping every time she saw her reflection, so sure someone was hiding among the crooked trees.

She'd have to take the blankets down if she knew the landlord was going to be stopping by. She wasn't letting the outside in, she knew, and that would make mother very upset. She ran her hands along her bare arms, feeling the goosebumps there despite the heat. Was she angering the ghosts by sealing up the windows? Harriet eyed the corners of the room, waited for something to move, to rattle. Nothing. At the very least, she hadn't angered Mr. Morrison yet. She'd mailed her rent check on time, avoiding an in-person interaction and draining her bank account.

The truth was, she was burning through money fast. Though she was making decent money at school, and had reaped a couple hundred bucks from Serenitea, she wasn't able to keep up with both rent and the tea. She was drinking a box every three days. It was worth it, though, to feel this serene, this calm. A few years back, she'd been prescribed some anti-anxiety medication, some antidepressants, and all they had ever done was make her face break out. The tea was better— the only side effect a glaring lack of money.

She'd have to sell more. Recruit more. There was no other way out of this. She could call her parents, ask for help, but that was more humiliating than shilling pyramid scheme tea. At this point, she didn't even care about her status in life, her reputation. Maybe she could stoop to selling, after all.

Harriet walked from blanketed window to blanketed window, peeking behind the makeshift curtains. It was gloomy out there—the panes were speckled with rain. That was good. *Lucy would never let herself get soaked*, she thought. She'd melt, pink and blue cotton candy.

She spat out a puff of air. Lucy had been scared the last time they'd talked. Harriet threatened her with the law. The windows were covered. There was no reason to think the woman was still stalking her. And yet she couldn't shake that feeling of being watched.

She leaned her head on the greasy wall, breathed in the sour scent of cooking oil and smoke. Her heart was racing and she put one hand on her breast. She was hyper-aware of the slightest exertion now, the faintest of jitters. When your baseline is deathly quiet, it's easy to hear the mildest noise.

She needed tea.

The kettle was still in the box, and she tore it back open, exposing the gleaming hull. It was an elegant thing, utilitarian yet beautiful, and it looked so goddamned out of place in her brown and musty home that she giggled.

Harriet rinsed the kettle out with warm water, not bothering to add soap or scrub it. It was probably fine. Besides, she'd been guzzling unregulated tea—what were a few germs, a few hard metals? She filled it with cool water and set it on the stove.

Chapter Twenty-Nine

Harriet checked the mail once a week, never expecting to receive anything. The mailbox was at the end of her long driveway, facing town, and she always felt vulnerable and exposed when she burst from the woods to swing open the box. It was awkward and she avoided it.

But she'd gotten a text from her mother—she sent something, a surprise. So she'd been checking the mailbox almost daily, waiting to see just what it was her mother had mailed. Most days the mailbox sat empty, a dark maw into which she stuck her hand, felt for paper. Somedays there was an ad. On this day there was mail.

Her heart leaped at seeing her mother's handwriting scrawled across the creamy envelope. She hadn't realized how much she missed her parents until that moment, and she vowed to go visit them soon. It might be nice to leave Bentwood behind for a few days, forget about Serenitea and stalkers and ghosts.

Beneath the letter from her mother was another envelope, this one crinkled and stained. Big, sloppy letters spelled out her name there, indented the paper with the force with which it was written. She slid this ominous letter out, held it away from her. There was no postmark, no stamp. It had been placed in the mailbox by hand. She shivered, looked behind her, up and down the street. There was no one there. Main Street was empty.

She tucked the envelopes under her arm and set off back down the driveway. She tried to act calm, nonchalant, but the letters in her armpit seemed to burn with strange energy. She could feel them, hot and expectant.

She ripped the one from her mother open the moment the door swung shut behind her. A note, written on pink floral stationery, fluttered to the floor. She was left holding a glossy McDonald's gift card in her hands. She stooped, picked up the note she'd dropped.

Not sure what restaurants you have in town. It read. *Hope this is alright!*

Harriet smiled. McDonald's was hardly a treat, but she could imagine her mom and dad sitting across from one another at the kitchen table, deliberating which sort of gift card they should buy. It was thoughtful and couldn't come at a better time. She'd have to give her mom a call.

She set the note and card aside and turned her attention to the second envelope. She ripped open the flap and removed a crinkled sheet of wide-ruled notebook paper. For a second, Harriet thought it was a letter from one of her students, but then she began to read.

Harriet,

I know you probably hate me. If you want to call the police on me, so be it, but I want you to know this. I've tried to tell you so many times before but it never came out right. The Serenitea women you've been hanging out with aren't human.

They prey on their downlines. Haven't you noticed how perfect they are? How they seem ageless? That's because they are. They're <u>vampires,</u> Harriet. The tea is just a tool they use to reel in their victims.

Please, don't go back to them.

Lots of love,
Lucy

Harriet laughed. She hadn't laughed like that in so long. Lucy's jealousy was hilarious, and Harriet laughed so hard she thought her lungs might explode. She wadded up the note in one hand and tossed it into the trash.

It was true the Serenitea women had supernatural beauty, but that was a side effect of good genes and wealth. If Harriet had that kind of money, she'd look good too. A personal trainer, a plastic surgeon. It didn't take much.

She pushed her hair out of her eyes, giggled out the remnants of Lucy's disturbing letter, and put on a kettle of tea.

Chapter Thirty

She slept sound, peaceful, carried by a soft current of tea. She dreamed of being a child, of the sun's warm caress on her cheeks. It was all very stereotypical, but there was comfort in that cliché, and she smiled in her sleep.

Harriet awoke to her phone vibrating near her head. It was a deep, jarring sound, and she fought heavy eyelids to find it, to see the screen.

Angela Monroe. The name glowed in the dark. She fumbled with the device, swiped to begin the call.

"Hello?" she asked with a weighty tongue.

"Harriet!" Angela's voice was bright and energetic. "I hope I didn't wake you."

Harriet rubbed an eye. "No, no," she said. She pulled the phone away from her head, glanced at the time. 11:45. Nighttime. Dark. She thought of bats unfurling their wings, pointed teeth, and then she huffed, all the air rushing out of her nose. It was late, but not vampire late. It was ridiculous, the things that seeped into one's head when half asleep.

"I just *had* to call. I've been thinking a lot about our meeting the other day."

"Thanks for the kettle," Harriet said. "I use it all the time."

"Oh, you're very welcome." Angela cooed.

There was an awkward silence. Harriet scratched her leg.

"Have you given recruitment any thought? Anyone in mind to fill our void?"

"Erm, well…" Harriet began.

"No worries," Angela said. "I think I have the perfect person in mind."

"You do?" Harriet asked.

"Yes," Angela said.

"That's great," Harriet said. "You'll have no trouble recruiting them, then." She meant it. No one could resist Angela's charm, not even her with her staunch anti-MLM views and paltry paycheck.

"Me? Oh, no. I still need you to bring them onboard."

"What? Why?"

"Well, she's your friend, after all. You know her best."

Whatever sleepiness remained drained out of her. "Who?" Harriet snapped.

"Why, that woman who's always hanging about. At the coffeeshop? The market? The one with the, um, *exuberant* clothing."

"Lucy? You want Lucy to be part of your club?" It didn't make sense. Lucy was the antithesis of whatever the Serenitea ladies were trying to achieve with their understated garb and subdued demeanors. Harriet stood now, paced a few steps.

"Sure," Angela said. "She seems bubbly. Lively."

"That's the problem," Harriet said. She could see Lucy joining far down the line, at the bottom of the pyramid, but to be invited in to the inner circle? The sacred world of steamed yonis and supple flesh? She was too turbulent, too clumsy. She wasn't sure even she herself belonged there, let alone Lucy.

"Why's there a problem?"

"She's just," Harriet said, looking for the right words. "She's just different, is all. And I'm pretty sure she doesn't like Serenitea. Actively speaks against it, actually."

"She does?" Angela asked.

"Oh yeah, big time." Harriet thought about telling Angela about Lucy's vampirism accusation, but decided against it—she didn't need to give Lucy's ramblings any more time than necessary.

"So it'll be a challenge, then," Angela said in her sing-song voice.

"I don't think you're understanding," Harriet said. "This girl has an ax to grind. Besides, I uh, threatened her with legal action."

"Oh?" Angela asked.

"It's a long story," Harriet said.

"Well, make amends. Serenitea needs her."

"I don't know," Harriet said.

"I do," Angela said.

Harriet chewed on her lip.

"Listen, I have to go, but I'm confident you'll be able to bring her in. You're a smart woman. Figure it out. Bye bye now."

The line went dead and Harriet lowered the phone. Lucy? Really? It was true Lucy had a certain effervescence, but she also had a certain neuroticism. She had proved herself incapable of selling Mary Jane and, while Serenitea was by far a better product, Harriet doubted she could sell anything at all. She shivered thinking of the way Lucy had gone into autopilot at the "party", spouting off a presentation to an empty room with that weird, blank look in her eyes. If anyone was a creature of supernatural origin, it was Lucy, zombie-like and hollow.

Harriet sighed, threw herself back on the couch. She'd have to convince Angela that Lucy wasn't what they were looking for, because she knew she'd never convince Lucy to join Serenitea. Besides, there was an exclusivity to being in their small group that Harriet wasn't all that willing to share with someone as bumbling, as foolish, as Lucy. It felt strange to admit it, even in her head, but Harriet wanted the tea ladies all to herself.

Chapter Thirty-One

There were only a few more farmers markets left in the year, and Harriet managed to get out of working any of them. She was free to roam the bank parking lot at her own volition. She went straight to Kelsey's booth.

"About that class," she said.

Kelsey rubbed the back of her neck. "Well, it's full now, actually. We're coming up on the harvest and it books up fast."

Harriet frowned, studied Kelsey's tousled hair. She had been interested to see the bee hives, the place where the honey came from. She was afraid of bees, but Kelsey's promise to keep her safe had intrigued her. There was something about

Kelsey that attracted Harriet—an honestness, an openness. She liked the way her hands looked, work hardened and real.

"But"—Kelsey rushed—"I could take your name down for next year?"

Harriet nodded. "I'd like that," she said, even though she was disappointed to have to wait so long.

Kelsey must have noticed some of the despondency in Harriet's voice because she stood, chair screeching behind her, and held out a little jar. "Here," she said. "I want you to have this. It's from the bees I keep at my mom's place, my childhood home, and it's always a little more earthy. It's special."

Harriet wasn't sure what to say. She held the jar close to her chest.

"Listen. Why don't you stop by anyway? Forget the class. I'll give you a private tour."

"You'd do that?" Harriet's heart beat out an irregular rhythm.

"Sure. Why not?"

"Thank you," Harriet said. "I'd love that."

"How about this Wednesday? Evening okay for you?"

Harriet opened her mouth, but shut it again when she remembered: Wednesday brought another Serenitea meeting. But she could skip one…right? They'd let her off the hook for the farmers markets, what was one meeting? "Sure," Harriet said. "That works great."

Kelsey's face glowed in the morning sun. "Awesome.

6 p.m.? Here. My address is on my cards. I don't know if you have one or not."

Harriet slid the card into her back pocket. "Thank you. I'm really excited to see your bees."

"You'll love them." Kelsey smiled.

Harriet had never considered loving a bug before, but maybe there was a chance for her yet.

"You can bring a friend if you want?" Kelsey said, voice rising at the end, as if it were a question.

"No," Harriet said. "No friends. I don't have any." It sounded pitiful, but Harriet didn't want to bring anyone. She wanted this to be just for her.

Kelsey frowned. "Sure you do. I see you with those tea chicks all the time. And that one little miss with the clothes?"

"Oh god, no. Those aren't my friends," she said. Lucy *definitely* was not her friend, and though she felt more at ease around Angela and her brethren, she wasn't sure if what they constituted a friendship. She still felt a little used, a little pushed around. If it wasn't for the tea, she wouldn't have anything in common with them.

"Okay." Kelsey smiled. "I don't really do MLMs."

"Me neither!" Harriet cried.

Kelsey cocked her head. "But the bug pants, the tea booth."

Harriet's face turned red. "I get myself into these ridiculous situations but I swear to you I am against pyramid schemes all the way. They're predatory and hurt actual small businesses and—"

"Hey, no need to get worked up." Kelsey soothed.

Harriet was embarrassed. She had hoped Kelsey had somehow forgotten seeing her staff the Serenitea booth, the awkward way she'd thrust the mosquito leggings at her so many weeks ago. "I guess I got myself caught up in something," she admitted. "And I'm not proud of it." Saying it aloud made her realize it was true. She looked down at her sandals. She just wanted Kelsey to like her.

"Come by Wednesday. We'll figure something out," Kelsey said.

"Okay," Harriet said.

Kelsey gave an encouraging smile, nodded, turned away. The farmers market was busy now, vibrating with people ricocheting from one stall to another. Lucy's table still sat empty and a line had formed at the Serenitea booth where Georgiana poured samples with delicate grace. Harriet watched for a moment, then went home.

Chapter Thirty-Two

She wouldn't drink any tea tonight. She couldn't get her own words out of her head, repeating again and again with increasing clarity. They weren't her friends. She didn't like MLMs. Kelsey didn't like MLMs. The tea was good, helped smooth over all the roughness of the day, but she thought of the awkwardness enshrouding her—the constant demands of the tea ladies, the whole stalker situation with Lucy—and realized she could just end it all. She could just walk away. It would be easy. Kelsey would be proud.

Harriet rinsed out the kettle, dried it with a rough towel, and slipped it into a cupboard. If she couldn't see its metallic gleam, she thought she'd be less inclined to use it. The tea itself went into the pantry, the boxes piled against jars and cans, haphazard, messy. She had held it all above the trash can, for a moment considering dropping it all in, but it was such a lot of money to throw away. She hesitated, and that's all it took for her to keep it. Harriet knew she was weak for keeping it, but she hadn't ripped open a sachet in twelve hours. Surely, that counted for something.

Instead, she settled on the couch with a book and a cold glass of water. The ice cubes clinked together whenever she drank, and the sound reminded her of her grandmother sipping sweet tea on the porch in the summer. The evening sun rays shone through the golden liquid, making it glow. She had watched her grandmother's pendulous neck quiver when she swallowed. Sweet tea sounded awfully good, but she didn't trust herself to return to the land of steeped beverages just yet.

The book was a new one, one she ordered online, and she creased the paperback's spine as she read. She wasn't one for keeping her books pristine—they should be read, loved, used—but she did treat them with a sort of reverence. She never dog-eared the pages, but she would write a note in the margins in pencil if something struck her. There was a method buried there somewhere, though she herself didn't know it.

It was a pretty edition of *Carmilla*, thin with red glossy letters on a matte cover. She hadn't read it before, but she knew it was a story about a woman vampire. She'd purchased it before Lucy's letter, before all the nonsense had ensued, and it tickled her to read it now. She was laughing in Lucy's face. Carmilla seduced a young girl on the page, and Harriet smiled.

Carmilla was written well before *Dracula*, but Harriet had no trouble keeping up with the language, the quaint dialect. It made her feel smart. She was smart. She taught Gifted Ed, was escaping a pyramid scheme, and had a date with a new friend on Wednesday. The words breezed by.

And then she was screaming, the book falling from her lap onto the floor, the water trickling down the arm of the couch. A hollow sound, like restrained thunder, pounded through the house. Harriet hugged herself tight, took deep, gulping breaths. She listened hard over the rasp of her breathing. It was quiet now.

Could it have been thunder? She went to the window, threw the blanket to the side. She could see slivers of the sky between branches. It looked calm. The boughs hung still and dry. It wasn't storming.

It came again—a low rumble—and this time she didn't scream. This time she cocked her head, ear angled toward the sound, and crept toward what she thought was the source. She was afraid, but she was defiant too. She was smart. She'd figure this out.

The sound died away by the time she neared the pantry door, but she was certain this was the origin. She waited for a while, hand pressed against the slick wood, and wondered if it would happen again. It didn't. She pulled the door open.

The tea spilled out as she swung the door, boxes cascading over boxes, bags escaping through bent and opened lids. The pantry was full of tea. The boxes tumbled out onto her feet and she shuffled backward, the pile around her coming to her knees. The tea had multiplied. *How?* Her hands trembled.

It didn't make sense. She could no longer see the mysterious jars of preserves, or even the shelves themselves. It was nothing but a wall of tea, white and imposing.

Harriet kicked at the boxes at her feet, sending them flying back into the tiny closet. She pushed the door shut and struggled against the massive crush of boxes on the other side.

She shoved a rickety chair beneath the doorknob, jamming it shut. Just in case.

The mosquitos pierced her skin and gorged themselves on her turbid blood, but she sat outside all night. She sat on her doorstep and cried and waited for morning to come.

Chapter Thirty-Three

She made a cup of tea. She had to. She needed to still her shaking, the tight clench of her jaw. There'd be no way she could face work without it.

Venturing back inside the house was hard. She half expected to open the front door and find the living room stacked with white boxes, but it seemed the multiplication had taken place only in the pantry. It felt wrong, fishing through those ill-born boxes for the perfect sachet, but wrong wasn't something she'd shied away from.

Nerves calmed, Harriet washed her face and put on a fresh outfit. She hadn't slept, but calling off work wasn't something she was interested in. Where would she go? What would she do? Sleep in the room next to the cursed closet? She stuffed her feet into some shoes and let the door slam behind her. She carried a full thermos, tea bags bobbing inside.

The day passed in a dream-like haze, students flitting before her eyes, Harold waving a summer sausage under her nose. It all seemed so far away. Like it was happening to someone else. She roamed the halls between classes, bumping into lockers, stepping on gum. It didn't matter. The only real thing was the thunder—the sound of boxes collapsing against themselves, pelting the door. The only thing real was Serenitea.

Her thermos ran dry, her stomach hurt. The pain induced a sort of clarity, an awakening, and Harriet looked around. At the students bent over quizzes. Wondered just how she'd gotten there. Panic burbled up within her. Something terrible had happened, something was wrong. She needed help.

She dug through her bag, pushing aside old Chapstick and crumpled pads, and pulled her wallet from the depths. She'd stashed the card in there, in the section where paper money was supposed to go.

Goldenridge Farms. It read. *Kelsey Roberts.*

She looked up, ensured no students were paying her any mind, and slipped her phone from a pocket. She tapped it to life and began typing.

Kelsey. She wrote. *It's Harriet. From the farmers market. I was wondering if maybe you'd like to meet sooner. It's alright if you don't have the bee stuff ready. I really just need to talk to some-one. Sorry to throw this at you like this. It's fine if not. Wednesday is fine.*

She pressed send, covered her screen with both hands.

"Just a few more minutes left," she announced to the room. The sound of pencils scratching paper intensified.

The phone vibrated loud against the tabletop. The nearest students raised their eyes, looked at her in disgust.

Harriet ignored them and stared down at the text. *You can come by any time. Should I come to you? Is everything okay?*

The thought of Kelsey in her home made her dizzy. *No. I'll come there. This afternoon?* She wasn't known for being so forward, but desperation was spurring her on. Fear.

That sounds great. Are you sure you don't want to talk on the phone? Is everything okay? I can FaceTime you?

At work. She typed.

Oh, right. Sorry.

I'll come after school.

Sounds like a plan. Kelsey wrote. *Message me if you need anything in the meantime, okay?*

Harriet was stuffing her phone back into her pants when another text arrived.

You're behind on your recruitment, Harriet. I'm trying to be nice, but this is our livelihoods in your hands. Any progress with Lucy? Is that her name?

She buried her head in her hands.

Chapter Thirty-Four

She almost ran to her car, bag slapping her leg in a frantic rhythm. School had dragged on, time slowing, thickening into something tangible, something she couldn't push through. But now the last bell rang, and she was galloping across the pavement toward her little vehicle.

Harriet threw herself inside. She didn't care if she looked like just another student rushing away from the building. She had to go.

The car sputtered to life when she turned the key. She threw it in reverse, backed out of the spot without looking to see who or what was behind her. Lucky for Harriet, she escaped the parking lot unscathed. Lucky for everyone else, they had escaped Harriet.

She tapped her phone to life, the screen displaying

directions to Kelsey's farm. It wasn't far—fifteen minutes—but any distance at all felt unbearable, insurmountable. She blew through the school zone, past the center of town, and her driveway.

Bentwood proper dissolved in an instant, the storefronts ending abruptly, the houses sprouting farther and farther apart until, at last, whole cornfields stood between them.

"Your destination is on the right," her phone said.

Harriet slowed. The corn gave way to a manicured lawn, a house set way back on a slight rise. The house was old, but kept well. Its siding was covered in a fresh coat of white paint, and the plants on the sprawling porch—each in its own stoneware pot—looked healthy and lush. Harriet rolled up the driveway, stones crackling beneath her tires. She squinted up at the house, at the glistening black windows.

She stopped. Wondered if she should text Kelsey, make sure she had the right place. But she could see the hives from the car—an assemblage of boxes near the tree line. She threw open her door.

"Harriet!" a voice cried. "You made it!"

Harriet looked around, bewildered. The porch was empty but for the pots, and though it was Kelsey's voice she heard, she didn't see Kelsey anywhere.

"Over here. In the barn," Kelsey called.

Harriet flushed red. She felt silly, stupid. She swiveled, found Kelsey standing in the wide doorway of a white building.

"You made it okay?" she asked, taking big, easy strides toward Harriet.

Harriet bumped the car door with her hip, sending it shut. "It was only a few minutes from school," she said. "Hardly a long journey."

Kelsey shrugged. "You'd be surprised. Once people find themselves in all this corn, they get a little discombobulated." She pointed at her head, spun the finger in a circle, and screwed up her face.

Harriet laughed, then caught herself laughing. She forced her face into a frown. "My house is haunted," she said.

"Oh?" Kelsey said. She didn't look surprised.

"Yeah," Harriet said. "It's haunted and I was being stalked by a crazy pyramid scheme lady and, actually, I'm still being stalked by crazy pyramid schemes ladies, but different ones, from a different pyramid, and and and—" She hiccupped and the tears streamed down her face. She felt her nose run, a rivulet of snot touching her top lip. She was embarrassed, and that made her cry even harder.

"Hey, now." Kelsey soothed. She inched closer, pulled a handkerchief out of her back pocket. She stuffed it in Harriet's hand.

"A handkerchief?" Harriet flapped the thing in the breeze. "You actually use these?"

"Sure," Kelsey said.

Harriet blew her nose into the coarse fabric. "Thanks," she said.

"No problem."

Harriet wondered what to do with the handkerchief now that she'd gotten it all slimy. What was handkerchief etiquette? Should she take it home, wash it, and return it? Should she hand it back to Kelsey? She scrunched it into a ball in her hand.

"Here, over here," Kelsey said. She turned away, moseyed back to the barn.

Harriet followed, squeezing the handkerchief tight.

"Throw it in here," Kelsey said, holding up a woven basket. "Everything in here gets washed."

"Oh," Harriet said. She tossed the fabric and Kelsey caught it in the basket.

Kelsey smiled. "I like to use reusable things where I can. I keep a bunch of hankies for my classes. Some people think it's gross, but half the time people are just using them to wipe away honey from their hands." She shrugged.

Harriet looked up at the vaulted ceilings, the thick wooden beams holding up the barn. It was the fanciest barn she'd ever been in. It'd been converted into something resembling the set of a cooking show. There was a long table at the front of the room—from which Kelsey taught, Harriet guessed—with smaller tables lined up before it. The walls were covered with shelves, full of books, jars, plants, and bee memorabilia—statuettes, paintings. The air smelled sweet, mellow.

"This is amazing." Harriet sniffled.

"Thank you so much!" Kelsey put her hands on her hips, looked around the room as if she too had just entered for the first time. "It took a lot of hard work to get this old barn looking good."

Harriet nodded. "It's nice."

Kelsey slapped her leg, breaking the quiet spell they'd fallen under. "So, tell me about your ghost."

"What?" Harriet blinked. She hadn't thought about what to say, or why she'd even come to Kelsey's. She just knew she had to do it.

"Your house is haunted. Tell me about it." Kelsey guided Harriet toward a table with two tall stools.

Harriet pushed herself up onto the slippery stool seat. "Well... I guess I don't know. Do you believe me?"

Kelsey cocked her head. "Of course I do. I believe in spirits."

Harriet looked down at her hands held together on the lustrous wooden table. She wasn't sure if spirits were the same as ghosts, or if what she was dealing with was even a ghost. A poltergeist? A demon? She sighed. "Well, first of all, things I throw away just reappear. Like, early on, one of the first days there, Lucy—she brought me a brochure and I threw it away but it reappeared later that night. I know it sounds stupid."

Kelsey shook her head. "Not stupid at all. What kind

of brochure was it?"

Harriet wasn't sure why that mattered, but she told her. "Something about Mary Jane. Their new line of clothes."

"Hmm," Kelsey said. "And they're an MLM, right?"

"Yes."

"Okay, carry on."

Harriet brushed a piece of hair out of her face. "Well, uh, then I always feel like something's watching me, you know? Like from the woods? I live in the woods."

"Sure. In the old Morrison place."

Harriet frowned. How did Kelsey know where she lived?

"It's a small town," she answered, as if she'd read Harriet's mind. "There are only so many houses up for rent."

"I guess," Harriet said.

"So is that all?"

She felt a little offended that Kelsey thought those problems, on their own, weren't spooky enough. She was hurt, in a way. She wanted to be spooky. She puffed up her chest. "My front door—it opened on its own in the middle of the night. Opening and banging shut, over and over."

Kelsey nodded, as if this were expected.

"Then most recently, last night, I put some boxes in the pantry. And there was a horrible sound. Like thunder or something, and when I opened the door, the boxes had multiplied. Like…exponentially."

"What do you mean? There were more boxes?" This, it seemed, had caught Kelsey's interest.

"Yeah."

"Did you count them?"

"What?"

"Before and after—did you count the boxes?"

Harriet shook her head. "No. You don't understand. I put *a few* boxes in the pantry, small ones, and when I opened it up again, the whole pantry was filled. Tumbling out. There were *hundreds* of boxes."

Kelsey's brows pushed together in the center of her forehead. "Empty boxes?"

"Well, no," Harriet said. "They're tea boxes."

"For that one company you're all mixed up in?"

Harriet flushed. "Yeah," she said. "I guess so."

"Hmm." Kelsey drummed her fingers against the tabletop.

"Do you happen to know if the house was haunted before? When Mr. Morrison's mother lived there?"

Kelsey leaned in, adjusted herself on her seat. "Nope. Never heard of anything like that. But the Morrisons have always kept to themselves."

"I wonder if it's her," she said.

"Who? Morrison's mom?" Kelsey asked.

"Yeah," Harriet said. "She died there, right? Maybe she's angry that I moved in, messed with her stuff."

Kelsey shrugged. "There's only one way to find out."

Harriet's skin prickled. "What's that?"

"We have to contact them." Kelsey slid off her stool.

"We do?" Harriet followed, slipping down off the tall seat.

"Sure," Kelsey said, placing her hand on Harriet's lower back, guiding her toward the barn door.

Her hand was warm, solid. "How? Why?"

"I'm not sure yet. I need to think about this," she said. "But for now, let me give you a tour."

Harriet felt good, despite the looming threat of demons and the fact she hadn't even begun to explain the situation about the pyramid schemes. The sun was warm on her face, her arms. Kelsey's hand on her back was reassuring and real. Kelsey was in control, she'd figure it out. Harriet smiled and nodded as Kelsey showed her the hives, the field of wildflowers from which they fed.

Chapter Thirty-Five

Harriet returned home, flicked the lights on. The improbable boxes of tea were still there, straining against the pantry door, and there was the ever-present and ominous air of decay, but she ignored them all. Kelsey was right—this could be dealt with. This WOULD be dealt with. And while the "encounters" thus far had been horrifying, none of them had hurt her. Not really. Not physically. She would survive this.

She pulled her feet up underneath her and settled into the couch cushion, iPad on her lap. She'd watch something before bed. She'd show those ghosts, demons, poltergeists—whatever they were—she was not afraid. Maybe they'd get bored, go somewhere else. She tapped the screen.

The room dimmed as the sun set, but Harriet didn't mind. Her body was aglow in the light of the tablet, flickering and warm. She grew drowsy, a pleasant, heavy feeling, and was content to realize she'd entered the state without the aid of tea. She could do this. She *would* do this.

Morning shone clear and pleasant. She'd slept through the night without incident, without even getting up to pee. She stretched her legs, twisted her arms above her head. It felt like nothing could ruin this day. Even the sun was shining.

She yawned as she leaned over to check her phone. 99+ messages. Her mouth, hanging open because of the yawn, stayed open long after the yawn ended. The tea ladies' names scrolled by in her notifications. Her phone screen stalled, froze; it was too much action for her outdated model. When the screen jumped to life again, more texts rolled in. They weren't stopping.

Harriet flicked through the notifications, trying to get a sense of what was going on, where to start. The texts were panicked, misspelled, strewn with sad face emojis and broken hearts. Harriet frowned.

What are we going to do? I think we need an emergency meeting. Georgiana wrote.

I can't believe she's gone. Shannon typed.

Gone? Harriet's stomach dropped like she was rocketing over a rollercoaster's peak. Who was gone? She clicked the group message, scrolled as fast as her ancient phone would allow.

The answer came in a text sent well past midnight: *I tried to call everyone I could but not everyone answered. I hate to do it this way, but all of you deserve to know. You were her sisters. Angela died this evening.*

Harriet's hands trembled and her phone fell, slipped its way between the couch cushions. She didn't dive after it. She didn't do anything. She just stared down at her empty hands.

Angela was dead.

How? She knew the answer could be found somewhere in the stream of texts, but her hands weren't working. She couldn't hold the phone, let alone scroll. She bit her bottom lip. She'd have to get ready for work soon, force herself into the shower. She knew Angela's death wouldn't warrant an absence from school, but what else were you supposed to do when a woman that beautiful, that elegant, died?

"Oh, shit," she said, remembering the woman's son, Calvin. She'd been teaching him for weeks now, how could she have not thought of him straight away? She felt guilty. She'd go to school in his honor, to help the rest of the class understand. He wouldn't be there, but there might be something she could do. She pushed herself up off the couch.

She showered, barely running the soap over her arms. She felt the need to rush, but she wasn't sure what she was rushing toward. Panic was needling her on, and she wanted more than anything to sit down with a warm cup of tea between her still-trembling hands. She had thought she and Kelsey could fight her demons, literal and metaphorical, together, but this was too much. She needed the tea.

Her breathing evened out and she climbed out of the shower. She didn't wait to get dressed. The water heated up fast in the kettle and she was soon pouring it over a fresh tea bag. She took a big drink, the liquid scalded her tongue.

Her phone was still buzzing and flashing, new messages pouring in. She pulled on clothes, muted and modest, and at last began to type. *I'm so sorry. I just woke up. How did this happen?*

Unsure as of now. Someone wrote, whose name she didn't recognize.

Her husband found her in bed unresponsive, Georgiana typed.

We'll find out more later.

How horrible. Harriet wrote.

The messages continued to come, but Harriet shut her phone off, slid it into her bag. The thermos was warm against her hand.

Chapter Thirty-Six

Calvin wasn't at school, just as she'd predicted, but there was no mention of the boy's mother. There was no assembly in the auditorium. There was no crying between classes. Everyone just assumed Calvin was out because he was sick or had a dentist appointment. No one knew, or, worse yet, no one cared. Harriet had the impression that Angela was integral to the small Bentwood ecosystem—the mother who always volunteered, sent in gifts during teacher appreciation week— but life was buzzing on without her. It was strange.

She had turned on her phone between classes and was quick to turn it off again. The texts were still coming. They'd never stop. She saw one from Kelsey flit by: *How are you feel-*

173

ing today? Any better? She'd reply later. She wasn't sure what she'd say. In truth, she was feeling better. She wasn't deathly tired, she wasn't afraid of her home. She knew, with Kelsey on her side, her problems would soon be resolved. Angela's death was sad and confusing, but there was a sick sense of relief there too. With Angela gone, maybe they'd leave her alone. She blushed, sitting in the teacher's lounge. She wasn't supposed to think like that. She took a sip of tea.

"Whatcha thinking about?" Harold asked. He looked up at her over the lid of his open laptop.

"Nothing," she replied, too curt, too fast.

Harold raised one bushy eyebrow. "Did you hear about that kid's mom? Blondie?"

"Blondie?" Harriet asked, even though she knew who he was referring to.

"Yeah," he said, leaning back in his seat. "That blond kid. He's in your class. Calvin. His mom passed away last night. It's a damn shame, too. A body like that."

Harriet frowned. "Aren't you married?"

"Well, yeah. But a man can dream, right? But not anymore, I guess. They're saying it was an overdose."

Harriet's stomach clenched, rose high into her throat. "Overdose?"

"Yeah. It's always the rich ones, isn't it? With those boutique doctors." Harold sighed, slammed his laptop shut. He rose, chair making an awful screech as it slid across the floor.

"Wait," Harriet said, reaching for his wrist.

Harold paused. "Yes, Miss Pendleton?"

She wanted to punch him, but she needed this information. "Did they say what she overdosed on?"

Harold shook his head. "It's too soon for all that. They're probably doing an autopsy and all the tests as we speak."

Harriet couldn't help but envision the scene—a body flayed on a gleaming metal table, thick, congealing blood. She pressed her fingers to her eyelids.

"It wasn't like there was a pill bottle on the nightstand or anything like that." Harold continued. "And no one thinks she was looking to off herself. Accidental. It's sad, really."

"How do *you* know all this?" she asked.

Harold shrugged. "It's all anyone was talking about this morning. You don't stop by the lounge first thing for coffee, do you? You're always drinking that tea." He frowned, glanced down at her thermos.

"I guess I only come in between classes. For lunch."

"You're missing out on all the best gossip then."

"Oh," she replied. She held one hand in her other, trying to hide her shakiness. Gossip. That's what Angela had been reduced to. A lurid tale to tell around the coffee machine.

"Well, I gotta get to class. Catch you later?" Harold left without waiting for her response.

Harriet stood and wobbled her way to the sink. Dumped out the thermos without ceremony, watched it gurgle down the drain. Tea splashed off the dirty mugs and onto her shirt. She wiped at the mess with a crumpled paper towel, but it didn't seem to make any difference. She wanted to cry.

Chapter Thirty-Seven

An overdose. Angela had died of an overdose. That's what Harold had said. Harriet had no way to know if it was true—the tea ladies weren't divulging any specifics. Maybe they themselves didn't know, but Harriet was suspicious. Their sudden silence, after hours of frenzied messaging, was telling. She kept checking her phone, but the messages had stopped.

Anyone hear anything? She texted. She knew it was crass to ask this way. No one else was begging for answers, but maybe it was because they all already knew, had been conspiring without her. *I'm just confused.* She wrote.

No reply.

She thought about texting Kelsey, just to share the

news with someone, anyone, but she wasn't sure what she wanted out of the woman beyond simple acknowledgment. Part of her, she knew on some primal level, needed to be consoled. Not over the death itself—she and Angela weren't that close—but over the cause. What could Angela have overdosed on if not the tea?

She doubted someone as "well" as Angela was taking anything illicit. She knew some of the well-to-do moms out West were micro-dosing mushrooms, acid, to add some color back into their beige, domestic days, but Ohio was far from the Pacific. Harold had mentioned boutique doctors, someone infusing the rich with prescription cocktails—Michael Jackson had been killed by one, why not Angela?—but she hadn't noticed any slurring of speech, a wobble in the walk. Angela had appeared as sober as any of them. The only alarming thing she'd ever noticed about the woman was her penchant for making the tea too strong. She'd passed out herself when swigging from Angela's draught. It was not, and would never be, approved by the FDA.

Harriet's face flushed hot and red. She had to do something, warn somebody. She thought of all the people who had signed up beneath her, the innocent passerby she'd ensnared at the farmers market. She punched her leg as hard as she could and gasped at the pain. Then she punched it again.

Her phone buzzed. With one hand rubbing her sore leg, she checked the text.

Valium. Georgiana wrote. *None of us knew she had a script, but it was all above board. Took too much, I guess.*

Harriet frowned. She googled Valium, saw that it could be used to treat anxiety and could be deadly when taken in the wrong amount or mixed with alcohol. Was Angela a drinker? She'd been offered wine at the wellness retreat at Angela's house, hadn't she? But she hadn't seen anyone actually drinking the stuff. Everyone had opted for the anesthetizing tea.

She googled Serenitea. Maybe there was an ingredients list somewhere, something more concrete than whatever Angela had told her—*"A proprietary blend of botanicals."* She tapped through one link after another, all clean, bright websites that funneled you to a page urging her to "Buy now". She swiped back to the search page and scrolled to the bottom. There was one link that wasn't a thinly-veiled sales pitch. In fact, it was the opposite. *"A Treatise Against Serenitea."* It read. She clicked.

It was scathing. It was well-written. It was just what she was looking for. She read the article once, twice. She added it to her bookmarks. It picked apart the company from the bottom up: first it criticized the dubious tea, it's strange effects. Then it declared the organization a pyramid scheme and detailed the different "tiers" one could ascend through. It called out Eliza by name, an early adopter, a warped crone. Harriet scrolled to the bottom in search of an author, certain that whoever had written this would be some blonde, blue-eyed ex-Serenitea wellness consultant. They knew too much to not have been in the dregs. But the writer was anonymous. There was no contact information. No links. Harriet didn't blame them for wanting to avoid Serenitea's ire, but it would have been nice to have someone to email.

Thanks for the information. She wrote in the group chat. *It's just so sad.*

Chapter Thirty-Eight

I've been thinking. She wrote. Her fingers trembled as she typed. She pressed the keys out of order, tapped "Delete", tried again. *You were right. And I'm sorry.*

She deleted that too.

She sighed, slid the phone back into her bag.

"Does anyone have any questions?" she asked the room.

A few students looked up, but most, preoccupied with their projects, ignored her. She lingered over Calvin's hunched form. He was diligent as ever, writing and studying, head tucked beneath his shoulders. She was both surprised and unsurprised to see him back in class so soon. On one hand, he had always been a top-performing student. She imagined he found comfort in the routine, in the smell of just-sharpened pencils. But didn't he need time to grieve? Wasn't it improper to return so soon? She wondered if Angela had even been buried yet, and shivered.

"Calvin," she said, voice soft and low.

He tilted his face toward her, expectant.

"After class?" she asked.

He nodded once and returned to his work. Harriet knew she couldn't be the only teacher pulling him aside today, checking on him, showering him with platitudes and sympathy and offers of shoulders to cry on. But it felt wrong to let him leave without some word, some acknowledgment. She had so few students. She'd make him feel special.

The bell rang and the students tumbled out of the room. Calvin took his time, packed his bag with leaden ceremony. When the last pencil was tucked away, he turned toward her. "Yes, Miss Pendleton?"

"I just wanted to see how you're getting on," she said. "Make sure you're okay."

He chewed his bottom lip.

"Um... Are you?"

"Am I what, Miss Pendleton?"

It wasn't like Calvin to be so dense, and she had the strange feeling he was toying with her, drawing the conversation on for some reason. His features didn't betray any emotion at all. Maybe he was that lost, that shrouded in haze. "Are you okay?" she asked.

"Oh." He blinked. "Yes, I am. Thank you for asking."

"You know"—she paused, uncertain of what she'd say next—"I'm, uh, here for you, you know. If ever you need anything, you can count on me."

He nodded, scratched his leg with the opposing foot.

"I'm very sorry." She offered, but her voice broke with emotion imaging his loss, her loss, the world's loss.

"It'll be okay," he said. "There's no reason to be sad."

She frowned. "Calvin," she said. She wiped at her eyes.

"Really, Miss Pendleton. It's all okay."

"You don't have to pretend to be strong. I mean, you are very, very strong, but it's okay to cry."

He nodded. "You can cry."

"What? No. I'm talking about you, Calvin."

The corners of his lips turned upward in a half smile. "I don't know why everyone thinks I'd be so sad."

Harriet took a sharp breath in. This was unlike Calvin, it was unexpected and callous. Was he—was he happy to see his mother dead? Her brain felt like an old TV, flipping through stations at random. Flashes of shows, bursts of audio. Was he being abused? Did he kill her? Slip something into her drink? "I... I—"

"I'm sorry," he said. "I shouldn't have said it like that."

She lifted a hand to her face, felt her quivering lower

lip.

"I'll see her again," he said.

"You what?" She was far away, somewhere else.

Calvin smiled up at her, beatific.

"Erm," she said.

"In Heaven."

The final bell rang and he dashed away, bag flapping against his back. She stood, stepped toward the door, and then stopped. The Monroes hadn't struck her as the religious sort, but perhaps that's what Calvin was clinging to—the promise of an afterlife, of reunion. Her eyes filled with tears. Her phone buzzed against her thigh. She rummaged through the bag, brought it up to her face, tried to focus her eyes through the blur.

Congratulations! You have a new descendant.

Harriet sighed, tapped the email so it'd be marked as "Read."

Sometimes, the girls who signed up beneath her updated their profiles right away, adding pictures and fun facts, and some just left them blank. This person had already decorated their profile with an abundance of emojis, had added a picture, which appeared in the email's body. Harriet squinted. A lopsided smile, a swath of bright fabric. It felt like the floor had dropped out beneath her.

Chapter Thirty-Nine

She locked herself in the teacher's lounge bathroom. It smelled of cherry-sweet deodorizing spray and the acid tang of urine. Harriet didn't notice. She sat down on the toilet, pants still pulled up high, and stared down at the phone in her shaky hands.

Lucy had joined Serenitea.

Bumbling, bubbling Lucy had bought her way into the marble halls. What about her resentment? What about the sign-on cost?

Harriet opened the message she'd sent earlier, the apology, and began to type. *Lucy? Is everything okay? I got a notification that you joined Serenitea.*

She deleted it and began again. *We need to talk.* She sent the message.

Sure! came the reply.

Harriet's phone began to buzz, a new call coming in. The sound echoed in the stinking chamber. She tapped "Decline". *No, in person.* She wrote.

Oh, sure! Lucy replied. *Just name the time and place and I'm there!*

Harriet breathed hard through her nose. The flippancy was troubling. *How about the Grind House at six?*

The reply was almost immediate. *Works for me! Can't wait to see you!*

Harriet shut her eyes for a moment, then tossed her phone into her bag. The last thing she wanted to do was to meet Lucy at the coffee shop, but she didn't think what needed to be said could be said over the phone. Lucy had a way of making her voice singsong sweet, no matter the circumstances. She needed to see Lucy's face, to examine it for any breaks, any cracks in character.

Someone knocked on the door.

"Coming," she said.

She stood, flushed the toilet despite not having gone. She went to the sink, turned it on for a moment, and then turned it off again, pretending to be a normal person. She looked at herself in the mirror, bloodshot eyes, sallow skin beneath fluorescent lights. She turned away.

She swung the door open and almost ran into Harold.

"What are you still doing here?" he asked.

She looked down at her feet. "Just catching up on some grading," she said. "It's hard to concentrate at home."

He nodded. "I can understand that."

Could he? Did gym teachers even grade papers? Wasn't his just a world of attendance, participation? She frowned.

"Is everything alright?"

She stepped out of the doorway, allowing him entrance to the bathroom. "Oh, I'm fine," she said.

He didn't move. "Listen," he said. "About the Phys Ed offer. I—"

She shook her head so hard her hair lashed her face. "Nuh uh." Whatever he had to say, she didn't want to hear it.

"No. I think you misunderstood, or I said it wrong. I don't know."

She adjusted the bag on her shoulder.

"I know sometimes I can be a doofus, say things that aren't funny. But I just meant if you needed a jogging partner or something, I'm here for you."

"Jogging?" She'd never jogged a day in her life. "What are you talking about?"

He ran a meaty paw over the back of his neck. "I guess I don't know." He smiled.

"I have to go," she said. She took a step toward the teacher's lounge door.

"Wait," he said, hand shooting out between them. "I just feel like you'd like it. Jogging, playing tennis. Something

187

like that. With me."

She almost laughed.

Maybe he could see the way her lips twitched because he frowned, shifted on his feet. "What do you do for fun?" he asked.

Whatever she thought was funny before suddenly flipped over, inverted itself into something sad, something lonesome. What did she do for fun? She ran the past few weeks through her mind. She listened for ghosts with a knife in hand, she watched reruns on her laptop, she joined pyramid schemes and she—"Farmers market," she said. "I like to go to the farmers market."

"That's good," he said. "I've been a few times. But what do you do on the days that's not going on?"

"Well, I work," she said, knowing it wasn't a very good answer.

"That's not a hobby."

She bit the inside of her cheek. What had happened to her? She used to go out with friends, try new restaurants, she even took up cross-stitch for a while in remembrance of the grandmother who'd taught her as a child. Bentwood had hollowed her out, cored her like an apple. There was nothing left of her but anger and fear. She clenched her fist.

"I just—It seems like you're lonely." He confessed. "And it makes me sad in a way I can't really articulate. And I wanted to know if you'd like to do something sometime. Hell,

I'll bring the wife and kids. We can go for a walk."

"Why… Why do you care?"

"You're my friend, Harriet," he said, voice filled with an uncharacteristic softness.

She blinked at his words. "I am?"

"Well, yeah." He chuckled.

"Um, thank you," she said. She didn't know she was anyone's friend in this godforsaken town. Lucy might have considered her one once, but she wasn't sure where that relationship stood now that she'd threatened to call the cops on her. She supposed she'd find out at six.

"Think about it," he said. "You'd love my wife. The kids are kind of annoying but they're not all bad." He winked.

"Uh, okay," she said. And she would think about it, whether she liked it or not. "I appreciate that?"

He smiled wide, patted her on the shoulder, and disappeared into the bathroom. She heard the lock on the door click.

She lingered for a moment, heard the vigorous stream of his urine hit the toilet water. It'd been a strange day.

Chapter Forty

The Grind House was busy for six in the evening. Teenagers sprawled over tables, pretending to do homework as they sipped their sugary drinks. A middle-aged man stared at his laptop screen. Harriet stared at her fingers. She had bought a latte, but it was too hot to drink.

The door swung open, and Harriet looked up, expecting to see Lucy, but it was just another teen. Those assembled at the table whooped in greeting and the newcomer joined them.

Lucy was late. It didn't seem like her. Did it? Did she know Lucy well enough to know what was typical of her? Harold's words still rang through her mind. He had Harriet said looked sad, lonely, and he was a friend. Lucy had once asked to be her friend, Harriet wondered if the offer still stood.

At last, with a loud chime, the door opened again. Lucy peeked around the corner. Her face broke into a big smile when she saw Harriet. She waved.

Harriet lifted her hand in response. Lucy cleared the doorway and began to weave through the busy café. Harriet couldn't believe what she was seeing. Instead of her usual bright garb, Lucy was wearing a muted, linen sundress. It was wrinkled and a size too big, but it was elegant in a way she hadn't thought possible for Lucy.

"Uh, hi," Harriet said.

Lucy threw herself down in the seat opposite. "Hi!"

"Do you want a drink?" she asked. "It's on me." She remembered the frozen concoction she'd seen Lucy purchasing the day she'd caught her with Angela, the day she signed up for Serenitea. Her face flushed.

"Oh, no. Thank you, though." Lucy hoisted her tote bag onto the table and removed a thermos. "I brought my tea." She winked.

Harriet's stomach squeezed tight. "About that," she said.

"I wanted to apologize," Lucy said. "I've been so weird about Serenitea. I guess I was just jealous."

"Um, it's okay. It turns out—"

"It's so good. I feel great."

"But, Lucy, you were right. You were *always* right. It's not good for you." Harriet touched her latte cup, testing the temperature. Her fingertips burned.

Lucy laughed, high-pitched and loud. "All the best things are."

"Are what?"

"Not good for you, silly!"

Harriet rubbed at her face with an aggression that surprised her. "No," she said. "I mean really bad. Kill you kind of bad. Angela died, Lucy."

Looking around, Lucy leaned in, mouth half covered by her hands. "I heard it was drugs," she whispered.

Harriet shook her head. "It wasn't. I mean, that's what I was told too, but I think it was the tea. She always made it too strong. I passed out when I was at her house. The day you, uh…"

"Stalked you." Lucy completed.

"Yes," Harriet said. She fidgeted in her seat.

Lucy sighed, her shoulders fell as she exhaled. "I don't know," she said. "Are you sure it isn't because you hadn't eaten? Because of all the steam in the room?"

A shiver ran down Harriet's arms. "How do you know that?"

The color of Lucy's cheeks deepened. "Well."

"You're talking to them, aren't you?"

Lucy took a sip from her thermos. Harriet could smell

the deep sapidity of flowers, of earth. Her mouth watered.

"Kind of," Lucy said once she'd swallowed.

"Why?" Harriet asked. "How?"

Lucy cocked her head, looked close at Harriet. "Well, Shannon came by the house a few days ago. She brought some tea and we had a really good talk."

"What'd you talk about?" Harriet's voice was hard.

"You, mostly."

"Me?"

"She said you needed my support and that if I signed up, you'd talk to me again. And here we are." She giggled.

Harriet rubbed her brow, annoyed. "But you wrote me that letter. About them? You called them vampires, not normal women?"

Lucy scratched her arm with a stubby fingernail. "Like I said, I was jealous. I'm embarrassed, but they stole my girls, my livelihood."

"But you said it yourself—they're perfect. Immortal, even." She thought of Eliza's taut skin, her radiant glow. "How do you explain that?"

Lucy looked exasperated. "They're rich, Harriet. We'd look like that too if we had personal trainers, Botox."

"I don't know. I quit drinking the tea," Harriet said.

Lucy pouted. "That's a real shame."

"Is it? Why?"

"Because I was going to invite you to come on the

cruise!"

Cruise? Hadn't Angela mentioned a cruise? It was a vague memory but it was there. She'd said something about earning a place on it. She frowned. "You're going on the cruise?"

She nodded. "Yep! They gave me Angela's spot! Isn't that amazing?"

The bitterness of jealousy bit into her and she winced. She didn't want to be jealous. She didn't want to be angry. But it hurt. Despite it all, she still wanted their approval. Tears welled. "Why?" she asked.

"I don't know," Lucy said. "I do feel bad about it. Taking a dead woman's spot, me getting it when you've worked so hard. But that's why I was going to take you! I have a guest ticket."

Harriet bit her lip. "Shouldn't you invite your husband?"

"Oh no. He would hate it. I want you to come."

Picking up her cup, Harriet swirled the blend of milk and espresso. "They wanted me to take my clothes off," she said.

"They did? Where?" Lucy's eyes were wide.

"At the retreat. And when I woke up, everything felt wrong."

Lucy took another sip of tea. "I'm sure it's just a misunderstanding. You were sick. You were tired."

Anger flared in her. She wasn't so sure. She still believed the tea to be dangerous, the women even more so. Something wasn't right. "Maybe." She lied, hoping to end the conversation. She just wanted to go home.

"So, you'll come on the cruise?" Lucy's voice was bright and cheerful.

Harriet took a sip of her latte, bitter and warm. She felt the warmth spread all the way down her throat, into her chest. She was angry at the tea ladies, betrayed by their acceptance of Lucy. It wasn't fair. But also she distrusted them, knew there was something more to their purity, their timelessness.

Smiling at her, Lucy kicked her feet beneath the table. Lucy would be eaten alive. If she, Harriet, had become addicted, passed out in their presence, there was zero hope for dumb old Lucy. She felt sorry for calling her dumb in her head. She'd been right, she'd tried to warn her. She'd go to protect her. She'd thwart whatever plan the tea ladies had in store for Lucy. Yes. That was good. That was reason enough. "I'll go," she said.

Lucy squealed and grabbed her hand. "I'm so happy!"

Chapter Forty-One

Harriet was surprised when her request for time off got approved so quickly. She knew it was hard to find subs, had heard teachers complaining in the hallways.

"Probably won't be able to take off another day this year." Harold tutted.

"You think so?" she asked.

Harold swished his water around his mouth before swallowing. "Yeah," he said. "Where you going anyway?"

Harriet fidgeted in the hard plastic seat. She didn't want anyone to know she was going on a pyramid scheme cruise, especially one as nefarious as Serenitea. "Just taking some time to relax," she said.

Harold's mouth bent up in the corner. "No, really. Tell me."

"There's nothing to tell," she said, annoyed.

"You got some kind of surgery or something?"

"What? No," she said. She turned her laptop off, slid it into her bag with care.

"Aw, come on. Don't leave."

She shouldered her bag and shuffled out of her seat.

"How come you don't drink that tea anymore?" he asked.

She froze. Harold was more observant than she gave him credit for. She couldn't figure the man out. He was brutish and crass, but there was something more there beneath the surface. She'd seen it before, when he talked about his wife, and she was getting a glimpse of it now. "I can't afford it." She lied.

"Hmm." He purred.

Harriet knew he wasn't buying it.

"What else do you know about blondie?" Harold asked.

"I don't know, you're the one with all the info. You knew it was an overdose before I did."

He smiled wide. "So I was right? Sweet!"

"Bye," she said. She pushed on the door and it swung open.

"You're going on that cruise, I bet."

She spun around, surprised, and the door slammed shut. "What's it to you? Will you please get out of my business?"

"I knew it! Tea lady going on the tea cruise!" He taunted. He tilted his chair back until it balanced on two legs.

"How do you know about all of this?" She took a step back toward him.

"If anyone would know when half the women from this town would be MIA, it's me," he said.

She had to give it to him, he was the expert in that. "Stop it," she said.

"For real, I'm on Facebook. I see those girls recruiting and trying to get their goals or whatever. The cruise has been all over their pages for weeks. You drink that stuff, you're taking off, the dates line up." He smiled, self-satisfied.

"It's complicated," she said, softening.

He nodded. "You never struck me as the type to get involved in something like that."

At first she felt angry. Wasn't she beautiful enough, serene enough, to be a wellness consultant? "Why's that?" She snipped.

Harold raised his eyebrows. "Woah there. I'm just saying you're smarter than all those girls. They pour their life savings into this thing and get what? A pittance in return? I don't mean to be offensive, but I've always thought you knew better than that. What's your angle?"

The rage died away and she adjusted the bag on her shoulder. "What do you mean?"

"Why do you do it, Harriet?"

The compliment had opened her up raw to him. She sat back down, spread her hands across the table. "Do you really want to know?"

"Yes," he said, leaning in.

"Do you promise to not make fun of me?"

"Of course," he said.

She turned toward the door, checking for intruders. Most of the other teachers went to the Grind House for lunch, snacking on light sandwiches and veggie trays. She was never invited. Neither was Harold, so it seemed. "It's long," she said.

"I'm ready," he replied.

She told him about her cabin, the strange noises, the multiplying tea boxes. She told him about Lucy and her sudden acceptance of the tea. She described Angela's gorgeous home and the sickness she felt upon leaving. She told him that the tea was making her sick, might have even killed Angela. She told him everything—almost. She kept Kelsey to herself. She'd protect that part of herself, for now.

When she was finished, Harold leaned back in his chair and whistled long and low. "Damn, lady," he said.

"I know," she said.

"Do you want my advice?"

She considered this. It was interesting that he'd ask before dispensing whatever guidance he thought he could offer. In her experience, men just told people what to do. "Sure," she said.

"I think you're right to go on the cruise, get out of that creepy-ass house for a while."

"Yeah," she said.

"But…"

"Yeah?"

"I've never got the warm and fuzzies from those women, if you know what I mean."

She nodded. She did know what he meant. They weren't welcoming women, sequestered away in their finery. And when they had invited her in, she'd felt dowdy and misshapen.

Harold glanced toward the door, lowered his voice. "I think you need to turn this into a recon mission. Blow this wide open."

"You believe me? That something bad is happening here?"

"Sure," he said. "Anyway, what's the harm? Worst case scenario, you have a few cocktails and get a sunburn."

"And what's the best case?" she asked.

"You find out who they really are."

A chill ran down her spine. "What do you think I should do about Lucy? She gets so invested."

He shrugged. "You cling to her," he said. "She's your

Trojan horse."

She frowned, imagining herself riding Lucy over the gangway of the ship.

"Obviously you've put up some resistance, right? Could that be why they didn't invite you to begin with?"

It was true, she'd never committed herself to the tea ladies. She'd been hesitant to sell, she hadn't bared herself. They'd been looking for someone bubbly and bright. "I wasn't what they had in mind," she said.

"Right. And that's ultimately a good thing, because that's how you're gonna get the upper hand here. But for now, you need to ingratiate yourself back into the pack. And there's no better way than to align yourself with Lucy. Pretend to drink the tea, wear the weird culty clothes. Straighten your hair."

She nodded. He was right. "And let's say I do find something out. Who do I tell?" In truth, she was scared. Not just to be stuck in the middle of the ocean with those ravenous women, but to be targeted if she exposed their secret, whatever it may be. They were powerful, blessed with money and beauty and, perhaps, something more. She coughed.

"We'll cross that bridge when we get there," he said. "It really depends on what the secret is, right?"

It was true. Exposing a group of women for bad business practices was a lot different than blowing the cover on an immortal, vampiric coven. "Okay," she said.

"Well," he said, rising. "Gotta get to class. How about you?"

"Oh, shit," she said. She scurried up. "I lost track of time." Her face was red.

"It'll be alright," he said.

"How do you know?" she asked.

"Because I'm on your side."

She would have rolled her eyes, but deep inside she did feel more confident. She felt stabler, braver. She wasn't alone. She had Kelsey and now Harold, however bumbling he may be. She was surprised to find herself wishing they could come along on the cruise. She shook the thought away. "Thanks," she said.

He nodded and turned toward the door.

Chapter Forty-Two

She had an old, deflated suitcase she used to take on trips with her parents. She thought of them as she packed. They took her to Disney World, the Appalachians. She'd never been on a cruise. It wasn't that her parents wouldn't have liked to go on one, but her father got seasick, throwing up over the railings on ferries and charter boats. She'd call them before she left, she decided. She'd let them know where she was should anything happen to her. She'd call Kelsey too.

She knew the large pile of panties she'd amassed was unreasonable, illogical, and she studied it for a moment. Sighing, she turned away from the panties—two for every day she'd be gone, just in case, which seemed reasonable enough when she thought about it—and tapped Kelsey's picture in her contacts. She listened to it ring.

"Harriet?" Kelsey sounded out of breath

"Everything okay?" she asked.

Kelsey exhaled into the microphone, a crunchy sound. "I was wondering the same about you. You're usually a texter, Hare."

Hare? No one had ever called her that before. She wasn't sure if she liked it. "Oh, sorry," she said. "I didn't mean to startle you."

"Not at all! I'm glad everything is good. How's it going?" Her voice had returned to its warm timbre.

"Well, I just wanted to tell you I'm going on a cruise," she said.

Kelsey paused for a moment. "Is that so?" she asked.

Harriet realized how weird it was to be calling Kelsey to tell her this. Her stomach burbled. "Sorry. I just wanted someone to know in case something happens to me," she explained. And it was true, kind of. Harold knew she was going, of course, and soon her parents would be too, but more than that Harriet just wanted to hear Kelsey's voice.

"Happens to you? On the cruise? Like you fall overboard or catch Norovirus or something?" Kelsey joked.

"I mean, maybe? It's not a normal cruise. It's with *them.*"

"Who?" Kelsey asked, voice echoing.

Harriet's face turned red, even though no one was around to see it. "The pyramid scheme."

"The tea one?"

It was embarrassing that Kelsey even had to ask which scheme Harriet was wrapped up in now. "Yeah," she said.

"Why would you do that?" Kelsey's tone was kind, but there was a trace of disappointment there too. Harriet wished she could see her face.

"Maybe we should meet." She offered.

Kelsey breathed into the phone. "Yeah, okay. That's fine."

Just fine? Harriet felt her eyes sting with tears. She was being emotional, she knew that. But she was scared. Maybe it was okay to feel this way when entering the lion's den. Harriet whimpered.

"Listen," Kelsey said, sighing. "Why don't I come over there? I'll help you pack and check out your ghosts and you can tell me all about it."

Harriet glanced at her worn panties in the suitcase, the holes, the faded prints. She did want Kelsey to come over, she did want her to glean something about the weird things that happened in her house. She just felt like she'd made a mistake, had exposed herself in some way that was unbecoming. She'd been impulsive in calling her. "I just feel stupid," she admitted.

"No." Kelsey cooed. "I'll be there in thirty, okay?"

"Okay," she whispered, letting the call end.

She tapped on Facebook, hoping the app would distract her from her awkwardness on the phone. There was a new friend request. They'd slowed down in recent weeks, having added most of the local tea ladies and their connections, so this was strange. She swallowed hard before clicking the notification.

Harold Warnike wants to be your friend.

She walked to the window and peeked behind the blanket she'd hung there. The day was dimming, mellowing into dusk. She sighed. She hit "Accept." Why not? The man had some issues, but he had proven himself to be a good listener with some interesting advice. He believed her, at any rate.

Harriet walked back to the place on the floor where she'd been staging her suitcase. She needed to hide her panties before Kelsey showed up. She flung the zippered top open.

Her breath snagged in her throat. The suitcase was empty. All the panties were gone. She stared down into the dark, musty maw of the thing and felt herself grow dizzy. She sat down hard on her butt. The suitcase was empty.

She sat, gaping at the hollow luggage, until she heard the crunch of tires on gravel.

Chapter Forty-Three

"Are you sure you want to do this?" Kelsey asked. She clutched a canister of salt.

"Yes," Harriet said.

Kelsey raised an eyebrow. "Okay," she said, tipping the can. Granules poured out and she walked around the room, a lumpy circle of white forming at her feet. "Stand inside."

Harriet was already at the center of the circle; Kelsey had traced it around her. "I am," she said.

"Good." Her voice wavered. She was nervous, Harriet realized. She could tell by the way her voice broke, the way Kelsey stared down at her shoes.

She was nervous too, but less about what they were

about to do than the pure fact that Kelsey was in her living room. Her hands shook and she held them clasped together, hoping Kelsey wouldn't notice. "What do you think will happen?" she asked.

"I dunno," Kelsey said. "But the circle will keep us safe. I think."

"You think?" Kelsey had seemed so confident in the barn, on the phone. She had a plan, it sounded like. Now, Harriet wasn't so sure.

Kelsey ducked, wiping her cheek on her shoulder. "I've only done this once before."

"That's reassuring," Harriet said.

Kelsey squinted at her.

"I mean it," she said. "I've only done this never."

A wary smile crept across Kelsey's lips. "Okay," she said.

"What happened? Last time, I mean."

Kelsey shook her head, toed some of the salt with her boot. "Not much, to be honest. Lights dimming, maybe some floorboards creaking. I was a kid," she said. "You ever play with a Ouija board?"

She had, at late night sleepovers while sugared up on soda and fruit snacks. The board spelled out the same name over and over: Harriet. She had giggled then, so sure that one of her friends was manipulating the planchette, but she shivered remembering it now. "Yeah, I guess so," she said.

"It's kinda like that," Kelsey said. "Are you ready?"

Harriet nodded, swallowed hard.

"Okay." Kelsey stepped toward the middle of the circle and held out both hands.

Harriet took them without question.

"Close your eyes," Kelsey said.

"Will you close yours too?" She didn't want Kelsey scrutinizing her at the best of times, least of all when she was scared.

"Yes," she said. "It only works if our eyes are shut."

Harriet closed her eyes, apprehensive. The room, dark now, was a shade lighter than the space behind her eyelids. "Okay, mine are shut."

Kelsey gave her hands a squeeze. "Mine too," she said.

They stood for a while, eyes shut, hand in hand. Harriet listened to her own breathing. "What now?" she asked.

She felt the woman opposite her shift her weight. "First we slow down, listen to the room around us."

Harriet held her breath, listened to the hum of the refrigerator, the muffled chirping of a cricket outside. She moved her head and heard her hair hiss past her ear. Her heart beat heavy—she could feel it in her neck.

"Good," Kelsey whispered. "Keep listening."

She strained to hear anything beyond the pulse of her own body. "What are we supposed to be hearing?" she asked.

"Shh!" Kelsey rasped. "There!" Her hands tightened

around Harriet's like a boa constrictor's hug.

Harriet wanted to pull away, to open her eyes, but she quieted herself. She listened.

A creaking, somewhere near the corner. It was as if someone stood on the warped flooring, rocking themselves back and forth. Her arm hairs stood on end, skin prickling.

"What is it?" Harriet gasped.

"Shh!"

"I'm scared." She tried to untangle her hands from Kelsey's, but the woman wouldn't let go. She opened one eye, stared hard at the corner. There was nothing there. The sound had stopped.

"Me too, but we have to see this through. Now, listen. Eyes shut."

Her eyelid flickered shut.

"I think there's someone here," Kelsey said. "I'm going to try to communicate with them."

"No!" Harriet squeaked.

"It'll be okay," Kelsey said.

"How do you know?"

Kelsey pulled her closer. Harriet stumbled. "Have you ever known anyone to be hurt by a ghost?"

"Um…" Harriet began. It was true that she'd never been hurt in the cabin; nonetheless, her psyche was scarred. And who's to say people that drop dead alone in their homes, supposed heart attacks and aneurysms, weren't slain by something nebulous and nefarious? She marveled at her own thought process. She'd always been a scientific person, she thought. Never one to speculate when cold likelihood stood in the way, but now? She wasn't sure who she was, or where her mind would lead her next.

"It'll be okay." Kelsey repeated, softer this time.

Harriet mumbled.

Kelsey cleared her throat. "Okay," she said. "We sense someone here tonight." Her voice took on a faraway tone, flat and clear.

Harriet listened for the creaking sound, but the room was still.

"If there's someone here, please make a noise. Anything—a knock on the wall, a footstep. We're ready."

Silence.

"Use our energy." Kelsey offered.

"What?" Harriet snapped. "Not mine." She envisioned herself being depleted like an old battery, crumpling to the floor. The memory of the shimmering room, yoni pots steaming, where she'd last collapsed flooded her mind.

"Use our energy." Kelsey repeated.

Did she feel lighter? Did she feel herself floating up and away?

The women stood silent, holding hands, in the middle of the dark room.

A click, like a tongue snapping against the roof of a

mouth, echoed through the room. Harriet screamed.

"Shhh." Kelsey soothed. "Could have been anything."

"That was someone's mouth," she cried, eyes open now. She scanned the room, couldn't see into the dim corners now. "There's something here."

"Yeah, that's the point," Kelsey said.

Harriet examined Kelsey's face. Her face looked calm, serene. Her nose was a little sunburnt. Her chapped lips curved upward in a half smile. "No peeking," she said.

"How'd you know?" Harriet asked, shutting her eyes once more.

Kelsey exhaled in amusement.

"No really," Harriet said. "Are you a witch?" She was only half joking. Her hands felt sweaty in Kelsey's.

"No. I think each of us has the ability to do something like this," she said. "To channel something. Someone."

"Well, I think I'm done now," Harriet said.

"Just wait," she said, holding tight. "We haven't figured out what they want, why they're here."

Harriet stiffened. "I don't know if I want to know."

"What's the point then?" Her voice came fast. "Don't you want to figure out how to help them leave? If we know why they're here, maybe we can figure out how to guide them home."

"Home?"

"Yeah," Kelsey said, gentler now.

Harriet did want to send them away, banish them to whatever Hell they belonged to. Because, she was sure, someone as chaotic and frightening as this deserved a place among the tormented, the damned. She'd never thought about Hell before, or the afterlife much at all. "Do you believe in Hell?" she asked.

"Oh shush," Kelsey said. "They're just lost."

Harriet sighed. "What do we do?"

Kelsey fidgeted. "Ahem," she said. "If you need help, please knock."

Nothing came.

"I always thought it might have been Mrs. Morrison." Harriet confessed "The landlord's mom. He has all these creepy rules about the windows because of her, and I thought I pissed her off by covering them."

"Mrs. Morrison?" Kelsey asked.

The room stayed quiet.

"Use our energy," Kelsey said.

"I think they left," Harriet said, relieved.

"You try," Kelsey said. "They're obviously very comfortable around you."

"Try what?" She was repulsed by the notion. She didn't want to interface with them one on one. Holding hands in a dark room in the middle of a salt circle was enough.

"Just talk to them." Kelsey soothed. "Say whatever comes to your mind. Let it be natural."

Harriet wanted to curse, to scream. She wanted to rip out all her hair and stomp around the room. She wanted to tell them to leave her alone. Instead, she asked them, "What do you want from me?"

They waited.

"Do you feel that?" Kelsey asked. "It's cold now."

Harriet squinched her eyes shut, tighter than before. She didn't want to admit it, but it was colder than it had been a moment before. It felt as if they'd ventured into a cold spot in a pool, a place where the sunlight didn't touch. "I guess," she said.

"Keep talking."

"Uh, I'm Harriet," she said, unsure why she was introducing herself. "And I live here now. This is my home. I work at the school, with gifted kids."

Her phone chimed on the couch and she jumped.

"That's good," Kelsey said. "Keep going."

She scratched her leg with her foot. She wobbled on one leg. "I'm just wondering what you're trying to tell me. With the brochure, the tea boxes, the door, the noises. I don't understand."

The cold deepened, the chill now something she could no longer ignore. She heard Kelsey gasp.

"The truth is, I'm scared. You're scaring me. If I can— if I can help you in some way, please, now is the time to let us know."

She heard a flapping above her head, a soft, tremulous sound like a bird stretching their wings, an unfurling. She shivered. "Kelsey." She hissed.

"Eyes shut! Keep talking."

"Oh god. Oh god." She moaned. "Please. I don't understand. Give me something concrete to go off. A sign. A word. Anything. Please." Her voice shook, tears threatening to spill.

Kelsey squeezed her hands with approval, reassurance.

"I just, well, I just want to understand." And she did, she realized. "Please."

Something brushed her arm. She jolted, screamed.

Kelsey wrenched her back to the center of the circle. "Eyes shut!" she called.

She cried openly now. Something was touching her, a thousand somethings, caressing her skin, falling down the length of her body. She angled her head up and something tumbled against her lips. "Oh god!" she screamed. She opened her eyes.

Scraps of fabric floated down around them, billowing as it caught the air. Her first thought was ectoplasm—the gauzy material she'd seen in the spirit photography of the 1800s. But that wasn't real. This was real. The stuff drifted to the floor. "Oh my fucking god," she said, realizing then what it was.

Hundreds of pairs of underwear, faded and period stained, meandered down from the ceiling. They pooled around their feet, they obscured the salt circle. The air had a faint smell like detergent, like her.

Kelsey tilted her head upward, letting the panties brush her cheeks, her hair. She smiled, eyes open now. "Isn't it beautiful?"

Chapter Forty-Four

They spent the rest of the night shoveling panties into garbage bags, vacuuming salt from between the floorboards. They didn't speak, but there was no animus between them. They were tired, they were in awe.

Harriet, well past embarrassment now, kicked a torn Victoria's Secret thong into a black bag. "What do you think it means?" she asked at last.

Kelsey was quiet, laden garbage bag straining between her hands. She stared down into the maw, contemplated what she saw there. "I'm not sure," she admitted. "But I don't think it means you any harm."

Harriet plopped down where the salt circle once lay.

She was exhausted, drained. Kelsey folded her legs and joined her on the floor. "I just don't understand what it's trying to tell me," Harriet said.

"Maybe it's not trying to tell you anything," Kelsey said. She ran a hand through her blonde, tousled hair. She looked exhausted too.

Harriet stared down at the craggy flooring, traced her finger over a large, pronounced knot. She just didn't understand why something would work so hard to get her attention, use so much energy, to do these outlandish deeds. There had to be a meaning. "Why is it trying so hard?" she asked.

"We don't know that it is. Maybe all of this is just, like, child's play. The bare minimum. We don't have any reference for what's 'trying hard' or not," she said.

Harriet wasn't sure that was true. If this was a ghost— or poltergeist or whatever—barely lifting a pinky finger, why didn't more people experience things like this? Why, after offering up their energy, did they feel so depleted? She picked at the skin around her fingernail. She wouldn't mention it—it wasn't important. She decided to focus on the most pressing matter. "We still don't know how to make it move on."

Kelsey leaned back, propped herself up on an elbow. "Maybe you should just let it stay."

It took effort to keep her mouth from flying open. She looked around the room, at the dingy walls, the water and sun-stained portraits hanging in tarnished frames. It might not look like it, but this was her home. "No," she said.

"Why not?"

"Is your house haunted?" Harriet asked. Kelsey's house had looked old, with its ornate cornices and lopsided porch. She reasoned that it had to be older than her cabin.

Kelsey shook her head. "No. I don't think it is."

"Then you can't understand," she said. "It's terrifying, being here. I hate it."

"When's your lease up?" Kelsey asked, picking at a piece of flooring with a stubby fingernail.

"Not until next July." Harriet frowned.

"Listen," Kelsey said. She pushed herself up until she was sitting. "When you come back from your cruise, why don't you come stay with me for a while? Just until we can figure out what to do."

Harriet's face prickled. Leaving the cabin behind, even just for a short while, would be such a relief. She'd be gone while on the cruise, but that was just diving into another murky realm of uncertainty. Maybe at Kelsey's she could relax, do some work, remind herself of who she was. "I'd like that," she said. "Thank you."

Kelsey smiled. "Maybe we can get you out of your lease early, or at the very least figure out a way to placate whatever's staying here."

"Honestly, I'd just like to leave. Being here makes me depressed," she admitted.

"Sure," Kelsey said, "we'll figure it out."

Kelsey was so confident, so stabilizing. Harriet wished she could be more like her, could harness Kelsey's golden energy in the same way the ghost had harnessed her own. It'd be nice to possess her, she thought with some surprise.

"So, tell me," Kelsey said, "what's up with this cruise anyway?"

Harriet sighed, embarrassed. "It's this Serenitea thing for top earners. Lucy got Angela's spot—she died, by the way—and Lucy is inviting me along as her plus one. I feel like I have to go, to protect Lucy, and to figure out what they're really up to."

"Wait, one of your girls died?" Kelsey's eyes were intense, shining in the dark.

"Yeah. A supposed Valium overdose, but I think it may have been the tea. I passed out when I drank it at her house—she makes it so strong."

"Damn. Please tell me you're not still drinking that stuff."

It felt good to have Kelsey worried about her. Harriet forced down a smile. "Oh no, I quit."

"And now Lucy is wrapped up in Serenitea too? How'd that happen?"

Harriet rubbed her eyes. "Well, she hated them with a passion. They stole all her downline, you know. But I quit talking to her when I found out she was stalking me and Serenitea told her I'd see her again if she joined. She did, tried the tea, and got hooked."

"Wow," Kelsey said.

"I know," Harriet said. "It's a lot."

"And why do you feel like you have to protect her? I thought you didn't like her."

Harriet looked down at her lap. "She was right all along. She tried to warn me. And she's not a bad person, just, well, not bright, and I feel bad. She told me they were vampires."

"Like, actual vampires?"

"I think so," Harriet said. "I mean, I can't be totally sure she didn't mean it metaphorically, but she said they weren't normal women."

"Why didn't you tell me this sooner?" Kelsey said, a hint of hurt in her voice.

"I didn't think you'd believe me. Hell, I didn't believe it. I thought Lucy was crazy, jealous. You know? And I was so preoccupied with the haunting. There's just a lot going on." She sighed.

Kelsey's hand found hers in the dark. "I'll always believe you, Harriet."

"Oh," Harriet said. The place where their skin touched pulsed with something akin to electricity.

Kelsey pulled her hand away, stretched with her arms above her head. "Well, I gotta get going."

"Oh," Harriet said, surprised. She'd just revealed she was going to be trapped on a ship with literal vampires and Kelsey was leaving her alone in a house full of ghost panties?

Kelsey helped pull her up off the floor. "You'll text me, won't you? From the boat if you can, and when you get home? We'll pack for real, then, get you out of here for a little while."

Harriet nodded, followed Kelsey to the door, a puppy dog in her wake.

Kelsey turned to face her at the threshold. She smiled.

"I'm scared," Harriet said, voice breaking. "I'm really scared."

"You'll be okay." Kelsey laid a heavy hand on her shoulder.

"How do you know that?"

Kelsey shrugged. "You're stronger than you give yourself credit for. Think of what happened here tonight. That was scary, but you survived it, didn't you?"

"So you were scared?" Harriet asked.

"Hell, I'm scared most of the time."

Harriet didn't believe her, but she smiled anyway. "I'll see you," she said.

"You will." Kelsey smiled.

Harriet stood in the doorway long after her headlights faded.

Chapter Forty-Five

Getting ready to board the plane. She texted Kelsey from the airport bathroom. She swiped over to Facebook, sent Harold the same message.

Harold was the first to reply. *School isn't the same without you, kiddo.*

She smiled, despite herself. She imagined him sitting in the empty lounge, protein bar in hand. She was surprised to note that she missed him, a little, and their daily chats. Having told him the truth, the extent of her predicament, bound them in some way. She'd keep him updated. Maybe he'd have some insight should something arise.

Her phone buzzed. Kelsey had replied. *Safe travels.* It wasn't as personable as Harold's message, but it heartened her all the same.

"Harriet?" asked Lucy from outside the stall. "Are you okay in there?"

"Oh. Um, yeah. Sorry." Harriet pulled her pants up, waited for the automatic flush.

She swung the door open to find an anxious Lucy rocking from side to side. "They're gonna call our boarding group. We gotta get back to the gate!"

"I just have to wash my hands," Harriet said, edging around her.

"No time!" Lucy squeaked. She grabbed Harriet by the sleeve and tugged.

"But my hands," Harriet said, imagining them crawling with fluorescent green germs. She held them splayed before her. "They're dirty."

"Nah," Lucy said as she pulled her toward the door. "We'll find some hand sanitizer on the plane. Let's go!"

Harriet followed, reluctant. Lucy was right—their boarding group was lined up in front of the entrance to the jet bridge. They joined the queue, and Harriet noted several other women wearing white. Most of the local Serenitea consultants had left the prior day for a night spent frolicking in Miami, but Lucy and Harriet were relegated to a flight the day of departure. They'd only have a few hours to get from the airport to the port. It wasn't luxurious by any means, but she wasn't the one paying for the flight, or the cruise, so she supposed she didn't have the right to complain.

They were seated near the back of the plane, near the bathroom. Harriet imagined she could smell the antiseptic tang of it. She thought about getting up and washing her hands, but the attendants were rushing up and down the aisle. She didn't want to get in their way. She leaned back in her seat.

The plane began to move, wheeling itself toward the runway. Lucy's hand clamped down on hers and Harriet started, imagined her germs traveling up Lucy's fingers, her wrist.

"I have a confession to make," Lucy said.

"What's that?"

"I've never flown before."

"Oh," Harriet said, surprised. "Well, there's nothing to be afraid of."

Lucy leaned forward, eyes wide. "I'm going to throw up."

Harriet extricated her hand from the sweaty knot they'd formed, and pulled an emesis bag from the seat back in front of them. "Try to make it in there."

"Oh god," Lucy said, eyeing the woefully small bag.

Harriet rose up in her seat, looked for a flight attendant. "Just shut your eyes," Harriet said. "Try not to think about it."

"Oh my god," Lucy said as the plane picked up speed. "I'm going to die."

"Don't say that," Harriet whispered.

The nose of the plane lifted and Lucy let out a scream.

"Shh." Harriet hissed. She grabbed the woman's flailing hand and Lucy stilled.

"Help me, Harriet." She moaned.

Harriet stroked Lucy's fist with her thumb. "Shh." She soothed.

Lucy shut her eyes, fell back into her seat. She kept her eyes shut until the flight attendants began their rounds. "I did it," she said, wonder in her eyes, at last letting go of Harriet's hand.

"You did it." Harriet confirmed.

The flight itself was uneventful. Three hours of sitting next to Lucy wore her out, and she never did get her hand sanitizer. She stared out the window as they landed, watching the ground rise up to meet them. Lucy clutched her hand once more, but she didn't cry out or threaten to spew. Harriet hoped the flight back would be even more uneventful.

They collected their luggage and waited outside of the terminal for an Uber. Harriet checked her phone.

"I've never taken an Uber before." Lucy confided.

Harriet looked at her, sidelong. "It's not a big deal." She'd taken Ubers before, in the city where she used to live. She couldn't imagine needing one in Bentwood. "Have you lived in Bentwood for a long time?" she asked.

"Only my entire life," Lucy said.

"Oh," Harriet said.

"Yeah," Lucy said as their Uber pulled in.

"That's us," Harriet said.

They loaded their suitcases in the trunk.

"This is going to be so fun," Lucy said.

Harriet studied her face, open and smiling. "I hope it is."

Chapter Forty-Six

It was disorienting from the start. A man whisked away their luggage before they even reached the gangway. While rolling the overstuffed bags had been laborious, Harriet felt naked without hers, defenseless, which was the exact feeling she was trying to avoid. She had wanted to present herself as steely, unwavering. She had wanted to let the tea ladies know she meant business.

Lucy clapped her hands together. "This is already so fancy!"

"That's one word for it." Harriet sighed.

They were shuffled through checkpoint after checkpoint. At last, they were set free on one of the lower decks.

"What should we explore first?" Lucy had hold of her hand again and was tugging it, the way a child might.

Harriet stood firm. "I was thinking about going to our room," she said. "I think I need to lie down."

"Oh come on." Lucy pouted.

Women in white streamed around them, some of them already carrying what appeared to be fruity drinks. Harriet was pleased to notice that not everyone sipped Serenitea. Maybe this wouldn't be so bad, maybe the other covens, from other towns, weren't as stringent.

"I guess," Harriet said, letting Lucy pull her along.

They strolled through deck after deck, gazing out over crystalline pools, water slides, even a small rollercoaster that wove around the ship's massive funnel. They retreated to the inside of the ship and found a small shopping mall comprised of luxury stores neither of them could afford, what seemed like dozens of restaurants, a movie theater, another theater for live shows, a comedy club, a spa. At last Lucy slowed, seemed tired. "There's so much here."

Harriet couldn't imagine that there'd be time to take advantage of everything the ship offered over the course of three days. She nodded. "It's huge."

"Wouldn't it be amazing to work here?" Lucy nodded at an employee scooting past in a maroon uniform. "You'd practically live on the ship."

Harriet didn't like the idea of being trapped at work

for eternity. She shrugged, checked her phone. She hadn't purchased the ship's cellular or wireless plans yet, but they hadn't
departed the mainland. She was still getting a faint signal, even
here in the belly of the boat. She hadn't received any messages.

"I think I'm ready to see our room," Lucy said.

Harriet was exhausted. "Good."

They found the cabins just as the ship pushed off from
the dock. She felt the floor lurch a little, pressed her hand
against a wall. The halls were empty, most people on deck,
watching and waving as the ship set sail. Lucy and Harriet
snaked through the labyrinthine hallways until they at last
came to their room.

Lucy scanned their keycard and the door unlocked
with a thunk. "Here we go!"

Harriet frowned as the interior came into view. Two
skinny beds, no windows, no ocean view, a small TV that
seemed like an afterthought.

"It's cute," Lucy said.

"It's small," Harriet said. "Claustrophobic."

Their bags were already inside, waiting for them, and
they seemed to take up half the room.

"Let's get to unpacking!" Lucy said. She dragged her
bag over to a bed. "I'll take this one." She unzipped her suitcase and began rummaging through her clothes.

Harriet hadn't intended to unpack. She was never the
type of person to hang her clothing in the provided closet at

hotels, stuff the drawers full. She'd live out of her suitcase. That way, should she need to run, she could grab it and go. Besides, it just seemed futile to spend all that time organizing and unpacking for three days' worth of clothes. Instead, she threw herself down onto the remaining bed and shut her eyes.

"There's a big meeting tonight," Lucy said as she worked. "In the auditorium. Everyone will be there."

"Oh?" Harriet asked.

"Yeah. Didn't you read the itinerary?"

Harriet rolled over, faced the wall. She had studied the itinerary for hours, looking for any hidden meaning, any danger. She had the thing memorized. "I glanced at it," she said.

"Well, I'm going to go get a drink. Doesn't that sound fun? Want me to bring you one? They're free!"

Harriet sat up. "I don't think we should split up."

Lucy frowned. "Why not?"

Harriet wasn't sure what to say. She didn't want to frighten Lucy, but she wanted to make her aware of the potential danger. "It's a big ship," she said. "Anything could happen."

"Psh." Lucy scoffed. "Buy the ship's Wi-Fi and download the map! We can message each other. It's no big deal."

Harriet marveled at this woman, so scared on the plane, now raring to be set loose on the boat. "No," she said. "We stay together."

"Well, come on then."

She sighed. She had wanted to take a short nap. "Let me buy the Wi-Fi and stuff before we go," she said. "I'm surprised Serenitea didn't pay for that too. How are we supposed to make sales with no Wi-Fi?" Harriet's voice was laced with sarcasm, but Lucy's eyes grew wide.

"You're so right. What an oversight!"

Harriet opened her browser, was greeted with a page on how to buy internet. She followed the steps, refreshed the page. The dial-up speed was excruciating. She went ahead and bought the cellular package, too. Just in case. A message came through from Kelsey: *Everything okay?*

I guess so. She wrote.

Following Lucy back into the halls, she was surprised to see they were bustling now, women having returned from the decks, now intent on checking out their cabins. "I wonder how many passengers there are," she said.

"No idea," Lucy said. "But there's a lot."

They took an elevator to a different level. "We're bound to run into a bar."

Lucy nodded. "We'll just walk until we find one."

They didn't have to go far. They wandered into an alcove where a Mexican-themed margarita bar sat. "Margaritas sound so good!" Lucy cheered.

Harriet hadn't intended to drink on this expedition. She wanted to keep her senses about her. Being drunk meant being vulnerable. She eyed the menu. "Oh, Jesus," she said.

Every drink was some variant on Serenitea: frozen tea slushies with a shot of tequila, iced tea with fresh fruit, vodka shots infused with tea. "What the fuck," she said.

"What can I get you ladies?" a short man in maroon asked. "We have a special menu for you this week."

"This is so amazing." Lucy cooed. "Look at them all. I can't decide."

"Can I just have water?" Harriet asked.

"Hot?"

"No, cold please."

The bartender smiled. "Just thought maybe you intended to make some of that tea."

"No." She scoffed.

"Harriet, you're no fun. I'll have the slushy," Lucy said.

"Sure thing!" the bartender said.

Lucy wandered near the edge of the room, examining photographs of the Sonoran Desert that hung there.

Harriet stayed at the bar, watched as the man dispensed the slushy from a whirring machine. He slid a perspiring glass of water her way. "What's with the tea, anyhow?" He leaned in close, conspiratorial.

"They sell it," Harriet said. "The girls."

"And you don't?"

"Not anymore," she said. Her voice was low, rushed.

The man frowned. "Why not? The whole ship changed their menu to feature it this week. Even the food's seasoned with it."

"Seriously?" Harriet glanced over at Lucy who was running a finger along a golden railing.

"Yep," he said. "Haven't tried it myself."

"Don't!" she said. "Don't try it."

The man raised an eyebrow.

"It's—It's dangerous," she admitted.

The man smiled. "But you're letting your friend drink it? What an interesting time you'll have this week."

Harriet sighed. "It's complicated. I don't want to scare her."

"Hmm," he said, as Harriet gathered up both drinks. "Have a nice evening," he said.

"Here," Harriet said. She handed Lucy the sweating glass. "Promise me you won't drink too much on this trip, okay?"

"Harriet, I can handle my liquor." Lucy smiled. "I didn't know you were a prohibitionist."

"What? I'm not. It's not the booze, Lucy. It's the tea. Angela, she—"

"Oh shush," Lucy said. "I'm here to have fun." She took a big gulp of the slushy, screwed up her face.

"What?" Harriet asked, frantic.

Lucy's face was red, eyes shut.

"What's happening?" Harriet asked. She looked at the bar, but the man had his back to them, seemed to be cleaning something. "Lucy?" She knew something bad was bound to happen on this cruise, but didn't realize it'd happen so fast. She touched Lucy's arm and her eyes sprang open.

"Brain freeze." She gasped.

"Fuck, Lucy." Harriet turned, walked up a ramp.

Chapter Forty-Seven

Harriet spent the rest of the afternoon in a daze, being pulled from one activity to the next. She held a putt-putt club, she flopped around in the rollercoaster cart while Lucy screamed and squealed. She drank water after water, refused to nibble any of the hors d'oeuvres offered poolside. Her stomach growled and contracted.

"You need to eat!" Lucy said, scarfing down a shish kabob dusted in a proprietary blend of botanicals.

Harriet shook her head. "Not hungry."

Lucy frowned. "But I can hear your stomach from over here!" Lucy lay on a lounge chair three feet to Harriet's right.

Harriet sat up on hers, refusing to relax. "That bartender, he said they're using the tea to flavor the foods."

"It's incredible," Lucy said.

Harriet pulled her legs up underneath her. "Lucy, it's disgusting. It's ridiculous." A pair of women walked by, and Harriet lowered her voice. "The tea is poisoning you."

Lucy laughed. "It's not poison!" She was so loud, so high-pitched. Harriet winced, glanced around to ensure no one was looking their way.

"Shh." She hissed. "Angela died drinking that stuff. I know you don't believe it, but I was drugged that day at her house. Drugged, Lucy. Against my will. And they did something to me while I was out. I don't know what but I felt so wrong, so—"

Lucy pointed her shish kabob stick at her. "Why did you even come?"

Harriet looked down at her lap, her trembling hands folded there. "I want to protect you. I want to get to the bottom of what they're doing here."

Lucy snorted. "I'm sorry," she said. "I don't need protection, Harriet. I'm the best I've ever been. I'm thriving."

"No," Harriet said. "You're not."

"What do you mean? I feel great, I look great. I'm actually making money off this thing. I'm getting well."

Harriet stared at her. She did have a certain glow about her, a ruddiness to the cheeks that wasn't entirely unattractive. She—without a doubt—looked better in the muted neutrals she'd been choosing over the garish Mary Jane. Her hair was shiny, healthy. She had a twinkle in her eye. "No. It's all a ruse," she said. She had once felt that way too—soothed, rejuvenated. But where had it gotten her? Where had it gotten Angela? She shivered, despite the sun.

"You keep talking about Serenitea like there's some massive conspiracy. But there's not, Harriet. It's just a lot of women getting well and supporting themselves with their own initiative. I don't know why you can't accept that." Lucy's voice was whiny, tinged with accusation. "I'm starting to believe you're not a feminist."

"What?" Harriet squinted her eyes. "Of course I'm a feminist." Harriet fancied herself a progressive in every sense of the word.

"You just seem to have a real problem with women-owned businesses, that's all."

Harriet leaned forward, spat out a laugh. "Are you talking about pyramid schemes? Because, yes, I do have a problem with them. They're predatory, Lucy. They're not *helping* women. They're *taking advantage* of them. They're designed to prey on women and their connections, their places in society. I can't think of anything less feminist, actually."

"Ugh." Lucy grunted. She pulled down her sunglasses on her head, hid her eyes behind the dark lenses. "I'm not going to fight with you."

Harriet huffed. "Whatever. I'm going to find the truth, Lucy, and then you'll see."

Lucy turned and Harriet could see herself reflected in her glasses. She looked misshapen, pale. Lucy sighed. "They told me not to bring you."

It hurt. It still hurt. Being rejected—even by a cabal of evil vampires—hurt. "That's because I'm on to them," she said, voice cracking.

Lucy held a hand to her forehead. "All of that... It's in your head."

"No, it's not," she growled. She pushed off the chair, stood and looked out at the horizon. She couldn't see land, but she could see a bank of dark clouds building. She was all turned about, didn't know what direction was which, but she wondered if they'd soon be beneath that ominous sky. She wiped a tear from her eye.

Harriet walked to the railing, put a hand there to steady herself. She would text Harold and Kelsey, she decided. They'd prop her up, remind her of her mission. She fumbled with her phone.

"Only an hour 'til the big conference and then dinner," Lucy said, perky and bright, as if nothing had transpired between them.

Chapter Forty-Eight

The sky grew dark, and large raindrops splattered against the deck. Women ran laughing into the inner sanctum of the ship, hands held above their heads. Their white dresses turned transparent in the rain, and Harriet saw an impressive number of nipples. But she wasn't in the mood for ogling. She picked at the skin on her finger. She was anxious. The sea swelled around them, the ship rising and falling and her stomach did the same. "I think I'm going to be sick," she said.

Lucy looked her up and down, her own pale nipples shining through her dress. "Eating might help settle your stomach. Everyone's eating in the grand ballroom after the presentation."

Harriet shook her head.

"Let's get to the auditorium," Lucy said.

Harriet let herself be led through the ship to a large room with rows of seating, an ornate looking stage. The seats were filling with waves of white dresses, smiling women, nipples. Their voices echoed in the cavernous space. Harriet held onto Lucy as the floor rolled.

"Oh look!" Lucy paused, waved up into the seats. "Hi!"

Harriet felt a thousand eyes on her and grew hot, prickling. Georgiana waved and smiled at Lucy. "Can we just sit down?" she asked.

"Looks like all the seats around Georgina are full," Lucy said. She spun, scanning the crowd with slow, needy eyes. "I can't find any of the other girls. They have to be around here somewhere."

"The back," Harriet said. "Let's just sit in the back, please."

Lucy shrugged and began the slow climb to the top of the auditorium. She pulled her dress up high as she walked, exposing thick calves. Harriet watched them as they mounted the stairs, wishing she had sturdy legs to stabilize her now.

At last, they found two seats in the very back. The lighting was dim and the stage was distant and small, but Harriet preferred it this way.

Lucy leaned back in her seat. "Can't wait to hear from

the Ascendants!"

Harriet sighed. She'd read in the itinerary that this was to be a motivational pep talk, a kickoff for their time spent on the ship. They'd offer goals to strive toward, details on the following days' events, blah blah blah. Harriet would listen hard for subtext, hidden meaning. She put her hands on her stomach and closed her eyes.

After a few minutes, the crowd quieted and Harriet opened her eyes to see that the room had darkened even further. A spotlight shone on a microphone on stage. She fidgeted, strained to see the women around her.

The ladies erupted into applause. A tall, blonde woman strode across the stage. She wore a white ballgown. The dress glowed in the light. Harriet could not see her nipples.

"Thank you," the woman said into the microphone.

The cheering didn't stop. Instead, it intensified, women rising to clap.

"Who is she?" Lucy asked, who clapped along.

"The founder," Harriet said. "Marissa Appleton."

Lucy looked at her out of the corner of her eye. "I thought you didn't care about this."

Harriet turned, opened her mouth to explain that she, in fact, cared a great deal, which was why she was here to tear it all down, but the woman was already talking, and Harriet shut her mouth.

"Welcome to the fifth annual Serenitea Wellness

Cruise!"

More cheering, more applause.

"I'm Marisa Appleton, founder of Serenitea. Wellness has been my lifelong passion, and I'm so happy to share this journey with all of you."

Harriet's phone buzzed. She tilted it upward, peeking at the screen. Kelsey: *Thinking of you.*

She felt her face grow hot. *Thanks.* She wrote back. *In a big culty meeting now.*

Lucy nudged her with an elbow. "Shh," she said, even though Harriet hadn't been talking aloud.

Be careful. Kelsey replied. *Any intel yet?*

All the food and drinks here laced with tea. Everyone's nipples are out.

For real?

For real. Harriet wrote. She tabbed over to the chat with Harold, wrote him a similar message. Marissa Appleton droned on in the background.

"Harriet!" Lucy hissed. "Pay attention."

Harriet dropped the phone on her lap. Right. She was supposed to be gathering information.

"That's why I want to bring up some of our Originators! Ladies?"

Three more women took the stage, all groomed to perfection, all in white. The consultants around her whispered, applauded.

"My name is Carrie Whitgrove," a thin woman, with voluminous black hair, said. "I've been Triple Ascendant for a year now, and—"

Harriet's phone vibrated against her thigh. *What the hell are you going to eat?* Harold wrote.

She sent back a shrug emoji.

Take pictures. He wrote. There was a pause, and then three dots bounced up and down in the chat. *Not only of the nipples, but of anything interesting. Might be useful down the road.*

He was right. If she was going to build a case, she needed evidence. She held up her phone, took a blurry picture of Carrie Whitgrove. She sent it to Harold and Kelsey.

Kelsey replied first. *Wtf. Everyone's in white? It's not just Bentwood?*

Another message rolled in, this one from Harold. *Creepy.*

You up for a call, honey? her mother asked.

Shit. In the excitement of the panty séance, she'd forgotten to tell her parents she was going on the cruise. Why did they want to call her now? *Not a good time.* Harriet wrote, ignoring Lucy's tsk tsk tsking from next to her. *I'll text when free.*

Her mother sent a thumbs up emoji.

Harriet stared down at her phone, a frown on her face. She was a horrible daughter, a horrible friend. She was going to make this right. She'd come out of this a hero, and everyone would forgive her for being absent, her mind elsewhere. And when she went home victorious, she would go straight to Kelsey's and not her dank little cabin filled with underwear and ghosts. It would be okay.

The ship lurched and Harriet cried out. A few women turned to look at her and she smiled, sheepish.

"Focus, Harriet," Lucy whispered.

She swallowed hard and looked down at the stage. The three women were holding hands now, heads bent. Were they praying? She held her breath as she watched. These women were triple ascendant, just like Eliza. Harriet wondered if Eliza was on board and, if so, why she wasn't chosen to grace the stage. Though, she thought she knew. Eliza was curt, sharp as a razor's edge. These women were rounded and wholesome and, despite their position at the front of the room, meek.

"We ask that you join hands," one of the women said.

Lucy found her hand in the dark and clenched it tight. There wasn't anyone to Harriet's right, but there was someone on Lucy's other side and she held Lucy's left hand. Harriet leaned forward, tried to see who it was.

"These are your sisters," the voice said. "Not through blood, but spirit."

Harriet perked up at the words "blood" and "spirit". No one seemed to be moving. The place was silent.

"Hold them now. Hold them close. We will become one during the next few days, transforming into something new. Something well."

Harriet rolled her eyes at the vague speech.

Then, the woman said something Harriet would play through her mind for the rest of the night: "Remember, we must all give something up. Wellness requires sacrifice."

Harriet's arms tingled as her hair stood on end. She wished she had recorded the speech. The women were cheering now, the ladies on stage backing away with little bows and curtseys.

"Come on." Lucy prodded. "Let's go to the dining room before it fills up. I'm hungry."

"But did you hear what they said?"

"Yeah. Let's go." Lucy yanked on her arm.

Harriet rose, swayed on her feet, but not because of the storm—that seemed to have abated—but because of her own swirling delirium. "Sacrifice," she said, dazed.

"Sure," Lucy said, pushing.

Harriet stared down at the empty stage, now dark. Perhaps if she could get close to Marissa Appleton and her select cadre of ascendants, she'd figure something out. But tracking them down on a ship full of women who looked alike, dressed alike, that would be a challenge. She let Lucy shove her once more and she stumbled forward, shocked and sick.

Chapter Forty-Nine

Harriet and Lucy followed a line of ladies to a dining room just off the auditorium entrance. They were shown to a table already occupied by four other women. Harriet frowned.

"Enjoy," the man who'd guided them there said.

Lucy smiled and cooed at the women, patted their bare arms. Harriet slouched in her seat.

"This is Harriet," Lucy said. "We're from the same town."

"That's wonderful," a brunette said. "I met these three this morning, but we're getting along alright." She winked.

The other women smiled, took sips of the tea before them.

"How does this work?" Lucy asked.

Harriet sighed. If she'd read the itinerary, she would know this was a three-course experience with everything pre-selected by the triple ascendants onboard. She could smell something savory wafting in from the wings and her stomach growled.

Lucy's new friends explained the menu to her, showed her the cards on the table where everything was laid out in curly gold script. "This is gonna be awesome," Lucy said.

Waiters streamed in from the sides of the room carrying giant silver trays. A large glass of iced tea materialized in front of Harriet, as did a plate of smoked trout croquettes. Harriet didn't like fish, but the little fried balls smelled so good. She rolled one around her plate with her fork, looking for traces of tea. A little mozzarella cheese leaked from one of the balls and she shut her mouth tight so she wouldn't drool on her dress.

"Oh my god these are delicious," Lucy said mid-chew.

The other women nodded, covered their mouths with their manicured hands.

"Is it—" Harriet didn't know how to phrase it without coming off as suspect. "Is there tea in the balls?" she asked.

One of the women shrugged.

"I can't taste any, but the flavors are so strong," another said.

Harriet stabbed one of the croquettes with the tines of

her fork and watched as a salty brine oozed out.

Lucy pointed at Harriet with her own dirty fork, a mean look of suspicion hewn across her face. "Why don't you eat?"

Harriet's face turned red. "I don't like fish," she said.

"Christ," Lucy said, reaching for Harriet's plate. She dumped all of Harriet's croquettes on her own plate, handed Harriet back her empty dish. Harriet stared down at it.

One of the women leaned in across the table. "The next course is chicken," she said, not unkindly.

Harriet nodded.

Soon, the waiters returned and whisked away their empty plates, refilled their teas. Harriet's glass sat untouched. She was so thirsty. She'd wait to go back to the room, she decided, and she'd drink from the faucet. That had to be safe, right?

The next course arrived with a flourish. Chicken marsala infused with the tea, wine, and sherry. Lucy tore into hers with an urgency Harriet didn't understand.

A man approached her from the side. "Would you care for a drink, miss?" he asked.

"Water?" She pleaded.

He frowned. "I have slushies."

"No slush," she almost shouted.

"Oh, wow, I'll take one. Those are so good," Lucy said. "You ladies need to try them."

"Oh, we've been drinking them all day." One of the girls giggled.

"Five slushies?" the man asked, staring down at Harriet.

"Five slushies!" Lucy cheered.

Harriet shredded her chicken with her fork, watched as the red juice pooled in the gashed breast.

"You need to eat." Lucy hissed. "You're embarrassing me."

Harriet looked up at the other women. They were staring now. "I'm not hungry," she said, while her stomach rumbled.

The women cocked their heads, chewed their meat.

"Are you a vegetarian, dear?" one of them asked. "There was an email. You could have replied back and said you have dietary restrictions."

"I—" She began.

"She's not a vegetarian." Lucy spat.

Harriet set down her fork.

"She's just being stubborn. She thinks the tea is poison." Lucy shook her head, chuckled, and shoveled another hunk of chicken into her mouth.

The women looked at one another, and then back to Harriet. She had trouble placing their expressions. Fear? Anger? Harriet broke out in a sweat. "That's not true," she said.

Their slushies arrived and, for a moment, the women

smiled. Then they focused their attention back on Harriet, faces flattening into mean glares.

"She thinks she's some kind of spy." Lucy laughed.

Harriet's stomach hurt with more than hunger. "That's not true. My stomach—it hasn't been right since the storm started. Maybe I'm sea sick."

"Storm's done now," one of the women said, gesturing toward a large bank of windows Harriet hadn't noticed before. It was dark outside, and she couldn't see anything beyond the railing, but it seemed calm outside. It wasn't raining, at the very least.

Harriet swallowed. Looked back down at her chicken. She picked up her fork, scooped up a few pieces of the wine-and-tea-soaked meat. Reluctant, she slid it into her mouth. She moved it around with her tongue, tasting the sweet juice, the sapid chicken. It was so good. She chewed, the flavors bursting in her mouth. Her face tingled with the intensity of it all and she shut her eyes.

"See?" Lucy asked. "It's good!"

Harriet cut another piece, popped it into her mouth. She ate the entire breast and most of the side salad. She sopped up the juices from the meat with the greens.

Having seen her eat, the women around her returned to their conversation. They sipped their slushies, their teas.

The room grew quieter as the night went on, and by the time dessert was brought out, the women were slouching in their seats, tired.

"I'm so glad I met you guys." Lucy slurred as she spooned cheesecake into her mouth.

"Mmhmm," one of the women said.

Harriet listened to the tinkling of silverware on plates, of ice in glasses, a few stray words spoken to one's neighbor. She felt a familiar calm descend over her, a mellow sweetness that numbed her senses. She ate the cheesecake, she called for a slushy. The women around her smiled, eyes lazy, dreamy. "Fuck it," she said, and they all laughed.

Lucy checked her phone and jumped up, sending her seat springing backward, crashing to the floor.

"What the hell?" a lady asked.

A waiter approached, extending a soothing hand.

"It's time for the chapter meeting. Oh my god. I'm late," Lucy said, gathering up her tote bag.

"Chapter meeting?" Harriet straightened in her chair, panic rising through the haze.

Lucy looked down at her. "Uh, yeah. You weren't invited? Guess I'll see you after!" She shuffled away, weaving between chairs and tables, bumping into waiters.

Harriet looked around, frantic. Everyone stared. "Bathroom," she squeaked, bumbling upward.

The world swayed, she placed her hand on a chair back to steady herself. Her body felt so heavy. She dragged her feet. She wanted nothing more than to return to their cabin and curl up in bed. Lucy was long gone, but she struggled onward. Every woman in white watched her halting progress. Tears fell down her cheeks, plopped heavy on her own white dress. When she at last exited the dining room, she almost collapsed in relief, but she had to keep walking. She had to find Lucy.

Chapter Fifty

She floundered through the hallways, onto dark and breezy decks. She peeked into every doorway. Some rooms held groups of workers in maroon, some held a few women in white, huddled together over laptop screens, notebooks, some held nothing at all. None held Lucy. She cried as she stumbled, vision obscured by tears, mind obscured by tea. She didn't forget her quest, though: find Lucy, keep her safe.

She called Lucy's phone over and over, sent countless, desperate texts. Lucy didn't answer.

Dinner had ended and there were women streaming down the hallways now, bumping into her, holding hands. They all seemed relaxed, at ease.

"Please." She reached out to one. "I'm looking for the Bentwood chapter meeting."

"What's Bentwood?" the lady asked.

Harriet dove away from her, grabbed the shoulders of another woman. "Where would a small group meet? A chapter meeting?"

The woman leaned away from her, looked down her nose. "There are private meeting rooms on the third floor."

"What floor is this!?" Harriet shook the woman.

"Four!" the woman shouted, pulling herself from beneath Harriet's heavy hands.

Harriet ran down the hall, pushing tea ladies out of her way. There were gasps and profanities, someone may have spilled their drink on their dress, but Harriet was headed toward the stairwell. She couldn't be stopped. *Wouldn't* be stopped.

The third floor, like all the other levels of the ship, was massive and strewn with restaurants, bars, inlets offering leisure activities, information desks. Most women were retreating to bed after their heavy meals, however, and Harriet seemed to have the floor all to herself. There weren't even workers here. "Hello?" she called out. Her voice echoed against the faux marble walls.

Harriet peered into a darkened shop window. She spied bottles of aspirin, sunscreen, and, best of all, packaged snacks. Nabisco cookies and Pop-Tarts. She would be okay.

She'd return in the morning and buy herself some tea-free food. She pushed off the window, leaving greasy fingerprints on the pristine surface, and wobbled away.

At last, the hallway narrowed down and lost some of the grandeur of the previous section. This area was subdued, lined with glass-encased rooms. These were the meeting rooms, she was sure of it. She ran as fast as her clumsy, drunken feet would carry her.

"Lucy?" she cried.

All of the rooms were dark.

She reached the end of the rooms where the hallway widened again. She collapsed onto the ramp, cried into her hands. Maybe it would be best to go back to their room. That's the one place she knew Lucy was sure to return. But what might have happened to her in the meantime? What would the tea ladies do?

"Miss?" A hand grazed the top of her head.

She looked up. A woman in the maroon work clothes she'd become so familiar with hovered above her.

"Sorry." Harriet sniffled.

The woman helped her to her feet. "Are you okay?"

"No." She confessed. "I'm not. I'm lost."

The woman gave a knowing smile. "It's easy to get lost on this ship. Can I help you get to your cabin?"

Harriet took her hand, warm and soft. It would be so nice to let this nice lady lead her back to bed like she was a child. She wanted it more than anything. She wanted to be mothered. "No," she said. "I'm looking for my group. They're having a meeting and I can't find it." She felt snot sliding down her lip.

"Hmm," the lady said. "They're not down the hall?"

"No. I looked. I looked everywhere," she cried.

The woman studied her puffy face, her bloodshot eyes, her dress, sagging and sad. "Let's go to your cabin, okay? You can catch up with your friends in the morning. I'm sure they won't mind." She put her arm around Harriet's shoulders.

"No." Harriet stood firm. "I need to get to this meeting. It's important."

The woman looked disappointed. "Well, there was a group that reserved the hibachi steakhouse. We're to keep it unlocked until two tonight. I don't know if it's your—"

"Where?" Harriet whipped around, grabbed the woman by the arms.

She shrank away. "Upstairs," she said. "Starboard side."

Harriet was a little sad that the woman didn't offer to lead her there, but she had shaken her around a bit. "Thank you," Harriet cried as she ran, rounding a corner. She didn't see the woman shake her head, sad and confused.

Chapter Fifty-One

The steakhouse—dramatic lighting, as if prepared to host a romantic dinner—had two entrances: one from the outside, one from the depths of the ship. Harriet approached from the inside, slinking low in the shadows. She peered through the glass front, gasped when she saw movement inside.

She saw the backs of their heads: Georgiana, Eliza, Shannon, Elaine, and a few others she couldn't recognize. She felt ashamed. She was a shitty spy. She crept closer. She didn't see Lucy's short frame anywhere among them. Where was she?

Their bare shoulders shone in the subtle lighting—skin smooth, unblemished. Harriet blushed when she realized they were naked. What were they doing, getting naked right where anyone could walk by and see?

Georgiana turned an inch, and Harriet ducked down. Her face glistened, streaked by tears. Shannon faced her, put a hand on her cheek. Eliza bent over something in front of her. Harriet couldn't see. She needed to get closer.

The door opened with a whisper, Harriet crawled through. She scurried beneath the nearest table, peered between the legs. No one seemed to have noticed the door swinging shut.

"It worked," Georgiana said, still crying. She dabbed at her eyes with a bit of cloth.

"Of course it worked." Eliza snapped.

Harriet crept to the next table, careful not to bump any of the chairs. She had a better view now, could see the girls gathered around one of the large hibachi grills—where chefs would slice and fling vegetables, exotic meats. She saw white fabric gathered there, a dress. Someone lay sprawled across the grill.

Harriet's heart was in her throat and her head swam, but she knew it was Lucy they clustered around. She couldn't crawl any closer without rousing suspicion. She lowered herself on all fours, like a mountain lion ready to strike, and weighed her options. She could wait them out, gather as much information as she could, and pray Lucy was alright at the end of it, or she could pounce, jump on Shannon's back, and slam her head into the countertop. She could rescue her friend. She breathed hard through her nose. She wasn't sure how she'd take down the other girls.

"When will she wake up?" a woman on the far side of the group asked. Harriet had trouble seeing who it was.

"Soon enough," Eliza said. She raised a hand, caressed the figure on the table. Harriet stifled a growl. "You must be patient."

"Oh." Someone gasped. "Look."

Harriet pushed herself as far out from beneath the table as she was willing to go. The fabric, glimpsed between naked girls, shifted, fell away. Harriet squinted. She saw naked flesh illuminated by studio lighting. The skin stirred and twitched.

The women murmured.

"Where?" a voice asked, muffled and confused.

"Shh," Eliza said, petting the exposed flesh, digging her fingers in as if in a repetitive massage.

"Eliza." The voice was stronger now, resolute, clear and steady. Totally unlike Lucy's burbling speech. Harriet gagged, swallowed down some vomit. It wasn't Lucy there on the table.

Angela sat up, her shining hair falling around her shoulders, her breasts. She smiled.

"Oh, thank you, Eliza," Georgiana cried.

Eliza shrugged, stared at Angela. Harriet saw her

clench her fists. "And how do you feel, my dear?"

Harriet fumbled with her phone, took one blurry picture. Her hands were shaking, rattling. She couldn't breathe.

Angela's eyes flitted down the length of her body. Then she turned to the women, lingered over each of their faces. "I feel well."

Chapter Fifty-Two

The women donned their dresses, pulling them up over milky shoulders. Shannon and Georgiana helped Angela into hers. Angela wobbled, but otherwise did seem "well". Her face had color, her lips were full and bent up in a smile. Harriet would have never known she was dead.

She shrunk down under the table as the women filed by, tucking her limbs beneath her. She watched Angela's bare feet, examined her manicured toenails. French tips. The women whispered to themselves.

The door shut, and Harriet was alone in the restaurant. She exhaled—a loud, sharp sound—and clambered out from under the table. "Fuck."

She woke her phone, pulled up the picture she'd taken. She had been shaking too hard and the long shutter speed had resulted in a very streaky photo. Ghost-like forms hovered above each woman, their own bare backs superimposed and smeared across the screen. There, in the middle of them, Harriet could just make out a blonde head, a specific curve to the nose. It was Angela. She sent the picture to Harold, then Kelsey. She waited a moment, but neither replied. They would both be asleep.

She also sent the picture to Lucy. Where was she? Harriet hadn't seen her at the meeting. The women never mentioned her absence. Though, it was possible they addressed it well before she snuck in. She tried calling her again. Voicemail.

"Hey, uh, I didn't see you at the meeting but some pretty crazy shit went down and we need to talk. Actually, we need to do more than that. We need to get out of here. Meet me at the cabin."

Maybe Lucy had gotten lost, just as she had, was still roaming the boat looking for the Bentwood girls.

Harriet stood at the grill where Angela had lain, spread her hand across the steel surface. It still felt warm. She couldn't comprehend what she'd seen. Something had happened before she arrived—some sort of ritual? Whatever happened, it didn't seem to cause Angela any distress. She'd said it herself—she was well. And where was Lucy? She remembered what the originator had said at the big welcome event: "Wellness requires sacrifice."

"Fuck," she said again. She didn't like where her mind was headed.

She exited the steakhouse and looked up and down the hallway. It was quiet still. She couldn't hear the Bentwood ladies, but she walked slowly just in case. She didn't want to meet them on the way to the cabins.

She'd told Lucy to go to their room, but that didn't stop Harriet from checking every open door she passed. "Lucy," she whispered into spas and empty bars. "Lucy."

At last, she came to their cabin. She listened, one ear against the door. She could hear hushed talking, laughter from other rooms, but their own seemed silent. She scanned the key and flung the door open.

Empty.

Harriet marched around the small room, just in case, checking under the beds, in the small shower. She threw herself down on her comforter, defeated. She checked her phone again, hoping to have heard from Lucy, from anybody. But there was nothing there.

She must have passed out because in the next moment she was opening her eyes, checking her phone. It was morning. "What the hell?" she asked.

She wanted nothing more than to bolt from the room and resume her search, but she looked at herself in the mirror and saw how disheveled, how unkempt, she looked. She threw her dirty dress on the floor and stepped into the shower. Though the warm water felt good on her skin, it wasn't very relaxing—she kept hearing phantom voices and screams, crying, in the white noise of the faucet. She climbed out. At least she smelled better.

She drank some water straight from the sink. She wasn't sure when she'd find untainted water again, so she drank long and heavy. It tasted good.

She dressed herself—another white sundress—and pulled on some simple sandals. Dark sunglasses hid her puffy eyes. She looked like every other woman there, and that's just what she wanted.

Her phone rang and she jumped. *Mom.* She'd forgotten to text back the night before. She couldn't ignore them again.

"Hello?" she asked.

"Harriet!" Her mother began. "I hope I caught you before school. It's just, we haven't heard from you in a while and your father is worried. Are you okay? Do you need anything?"

Harriet's throat constricted. Her voice came out all wobbly. "I'm alright," she said.

Her mother paused. "You don't sound alright. What's wrong?"

She cleared her throat, tamped down the tears. "No, really. I'm fine. I'm on a cruise."

"A cruise? Really? Why didn't you tell us?"

Harriet sighed. "It was kind of spur of the moment. It's a work thing," she said.

"In the middle of the school year?"

Harriet looked down at her yellowing toenails. "Okay, it's a pyramid scheme thing," she admitted.

"A pyramid scheme?" Her mother's voice was incredulous.

She heard her dad coughing in the background. She missed him. She decided she'd tell them everything. They deserved to know. "Are you sitting down?"

"Yes..."

She talked for fifteen minutes. She told her mother about Lucy, about Angela and Kelsey. About Harold in the teacher's lounge, and the way strange things happened in her house. When she was finished, she was crying. Her mom didn't say anything for a long time.

"Oh, honey," she said at last.

"I know," Harriet said. "It sounds crazy."

"Well..."

"But it's true, Mom. Now I'm stuck on this ship, looking for Lucy, all while an undead Angela prowls the decks and

I still don't know what it means, what they're up to."

Her mom took a deep breath. "When you land, I want you to come straight here. Don't even bother with work. We'll figure it out. Find you something close to the house."

It took a moment for Harriet to register what she was saying. "You want me to move in with you guys?"

"Yeah. Why not?" Her mother's voice was cheerful, but she knew she was worried about her only daughter, thinking she'd gone insane.

"I don't know," Harriet said. "Kelsey offered to let me stay at her place for a while. That way I could keep working and—"

"Don't you think you need a break?" Her mom interrupted.

Her phone buzzed in her hand, another incoming call. "I have to go," she said. "I'll think about it, okay?"

"Uh, okay. Love you?"

"Love you too," Harriet said as she mashed her finger on the screen. "Hello?"

"What the fuck, Harriet? Is that Angela?" Kelsey sounded angry.

"I think so," Harriet said. "I mean, yes. It is."

"How?"

"I don't know. And Lucy is *missing*. She didn't come to the cabin last night and I'm worried they sacrificed her to bring Angela back to life." Saying it aloud made it sound preposterous. She blushed, even though she was alone.

Kelsey was quiet for a long time. "For real?"

"Kinda?"

"Okay. How do we get you off that boat?"

Harriet looked at herself in the mirror. "I don't think I can leave until I find Lucy, or, at least figure out what happened to her."

"It's not safe there," Kelsey said. "Besides, if what you're saying is true, that means Lucy is gone. Come home. We'll figure out how to go to the authorities together, get the law involved."

"You believe me?"

"Kinda," Kelsey said.

"I wish you were here," Harriet said, surprising herself even as it left her lips.

"I don't," Kelsey said.

Harriet laughed. It felt good. "I'll call you later, okay? I'm gonna go look for her, hear what I can hear."

"Please be careful," Kelsey said. "Promise me you'll be careful."

"I promise."

"Okay," Kelsey said.

"Okay," Harriet said.

The line went dead.

Chapter Fifty-Three

She sat in an alcove, watching the women stream by on their way to meetings, seminars, meals, pedicures. She held her phone out before her, staring at the text she was about to send. Their group chat had gone silent, and Harriet suspected the tea ladies had created a new one without her. With Lucy in their clutches, they no longer needed her. She was about to revive the chat, raise it from the digital dead.

She took a deep breath, pressed send.

Hey ladies! It read. *Hope you're having as much fun as I am. My roomie, Lucy, didn't come back to the cabin last night and I'm just wondering if she went back with any of you, or said anything. Thanks!* She didn't expect anyone to reveal anything, but perhaps some would feign surprise and she could parse their messages for meaning, subtext.

A few girls viewed the message, but no one replied. Harriet sighed and slid the phone into her dress's pocket, which pulled the fabric around her neck. She rubbed the skin there, defeated. She'd been searching for Lucy for hours with no luck. She wanted to cry.

A message came through and her heart did a somersault. But it was just Harold, asking if she'd found Lucy yet. *Nope.* She wrote.

Have you told anyone, like, in command of the ship?

Harriet's mouth hung open. She hadn't even considered escalating the issue up past Serenitea. They were all consuming, all knowing. It hadn't occurred to her that there was another governing body here. She felt stupid.

I just wonder if she fell overboard or something mundane like that. He wrote.

Harriet hardly considered falling off a giant boat mundane, but she understood what he was trying to say. Maybe their problem wasn't supernatural. The ocean had been a little tumultuous, enough to upset her stomach. What if Lucy was near a railing when an errant wave came crashing through? She stood.

"Excuse me," she asked a passing worker. "Who can I talk to about a missing person?"

The woman raised an eyebrow. "Someone on board is missing?"

Harriet felt small beneath the woman's intense stare.

"Yes. I mean, maybe. I can't find my roommate."

"Let me take you to guest services. They're better equipped for this kind of thing. They can put out an announcement."

"Okay," Harriet said. "But what if she's not on the boat at all?"

The woman frowned. "Like, she didn't get on? You call her?"

"No, she was here."

"Come on." She sighed. "We'll let guest services figure this one out." The woman seemed exasperated and Harriet wondered if she thought she was drunk or off her meds or some combination of both.

She followed the worker across the ship and up a level. The woman didn't speak to her or check that Harriet still followed. She struggled to keep up. At last, the woman stopped. "Here," she said, gesturing to a bank of computers and more figures in maroon.

Harriet eyed them, breathless.

"They'll help you," the woman said. She turned, disappeared into a crowd, seeming far too happy to be rid of Harriet and her problems.

Harriet approached the desk, sheepish. "Uh." She cleared her throat.

"Can I help you, ma'am?" A young man smiled up at her.

"Yeah," she said. "I can't find my roommate."

He nodded. "When did you get separated?"

"Last night," she said.

His smile faded. "That long, huh?" He drummed his fingers on the countertop.

"I guess so," she admitted.

"And do both of you have the Wi-Fi and cellular package? You've called and texted and whatnot?"

"Yes," Harriet said.

"Try restarting your phone. Sometimes things get hung up."

Harriet shook her head. "This isn't a matter of things getting 'hung up.'" She huffed.

"Fine, fine," he said. "I can make an announcement over the intercom. Would that help?"

Harriet shrugged, told him Lucy's name. She knew deep down that wherever Lucy had gone, a simple announcement wasn't going to bring her back.

"This will play in all public spaces," he said to Harriet. The man picked up a device and a chime rang overhead. He inhaled, cleared his throat. He requested Lucy's attendance at the guest services kiosk on floor three. He nodded at Harriet and smiled, pleased with what he'd done.

"Now what?" she asked.

"Well, you just hang around here until she comes back. Might take a while, though, depending on where she's at. Grab a drink, have a seat."

"What if she doesn't come?" Harriet asked.

The man smiled and blinked, face blank. "Why wouldn't she come?"

"Well, I mean, what if she fell off?"

"Fell off?" The man's stupid smile persisted.

"I think she might be dead," Harriet said.

"*Dead?*"

"Listen,"—Harriet leaned over the desk until their noses were almost touching—"she either fell overboard or got sacrificed by a group of wellness vampires. What do you propose we do?"

"What was your name, Miss?"

"Harriet Pendleton," she said.

"Right." The man typed on his loud keyboard. He paused, looked her up and down. He took a step backward. His hands shook as he unclipped a walkie talkie from his waist. He raised it to his mouth. "Requesting Charlie at GS3. Maybe Alpha, too."

"What are you saying? What does that mean?"

"Just have a seat, Miss." His finger trembled as he pointed to a line of cushioned chairs. "Someone will be with you in a moment."

"But I don't want to have a seat. I want to find my roommate." The man's lip quivered. He was afraid, she realized. "What did you tell them?" she asked.

"Please." He begged. "Have a seat."

Harriet pressed herself against the counter. "What did you tell them? All those code words—what did they mean?"

The man shook his head. "Someone will be here to help you shortly."

A man, not wearing the maroon she'd come to associate with workers but a very official black ensemble, approached from the left. His own walkie talkie, dangling from his pocket, hissed.

"Hello," he said, sidling up next to her. "What seems to be the problem?"

Harriet didn't like the looks of him. "No one is helping me."

"Well, I'm trying. What's wrong?" He was bald in a threatening way.

"I've lost my roommate. She might have gone overboard. Shouldn't we be stopping the boat?"

The man looked up at the whimpering guest services person. The worker in maroon shook his head, just one little jerk to the right, but Harriet saw it.

"What?" Harriet snapped.

Another man in black, this one with hair, approached from the right. He looked to the bald man.

"We can better help you below deck, in the med wing." The bald man's voice was soothing, practiced.

"Med wing? Like a hospital?" Harriet whipped her

head back and forth between the two men in black. Her stomach hurt. Why would they want her to go to the med wing? Her heart thundered in her chest. "Lucy—is she hurt?"

The haired man leaned in close. "This isn't the place to be having this conversation, Miss."

Harriet looked up. A crowd was beginning to form around them. "Oh," she said, suddenly faint. She let the bald man, threatening though he was, loop his arm through hers. He began guiding her toward a set of stairs. The other followed close behind. She could feel his breath on her neck. She shivered.

Her phone vibrated against her thigh. She slipped her free hand into her pocket, pulled out the device.

Harriet? Shannon typed. *Lucy isn't on the cruise.*

Chapter Fifty-Four

Numbness rolled over her like fog as the men guided her into an elevator. She knew Lucy had been there. She just couldn't believe Serenitea was trying to pull something like this. They were hiding something—something big. A sacrifice. A murder.

The elevator descended. "I don't think I want to go to the medical area," Harriet said, realizing they weren't taking her to an incapacitated Lucy.

The bald man glanced at her, tightened his arm around hers. "It's just standard procedure, Miss. Nothing to be worried about."

Her skin tingled as goosebumps formed. "Standard

procedure for what?" she asked.

The bald man looked ahead at the shiny elevator doors.

Harriet bent herself around, faced the man with hair. "Standard procedure for what?"

His cheeks turned red and he too stayed mute.

"Fuck," Harriet whispered.

The doors parted and Harriet ripped her arm out of the bald man's embrace. The men grabbed for her, clutched at her flowing dress, but she tore away from them, began to run.

"Stop!" one of the men shouted, his voice a commanding bark.

Her sandals slid around on her feet and she stumbled, but regained her footing and bolted down the long, empty corridor. She glanced behind her. The men were fast, just a few paces behind. They swiped out with big hands, and she screamed.

She turned back around and ran straight into a man in a white coat. Her head conked against his and she went down, sliding against the length of his body. He grabbed for her, crumpled at his feet.

"I've got her," he said, calm and quiet. The men in black backed away.

"Let me go!" Harriet screamed. She thrashed against his feet, his hands. Tears stung her eyes and she couldn't make out the man's face.

People in bright scrubs emerged from a door Harriet

hadn't noticed before. They joined the man in the coat, held her down.

"Get off me!" she cried, kicking at a man in green.

"Shh." The man in white soothed.

Something sharp poked her in the side and she screamed. "Did you just inject me with something? What the fuck!"

"Just something to help you sleep," the man said.

"I don't want to sleep!" she roared. She reared up, twisted her limbs away from the many-handed creature that held her down, but there was a heaviness in her arms and legs that wasn't there before. It took extra effort to drag them around. She was slowing down. She cried, "No."

"Shh," the man in white said. "We're gonna take good care of you."

"I…don't want…"

"I know, I know." The man patted her hair.

She sat for a moment, gathering her strength. Then she hissed at him, spittle flying, rolling down her chin. He jumped back, and Harriet smiled. Her head was so heavy, but still she gnashed at their hands, their fingers, with her teeth.

"Another?" a woman asked.

"No," the man said. "It's working."

And it was. The world was yellow and warm, and she was so tired. Something warm trickled down her leg. "Uhh." She moaned.

"It's okay," the man said.

She felt herself being lifted, up and away. Her head lolled. The yellow world went dark.

Chapter Fifty-Five

When she came to, she was in a stiff bed with railings on the sides. She dragged herself upward, but her head swam and, reluctant, she laid back down. She looked down at her arms, her feet peeking out beneath the thin blanket. She didn't seem to be restrained in any way, there were no IVs poking out from her veins. She pushed herself up again.

"Harriet?" a tentative voice from the door asked.

She turned her eyes toward the sound. "What?" She drooled. Her heart thumped in her chest.

The man in the white coat entered the room, sat on a small rolling stool at her side. He carried an iPad and a stylus. "How are you feeling?" he asked.

"Bad!" She tried to claw him, but her arm fell heavy against her stomach.

"Hey, now. I need you to relax." The man seemed amused, a small smile playing on his lips.

She collected some spit in her mouth, tried to shoot it across the divide at him, but it just flopped onto her chest. She looked down at the blob and found she was wearing some kind of paper bag instead of her dress. "Where are my clothes?"

"You had an accident, we sent it back to your room. I hope that's alright. Someone is retrieving a new outfit from your luggage now."

"Stay out of my shit!"

The man smiled wide now. "We're just trying to help you, Harriet."

She didn't want these people rummaging through her cabin, her bag. She wondered how they'd know her stuff from Lucy's. "Oh shit," she said. "Lucy's stuff is in the room!"

"Hmm?" The doctor was scrawling something on his tablet.

"You think I'm crazy," she said. "You don't think I have a roommate, do you?"

"I don't think you're crazy. You're just having some kind of episode. Absolutely treatable, and actually happens more often than you think on these vessels. People forget their medication, drink a ton, gamble all their money away. It's easy to lose yourself here."

"But I haven't lost myself," she said. "I lost my room-mate. Lucy is real."

The man sighed, looked up from his tablet. "There's no one else assigned to your cabin."

"Call the person in my room. They'll see her stuff there. She brought a big ass suitcase. It was there when I left this morning. It'll be there now."

The man frowned. "How do I know you didn't bring two bags?"

Harriet blinked. "Oh, check my airline reservation! I only checked one bag!" She was excited now. She would make them see.

"I'll page the nurse we sent down to your cabin," the doctor said, sounding a little sad.

"Thank you." She eased against the pillow. "This is all a big misunderstanding. Lucy was here and she's lost. We have to try to find her."

The doctor sighed. "Try to get some rest. Would you like some water?"

"Yes, please," she said.

He nodded, brought her a big plastic cup marked with the cruise ship's logo. Ice rattled inside. "I'm going to leave the room for a moment and call the nurse, okay? If you need anything, just shout."

"Alright," Harriet said, feeling confident she'd soon be set free and could continue her search.

She sipped the ice water. It hurt her teeth, but it felt good sliding down her throat. She set the cup on the little tray hanging off the bed. She patted her pocket and then remembered that she had none. "Hey!" she shouted. "Where's my phone?"

A nurse in blue's head appeared in her doorway. "What?" they asked.

"My phone." She tried to sound calm, wasn't sure how successful she was. She had to prove to them she wasn't crazy. "It's gone."

"Oh," the nurse said.

"Yeah," Harriet said.

"All your personal effects are in a bag on the counter. Except for the piss dress, we sent that to your room."

"Piss dress?" Harriet frowned. "Is that what you're calling it?"

"Gotta call it something." The nurse shrugged, slunk from view.

Harriet twisted about, spied a plastic bag on the counter by the jars of tongue depressors and cotton balls. She forced her legs to move, spun them out of the bed. She sat up, but her head was whirling. She took a deep breath. *I can do this.* She put her feet on the floor, put some weight on her legs. Collapsed. The floor was cold and gritty. "Fuck!" she yelled. Her bare ass was cold, exposed to the air.

The doctor came back into the room. "Oh my." His

eyes roamed over her ass before he rushed to her side, helped her back onto the bed. "What happened?"

"I wanted to get my phone," she said. "It's on the counter."

"Oh, please don't try to walk yet," he said. "The sedative is *very* powerful. We don't want you bumping your head."

She sighed. "I didn't need to be sedated. Can you get my phone? Please?"

The doctor shook his head. "I don't think it's a good idea. Not until we figure out what's going on."

"But my mom." She lied. "She'll want to know I'm sick."

"We can call your mother for you," he said.

"No!" she shrieked.

He raised an eyebrow. "Harriet, I talked to the nurse we sent to your room. He got you a new dress, new underpants. But there was only one suitcase there."

"No!" she cried. "There were two!"

He looked down at his feet. "Harriet, there was one, and it was yours. You came here alone."

"Check the manifest! Isn't there a big list of everyone? Come on!" she shouted.

"We did. There's no Lucy onboard."

Harriet's breathing was sharp, hurried. "They did this."

"Did what? Who's they?" The doctor was in the stool again, had his iPad at the ready.

Harriet eyed him, suspicious. "Forget about it. You'll have me locked up in the looney bin."

"I won't," he said. "I promise I won't. I just want to understand." His eyes were big, pleading.

"Oh!" she said, an idea coming to her. "Check to see if there's an Angela Monroe onboard."

"What will that tell us?"

"She's not supposed to be here." She explained.

"Where is she supposed to be?"

"She's dead," she admitted.

His eyes grew even wider. "You're saying there's someone impersonating a dead woman on this ship?"

Harriet sighed. "Oh, fuck it. I'll just tell you. Angela IS dead. Serenitea may have sacrificed Lucy to bring Angela back to life. Check the manifest!"

He shook his head. "I can't breach someone's privacy like that."

"You just did it for Lucy!"

"That's different. Lucy isn't here."

"So you're admitting Angela is here?" She propped herself up on one elbow.

"No," he said. "I'm just saying we're done checking the manifest, Harriet. You're very confused. No one sacrificed anyone on this boat."

"Last night. In the hibachi restaurant."

He wrote something down. "So you're saying a sacrifice took place and a woman was brought back to life…in a hibachi restaurant?"

Harriet knew it sounded ridiculous, but she had to make him see. "Check the cameras! They were naked!"

He attached his pen back to the magnetic strip on the iPad. "Harriet, you've clearly experienced some kind of psychotic break. Have you ever experienced anything like this before? Maybe even something minor—a sound that wasn't possible, things seen out of the corner of your eye?"

Oh shit. She knew she couldn't tell him about her haunted cabin. That would get her institutionalized for sure. Her stomach lurched. He'd say that was all in her head, proof she was headed for insanity. She shook her head.

"Like I said, this environment can be a big trigger for many."

"But I have a picture," she said. "On my phone."

"Of Lucy?" The doctor perked up.

"No, of Angela. Here on the ship. With the naked ladies in the hibachi place."

He frowned. "I think the best course of action would be to get you off this ship."

Dry land—that sounded good. But she knew she needed to stay, to figure out the mystery. To find Lucy. "No," she said. "Won't you just look at the picture?"

He stood. "I'm not going to entertain your delusions, Harriet. I did too much asking about the suitcase. It isn't right.

I'll arrange for you to be medevacked back to Miami. We'll take you to a hospital there, somewhere better equipped."

"No!" she cried. "I have to find Lucy."

He shook his head, sighed. "I'll contact your parents."

"Don't!"

He left the room, not even looking back. She cried into her hands. They thought she was crazy. Her mother already thought she was, what with the way she reacted on the phone this morning. Getting a phone call from this doctor would only cement the idea in her parents' minds. She needed to talk to Kelsey, to Harold. They'd get her out of this mess.

She pushed herself up again. This time she felt steadier, stronger. She stumbled toward the counter. She breathed a sigh of relief when her hands fell upon her phone. She tapped the screen. Nothing happened. She squeezed the button on the side. The screen remained dark. "It's dead!?" she cried.

A nurse entered, grabbed her by the shoulders. "Honey, you need to stay in bed. You're woozy. You'll fall again."

Harriet tried to shove her, but the action threw her off balance and she fell, ass up and out once more. "My butt," Harriet said, reaching back to cover her rear.

The nurse sighed, said something into a device clipped to her scrubs. Another nurse arrived, this one wearing a nautical print, and the two of them lifted her, placed her back in bed. "There," the first nurse said. "Now just stay put or we're going to have to sedate you again."

Harriet shivered at the threat. She'd stay put. She nodded.

The ladies left. Harriet pressed and prodded her dead phone. They hadn't taken it from her. After her announcement, they knew it was dead. Tears slid down her cheeks. Maybe getting off this ship wouldn't be so bad.

The doctor appeared a final time. This time he stayed in the doorway. "I arranged for you to be taken by helicopter this evening. Around six. Your belongings have been collected and will accompany you."

"Helicopter? Who pays for that?"

"Well, your medical insurance should cover some of it."

"Mine won't, trust me." She rubbed her eyes. "Isn't this drastic? A helicopter? Can't I stay here?"

He frowned. "Harriet, you've proven to be a danger to yourself. You've already fallen twice."

"Oh come on." She growled. "The ship goes back to land tomorrow. I'll be good, I promise."

"I can't keep you safe here that long. You need something more than I can provide. This is just a first-aid station, Harriet. We're not equipped."

"Did they put you up to this? Serenitea? They know I'm on to them."

The doctor didn't say anything, just turned away.

Chapter Fifty-Six

They took her to the top of the ship where a helicopter sat waiting on a pad. The rotor spun, kicking up the air so that her dress, piss-free and not paper, whirled about her. She pressed it down against her legs, unwilling to show her ass a final time.

"I'm scared," she yelled over the thrumming roar.

"It'll be okay," the nurse gripping her arm said. "The pilot is excellent."

Another nurse followed, wheeling her suitcase.

"All set?" A man in a red jumpsuit climbed out of the helicopter, his hair whipping. He grabbed the bag, stowed it inside, then took Harriet's hand. "Restraint?" he yelled to the nurses who had brought her there.

They looked her up and down. "Nah," one shouted.

289

"She's not gonna bother you." They turned away, leaving her alone with the jumpsuit man.

"I'm scared!" she yelled again.

He smiled. "First time?"

"Well, yeah!"

He led her to the yellow helicopter, helped her up the step. It was impossible, the sheer loudness of it, vibrating through her so her teeth hurt. Inside, a few more jumpsuit nurses sat around a bed. They wore big headsets. "I'm scared!" she told them. They just looked up at her.

The first jumpsuit nurse helped her onto the bed. "Just lay back," he yelled.

"I want to sit up," she yelled back.

"Nuh uh," he yelled, easing her shoulders back until they touched the folded bed. He buckled a series of straps around her.

"I thought you said no restraints!" She writhed against the belts.

"These are just safety harnesses. You can undo them yourself, see?" He tapped a buckle. "You don't want to know what the actual restraints look like. Do you?"

Harriet huffed at the threat. She turned her head away from the man. There was a small window through which she could see the setting sun. The sea was tranquil, beautiful. She sighed. She would have never predicted her cruise would end like this.

The man slid the door shut and sat on a small precipice. He pulled on his own headset, said something into the receiver.

The helicopter rocked into motion. Harriet screamed. No one seemed to pay her any mind. They lifted off into the sky, swaying, rocking, defying gravity. Harriet strained to see out the window, but the angle was off and she wasn't able to see the women crowded on the decks below, gazing up at the helicopter as it rose. They lifted their hands. They waved.

Chapter Fifty-Seven

Landing was just as terrifying as taking off. Harriet didn't scream this time, but she wanted to. It was dark and the lights of the city rose up to meet them. There was a bump when the skids touched the pad. Harriet swallowed.

"See? That wasn't so bad!" yelled the man as he unbuckled her straps.

"It was bad!" she shouted.

He looked her in the eye. "We made it, didn't we?"

"I guess."

One of the jumpsuit nurses grabbed her bag and they all climbed out of the helicopter together. Harriet's hair lashed her eyes and she scrambled to get it out of the way. A team of new nurses stood there, waiting for her. She turned, but the jumpsuit nurses were already climbing back onboard. They didn't even say goodbye. She cried.

"Come," a large woman shouted, grabbing her by the wrist. She was so sick of people grabbing her, forcing her around. But she didn't fight. She was tired, scared of being further restrained. She had to make them see she wasn't crazy. She followed, the obedient patient. One of the other nurses wheeled her bag along.

"Where are we going?" she asked once they were inside the hospital, away from the pulsing thunder of the helicopter.

"Just downstairs," the woman holding her wrist said. "Psych will evaluate you. Maybe even let you go today."

Her heart thrilled. "That'd be nice," she said.

The woman nodded. "We're not in the habit of holding people hostage."

Harriet wanted to hug her.

They took her to a quiet wing of the hospital and deposited her in an office. A man with a mustache sat at the desk there, looking like a skinny walrus. Harriet smiled.

"What's so funny, Miss Pendleton?"

"Nothing," she said.

He slid paperwork across the desk at her. "Fill these out."

"What are they?" she asked.

He shrugged. "HIPAA statement, emergency contact,

insurance. The usual."

She frowned, signed her name on every page.

"Do you have a phone charger?" she asked. "Can I look in my bag for mine?

"The nurse on staff will have all that."

"Thank god," she said.

He nodded, as if he were the god in question. "The doctor will see you shortly." He rose.

"You're not the doctor?"

"I'm the intake nurse."

"Oh," she said. She thought all psychiatrists had mustaches.

She sat for a while in the quiet of the office, marveling that they'd left her alone here after all the sedation and restraints she'd just experienced. She could pick up the heavy brass decoration off the table and smash in someone's brains, she could bolt out the door, she could eat an entire box of tissues. She frowned. Maybe she really wasn't thinking straight.

At last, there came a knock at the door and a pretty young woman entered. "Hi, Harriet," she smiled. "I'm Dr. Almasi."

Harriet nodded. "Hi," she said.

"I understand you had a bit of an incident on a cruise ship this morning?" She sat in the seat opposite Harriet, unfolded a gleaming laptop.

"So they say," she said.

"I spoke to the medical staff onboard and they seemed to think you were a risk to yourself and others. Do you feel like you'll harm yourself? Someone else?"

Harriet shook her head, vigorous, angry. "No. Not at all." She meant it, too. She never wanted anyone to get hurt.

"I didn't think so," said Dr. Almasi. She typed something on the laptop.

"I want to go home," she said.

Dr. Almasi nodded. "I can make that happen. We just need to talk a little first, okay?"

"Okay," Harriet said, apprehensive.

"Have you ever experienced psychosis before?"

"No. Never."

Dr. Almasi typed. "Mmhmm. Okay. And do you ever find yourself doing things you know are risky, or don't totally jive with your personality?"

"Jive? What—"

"For example, you might find yourself driving over the speed limit for no reason. Or you spend more money than usual."

Sign up for pyramid schemes. Move to cabins in the middle of the woods. Go on cruises without any planning. "I guess," she admitted.

"Right," Dr. Almasi said. "Okay."

"What's that got to do with anything?" she asked.

"Well, I'm wondering if you had a bout of mania,

Harriet. Have you ever felt depressed?"

"Yes," she said it fast, she said it with conviction. She had been depressed many times.

Dr. Almasi nodded, a slow, deliberate movement. "Right," she said. "I'm going to prescribe you something today, but I need you to follow up with your doctors back home. Your GP is a good place to start, okay?"

"Okay?"

A nurse came in, checked her blood pressure, her oxygen levels. Dr. Almasi typed.

"You're all set. You can pick up your prescription in the pharmacy downstairs in about half an hour."

"That's it?" Harriet stood, incredulous.

"Yes," Dr. Almasi said. "Do you need something else?"

"Well, no. I'm just confused because they helicoptered me off the cruise ship. I was sedated. Against my will! And now you're just writing me a script? Sending me on my way?"

Dr. Almasi raised an eyebrow. "Do you want to stay?"

"No!" she shouted. "I'll go. I just…" She knew she wasn't crazy. She knew she should be allowed to walk free. She was just shocked. The medical system in America confounded her, confused her. They were just going to let her go?

"I'll have a nurse take you downstairs," Dr. Almasi said. "It was nice meeting you." She scooped up her laptop and walked out of the room, her high heels clicking.

Another woman entered, waited by the door. "We'll

go downstairs," she said.

Harriet rose, grabbed the handle of her suitcase by the door. "Do you mind if I dig through my bag? Get my charger?"

The woman frowned. "Do that on your own time, Miss."

"Oh," Harriet said, taken aback.

She followed the nurse to the pharmacy, not speaking the entire way. The woman left her with a curt little nod and Harriet feigned walking into the pharmacy, even stood in line for a moment. Then, when she was sure the nurse was gone, she wheeled her suitcase back out the door.

She roamed for a while until she came to a waiting room. A few people sat reading magazines, gazing down at their phones. Harriet parked herself in a seat next to an outlet and unzipped her bag. Her phone charger was on top of the tightly tied plastic bag she suspected carried the piss dress. She plugged it in, waited.

She knew she needed to call for an Uber to take her to the airport, and she needed to talk to the airline about changing her flight. And she needed to call her mom—they'd probably heard all about her episode by now. And she needed to call Kelsey, and Harold, and Lucy. *Oh, Lucy.* She stared at her reflection in the dark screen.

At last, the phone booted up. The missed call notifications and texts streamed in. She rubbed her eyes, tired.

Chapter Fifty-Eight

She had Kelsey pick her up from the airport. They embraced, a tentative, hurried hug, and then Kelsey ushered her into the passenger seat of her truck. "What the hell happened?" she asked, even though Harriet had told her the story over the phone.

"They gaslit me. They tried to make me believe I was crazy, that Lucy was never on the ship."

Kelsey looked at her sidelong. "And what did the doctor say?"

Harriet grumbled. "I'm not crazy, Kelsey!"

Kelsey merged onto the highway. "It's just so weird."

"You're telling me," Harriet said.

"Why don't I take you straight to my place? You can get a nap and we'll go get the rest of your stuff from your place later."

Harriet had almost forgotten she'd agreed to move into this other woman's house. She had also told her mother she'd consider moving in with her. They'd talked again while she waited for her flight. Her mother was adamant that Harriet move in with them, was very disappointed when Harriet insisted on going back to Bentwood. They vowed to intercept her there, drag her home. She sighed. She'd sort it all out later. "We need to go to Lucy's."

"Now?" Kelsey tapped the brakes.

"Yes. I need to see if she's there."

Kelsey slowed, looked at Harriet. "So you admit she might not have been on the cruise?"

"What? No. Kelsey, are you seriously doing this to me right now? I have the picture of Angela on my phone. She came back from the dead. You saw it yourself. It happened."

Kelsey nodded. "You're right. It happened. I'm sorry. I'm just so confused."

"When the cruise is over, we need to go to Angela's house."

"And do what?"

"See if she's there!" Harriet hissed.

"Christ. Can you just, you know, relax? Take it easy. We're not even home and you're already going on another crusade. The last one didn't turn out so well. These women—they're not something to mess around with."

"Take me to Lucy's."

"Ugh," Kelsey said. "And what are you going to do if she's there?"

Harriet paused, looked at the hangnail on her finger. "I don't know."

They rode in silence. Harriet didn't speak again until they'd entered Bentwood and only then it was to give Kelsey directions. "Turn left here," she said.

They inched into Lucy's neighborhood.

"Fuck, I forgot which one's hers." Harriet scanned the row of houses.

"They all look the same," Kelsey said.

"Wait. Just pull over." Harriet turned her phone on, opened Facebook. She searched for the invitation to Lucy's Mary Jane party and was relieved to find it still existed. "Okay, got it," she said.

They drove on.

They pulled in behind Lucy's car, still stuffed to the brim with Mary Jane. "Car's here," Kelsey said.

"It was here when we left," Harriet said. "It doesn't mean anything."

"Alright," Kelsey said, putting the car into park.

Harriet jumped out of the car, ran to the door.

"Wait!" Kelsey yelled. "Wait for me."

Anxious, Harriet shifted on the front step. Kelsey climbed the stairs. "Okay," she said, as Harriet rang the doorbell.

They waited in silence, staring at the door, willing it to move, or not move—Harriet wasn't sure what she wanted to be true. At last, it cracked open. A puff of candle-scented air escaped.

"Hello?" a man asked. Harriet recognized him from the pictures Lucy had shown her in her home. He looked apprehensive, confused.

"Is—We're looking for Lucy," Harriet said.

"Oh," he said. "Well, she's not here."

"See!" squeaked Harriet, grabbing Kelsey by the arm. "She's not here!"

The man squinched up his eyes.

Kelsey pushed Harriet out of the way. "Uh, sir, could you tell us when she'll be back?"

Lucy's husband looked Kelsey up and down, glanced back into the house. "Friday," he said. "She's on a cruise."

"SEE!" Harriet jumped up and down, jiggling Kelsey along with her.

"Have you heard from her at all?" Kelsey asked.

The man gave them a disdainful look. "What's this about?"

"We think—" Harriet began, but Kelsey cut her off.

"Nothing," Kelsey said. "We're just, um, consultants, that's all. Thought she'd be in. We'll catch up with her another time."

"Ack, you consultants. She's always getting wrapped up in something. Why don't you just let my wife be? We don't need another scheme."

"Yes!" Harriet bounced around.

The man looked like he smelled something nasty. He shut the door.

"What the hell were you doing?" Kelsey whispered.

"Celebrating!" Harriet said.

Kelsey held her by the shoulders, steered her back to the truck. "Celebrating that she did go missing on that cruise?"

"Celebrating that I'm not crazy! Hey, do you think we should have told him?" Harriet stopped her happy quivering.

Kelsey shook her head. "No way. Not yet."

Harriet buckled her seatbelt. "I can't wait until Friday."

"Why?" Kelsey turned the key.

"Well, it'll be obvious she's missing, that's one thing. But Angela will be back then too."

Kelsey didn't look at her as she backed out of Lucy's driveway. "You think she'll just come waltzing back into her old life?"

"No." Harriet blinked. "I don't. I think they'll keep her hidden. But we can find her."

"And then what?" Kelsey asked.

Harriet looked out the window, watched trees and houses and sidewalks zip by. She knew what had to be done.

Chapter Fifty-Nine

She sat on Kelsey's front porch, watching the sun set in the field. "It's nice here," she said.

"Mmhmm," Kelsey said. She sipped a glass of iced tea.

"My stuff," Harriet said. "All I have are these stupid cult dresses." She gestured down at her garment.

Kelsey glanced at Harriet's dress, wrinkled and dirty. "We can go to your place tonight if you want."

Harriet sighed. "I think my parents might be there, waiting for me."

"Shouldn't we go talk to them?" Kelsey set down her glass.

"No," Harriet said. "They think I'm crazy. The doctor on the ship called them and I had just told my mom everything, about the underwear ghosts, you, everything. And now she thinks I'm insane. Really. If they get a hold of me, I'm never coming back."

Kelsey frowned, chewed her lip. "Okay," she said. "I guess you can wear some of my stuff until we figure out what to do."

"Thanks," Harriet said. "I'd like that."

Kelsey didn't say anything.

"Uh, Kelsey?" Harriet asked.

"What?"

"I also have a bag that's got a piss dress in it."

Kelsey scrunched up her face. "Piss dress? What's that?"

"Well…I peed. On my dress. And the people on the ship bagged it up and I'm scared it's getting ripe in there." She thought of the snotty hanky she'd deposited in Kelsey's basket that day in the barn.

"Throw it away," Kelsey said.

"Oh, yeah. Right," Harriet said. She looked down at her foot. Kelsey seemed troubled, not her warm usual self. But Harriet didn't know her well enough to interject. She turned her foot in the light, examined her toenails. "I'm pretty tired," Harriet said, the weight of the last twenty-four hours beginning to fall on her.

"Okay," Kelsey said. "Let me show you your room."

They'd left Harriet's bag by the door, and Kelsey hefted it up now, impervious to its weight. They climbed the stairs.

"This one's yours," Kelsey said, toeing open an old wooden door. The bedroom inside was bare but for a small bed, a table with a lamp, a window—curtained and covered—on the wall. "I cleaned it out while you were gone."

Harriet looked at her, saw her cheeks glowed red. "Thank you," Harriet said.

"I'm just down the hall," Kelsey said. She tipped her head. "Bathroom's back there too."

Harriet nodded. "Goodnight, then, I guess."

"Goodnight," Kelsey said.

Harriet took the bag from Kelsey, gave her a weak smile.

When Kelsey was gone, Harriet shut the door, stripped off her dress. She'd ask Kelsey for some of her clothes in the morning. For now, she could sleep in her underwear. She plugged her phone in near the bedside table and slid between the rough sheets of the bed. She wanted to cry. She missed her parents, she missed her musty cabin, she even missed Lucy. Her eyelids drooped and she fell asleep thinking about what she'd do to get her back.

Something touched her face, played across her nose. She yelped, eyes open now. There was nothing there, just a hair bouncing in some unseen air current. She smoothed it down, tried to calm her breathing. Sleep didn't come easy the second time around.

She turned over to face the little window she'd spied when first came into the room. Sometimes switching sides reset her brain, allowed her to find rest. She flopped unceremoniously, looked at the window. The curtains billowed, just as her hair had blown. Harriet wondered where the air vents were in the room. She yawned. This side wasn't doing it for her either, she turned back around.

Lucy's face hovered inches from her own. She could feel the heat of her skin, of her breath. Harriet screamed, throwing herself out of the bed. "What the fuck!" She pressed herself against the wall, but Lucy was gone. "Fuck fuck fuck." She breathed. She shook her hands and arms as if flinging the vision off and away. "What the fuck…"

She heard footsteps in the hall and scrambled to her suitcase, looking for something to throw on, but it was too late. Kelsey stood in the doorway.

"What happened?" She wore a baggy shirt, baggy shorts, sleep in her eyes. Her hair was in a low, messy ponytail.

"It was nothing. I thought I saw something. I don't know." She tried to cover her body with her trembling arms.

"What did you see?" Kelsey entered the room, crossed it in big easy strides. "Are you okay?" She put a hand on Harriet's bare shoulder.

"I'm fine," Harriet said. "I think. I don't know. I

thought I saw Lucy." She took a step away from Kelsey, slid out from beneath her hand.

"Really? What was she doing?"

"Just staring. I don't know. I turned over and she was just there."

"Hmm." Kelsey mused.

Harriet gave up on modesty, threw herself back on the bed. "Do you think it means she's dead?"

"Why would that be?"

"I saw her ghost."

Kelsey sat next to her. Their thighs touched and Harriet didn't pull away. "I don't know," Kelsey said. "I guess she could be dead. Do you think she's dead?"

Harriet shrugged. "Yes. No. I don't know. I thought Angela was dead once too."

"That's true," Kelsey said. "Nothing is as it seems with these damn pyramid schemes."

Harriet laughed, even though she wasn't sure if Kelsey intended her words to be funny. She couldn't stop laughing. It was absurd, wasn't it? These damn pyramid schemes...

Kelsey looked surprised, maybe a little hurt, but soon she smiled too. They both laughed. Harriet pressed her lips to Kelsey's, snuffing out the laughter.

They both had their eyes open, shock and wonder and dismay all rattling around their skulls. Harriet couldn't help but laugh again, lips vibrating against Kelsey's teeth. Kelsey didn't move, just stared while Harriet giggled into her mouth.

"Come on," Harriet whispered, lips still touching. "Kiss me."

Kelsey shut her eyes.

She leaned in.

Chapter Sixty

Harriet woke in Kelsey's arms. They didn't really fit in the little guest bed, but they'd figured it out. It involved being as close as possible, it turned out. Harriet enjoyed being the little spoon, and Kelsey's arm draped over her somehow felt like home. Despite that, Harriet sat upright, and Kelsey stirred. She looked down at Kelsey, at her sun-kissed skin, and felt an immeasurable sadness.

"Hm?" Kelsey asked, wrapping her arm around Harriet's midsection.

Harriet untangled herself, sat on the edge of the bed.

"What's wrong?" Kelsey asked.

Harriet shook her head, hair falling lank around her,

and looked down at the floor.

"Oh, seriously? You started it! You—"

"It's not what we did," Harriet said, "it's what we're about to do."

"What are we about to do!?" Kelsey was sitting up now, blanket drawn up over her breasts.

"I dragged you into this mess and it's only going to get worse. I should go."

"No. Nuh uh," Kelsey said, poking her in the arm. "You don't get to back out now. Now tell me, how does this end?"

Harriet looked at her, frowned. "We have to find Angela. We have to kill her."

Kelsey's fingers tightened around the blanket. "And what will that do?"

"Bring back Lucy."

"How do you know this?"

"I don't," Harriet said. "It's just this feeling I have. This hunch."

Kelsey nodded. "That's more than I've got."

"When I saw Lucy last night, I couldn't help but wonder if it was a plea for help, you know?"

Kelsey placed her hand on Harriet's. "Yes."

"I want to kill Angela as soon as possible. I don't understand why they brought her back, but she must be important to them in some way. She's powerful."

"Uh huh," Kelsey said.

Harriet sighed, angled her body toward Kelsey's. "We should get Harold."

"What's a 'Harold?'" Kelsey asked.

Harriet stood, shook out her hair. "He's the gym teacher at the school."

"Uh, and we want him involved why?"

Harriet twisted a lock of hair around her finger. "Well, I've been talking to him too."

"He knows?" Kelsey was incredulous, rising out of the bed.

"He knows everything. He knows everything except about you."

"Why didn't you tell me?"

"I didn't think we'd… Well, I didn't know it'd become so serious."

Kelsey leaned against the back of the door, looked up at the ceiling. "Okay, so there's someone else on our side. Okay. Who else knows?"

"My mom. My dad. The guest services person on the cruise ship. The doctor."

"Harriet, there are a lot of people involved in this murder plot."

"I know." Harriet grimaced. "But she's already dead, right? So we can't get in trouble."

Kelsey bit her lip. "Why didn't you tell him about

me?"

Harriet blushed. "He's, well, he's kinda a perv. And I wanted to protect you."

"So we're gonna go get this pervert gym teacher and storm Angela's house?"

"Yeah," Harriet said.

"Christ," Kelsey said.

"Except we need to be prepared. Lucy said they were vampires so I don't know if we need to get holy water, wooden stakes—"

"Wait, are you being serious? Are you joking?" Kelsey squinted, looked deep into her eyes.

Harriet looked away. "Well, yes. I told you about the note she wrote me…"

Kelsey sighed "Okay. So we get the pervert, some wooden stakes, and go fucking wild."

"And garlic. Garlic, too."

"Okay…"

"Do you still want to do this?" Harriet asked.

Kelsey considered for a moment, bunched up her lips. "Yes," she said at last. "I do."

"Thank you." Harriet breathed. She took Kelsey's hand.

Kelsey nodded, tried not to cry.

They stood in front of Kelsey's closet. "I guess you can wear anything here. I don't know if it'll fit, though."

Harriet looked at the earth-tone corduroys, the worn t-shirts. She knew the shirts would fit—they were oversized, men's cuts. But Harriet was curvier in the waist and thighs than Kelsey. She wouldn't be able to fit into her stiff jeans. "Do you have any loose pants? Maybe something stretchy?"

Kelsey's eyes lit up. "You know what? I do." She bounded to a set of drawers near her bed. She rummaged through it for a while. Harriet watched her shoulders rise and fall. At last, Kelsey surfaced, holding a pair of leggings up high.

"Oh, no," Harriet said.

Kelsey smiled wide, handed Harriet the bug pants.

"You kept them?"

"Of course I did! They were from you!"

Harriet unfurled them and the neon green mosquitos hurt her eyes. "Damn," she said. "Mary Jane to the rescue, I guess."

"If you don't want to wear them you can wear these pajama shorts, or I can go buy you something."

Harriet shook her head. The nearest Walmart was twenty-five minutes away and Harriet wasn't sure she wanted to be separated from Kelsey for that long. "I'll wear the bug pants," she said.

Kelsey watched as Harriet pulled them on. "Why did they put a mosquito right on the crotch?" she asked.

"Bad quality control," Harriet said, rifling through the closet for a shirt. "Can I wear this?" She held up a beige t-shirt so old and thin it felt like it would fall apart in her hands.

"Sure. That's just a work shirt, though. There are better things." Kelsey stuck her hand into the closet, began sliding the hangers around.

"I don't want better things," Harriet said. "I want this."

She'd already pulled the shirt on, and Kelsey looked at her for a moment. "Okay," she said.

"Now what?" Harriet asked, turning away from a mirror.

"You're asking *me*?" Kelsey said. "I was hoping you knew."

Harriet frowned. "I kinda want to go to her grave."

"Whose? Angela's?" Kelsey asked.

"Yeah, but I don't know where it is."

Kelsey nodded. "I do."

"You do? Why?" Harriet was surprised, and a little suspicious too.

"Bentwood only has one cemetery, Hare. We just go in, look for a fresh plot. Easy."

Hare—there was that name again. Harriet felt weird. "Oh," she said.

"Yeah. So, when do we go?" Kelsey sat on her bed.

Harriet joined her, sitting thigh to thigh once more. "I feel like we need to bring Harold, right?"

Kelsey shrugged. "You're leading this thing. If you feel like we need to get the pervert, we get the pervert."

"He's in school right now," Harriet said. "I could message him, but he wouldn't be able to join us until three at the earliest."

Kelsey considered this. "In the meantime, do you want to help me tend to the farm? It might be nice to get our minds off of this for a while."

"Yes," Harriet said, though she had hoped they'd pass the time in a different way. But she understood that Kelsey had responsibilities, live creatures to care for, even though they were bugs. "That'd be nice."

Kelsey stood, stretched out a hand. "Let's go."

Chapter Sixty-One

They stood at a mound of dirt bulging from the surface of the Earth. "You think this is it?" Harriet asked. There was no headstone yet, just a plastic number pegged to the ground where the feet would be.

"Gotta be," Kelsey said. "Unless they cremated her and kept the urn or something like that. There's only one fresh grave here." She gestured around her, at the dense field of headstones, stuffed animals, fake flowers, and solar lights. It was cluttered. It was tacky. Angela would have hated it.

"I don't know," Harriet said. "It's just so…pedestrian. You know?"

Kelsey walked over to another grave, bent over the pile of pennies left there. "I think it's kinda cool."

"It is cool. Just, Angela wouldn't think so."

A car door slammed in the distance. Both women straightened, turned toward the sound.

"Who's that?"

Harriet sighed in relief. "Harold!" She raised a hand.

"Christ, he's huge," Kelsey said.

Harold wove through the headstones, making slow progress toward them.

Kelsey sidled up next to her, snagged Harriet's hand with her pinky. "I want him to see this," she said.

"Umm, okay," Harriet said, grasping the woman's hand.

Harriet's phone buzzed. She'd wedged it in the waistband of the leggings. She patted it with her free hand. Her mother had been calling all morning, leaving desperate voicemails. They were still at her house, waiting for her. They'd wait forever, she said. She said they'd notified the police of her absence. Please come home. Harriet felt bad leaving them waiting on her doorstep, but what was she supposed to do? She was sure they'd institutionalize her if she went back. She put on a fake smile for Harold.

"Hey!" Harold said, jogging the rest of the way. "Glad to see you made it off that ship." He nodded at Kelsey, eyes lingering over the knot of their hands.

"They helicoptered me off. They thought I was crazy," Harriet said.

Harold's head bounced up and down. "There are

worse ways to leave a cruise."

Harriet laughed and Kelsey's lips cracked into a smile. Her protective hold on Harriet's hand loosened.

"This is Kelsey." Harriet explained. "She's going to help us defeat Angela."

"Blondie doesn't stand a chance," Harold said. "What's with the pants?" He eyed her crotch with suspicion.

Harriet blushed. "I can't go home and get my clothes. My parents are there and the police are looking for me. They think I'm a danger to myself."

"So why are we in a graveyard?" Harold kicked at the mound of dirt with his tennis shoe.

"This might be Angela's grave. We don't know for certain," Harriet said.

"Okay? And?" Harold said.

"Well, I don't know. I just wanted to scope it out, I guess. See if we could feel anything here."

"And do you? Feel anything here?"

Harriet shook her head. "No," she said. "Not really."

Harold glanced at Kelsey. "So, we're gonna go murder this bitch."

"I guess," Harriet said.

"It's a little more complicated than that," Kelsey said. "You see, Harriet thinks we need to slay her. Like, she's a vampire. Garlic, silver bullets, all of that."

Harold frowned, thought for a moment. "I can get

garlic from the grocery store."

"So you're just down for this?" Kelsey asked, confused. "You're just gonna go along with this? Risk your life? Why?"

Harold looked from woman to woman. "My wife," he said.

"What happened to your wife?" Harriet's eyes were wide, fearful.

"Well, she's been distant lately, you know. Just not always there. And I figured it was her period or something but—"

Kelsey sighed.

Harold frowned, but continued his story. "I was doing the dishes—"

"You do the dishes?" Kelsey asked.

"Well, yes." He blinked twice.

Kelsey stared at him and the man cleared his throat. "As I was saying, I was doing the dishes and I noticed this red residue on the cups."

"No!" Harriet gasped.

"She's all wrapped up in it, Harriet." His voice was sad, pleading.

Harriet ran a hand across her forehead. "I'm sorry." She didn't know what else to say.

He looked down at the toes of his sneakers. "So, when do you propose we do this?"

"I've been thinking about that," Harriet said. "I think

Saturday is our best bet. The cruise is supposed to come back tonight, but I want to give them time to get home. But not too much time, you know?"

Kelsey and Harold nodded.

"So we prepare in the meantime—pick up the supplies. I can train you girls. We only have a day, but tomorrow afternoon, we should meet in the gym and go over some combat situations."

"Combat situations? What do you know about that?" Kelsey asked.

"Well, nothing, to be honest. But I do have a punching bag."

The women looked at each other. "I guess it couldn't hurt," Harriet said.

Harold nodded. "So, want me to pick up garlic? Make some necklaces or something like that?"

"That would be great, thank you," Harriet said. "But won't your wife be weird about it?"

Harold shrugged. "Eh, I'll just say it's for school. She doesn't pay attention to me these days anyway."

"Okay," Harriet said.

"I don't know where to get silver bullets, but we can make some wooden stakes, whittle down some branches tonight," Kelsey said. "I'll build a fire. It'll be fun."

"Alright," Harriet said. "We'll meet up tomorrow then, Harold. At the school. We'll train."

Harold puffed up his chest. "We're gonna be so prepared."

Harriet wasn't so sure about that, but she smiled just the same. It was nice to have a plan, however strange it may be.

Chapter Sixty-Two

Harriet had blisters and calluses on her fingers from carving down the ends of the wooden stakes. She and Kelsey had sat up most of the night, whittling down branches Kelsey pulled from her brush pile. They made five stakes—two extras should one break. Harriet poked at a fluid-filled blister. "Should we bring the stakes to the school?"

"Probably," Kelsey said. "What if we want to train with them?"

Harriet nodded. She was nervous to return to the school. What if the police were looking for her there? It was one of the few places she went in a day—it made sense for them to monitor it. If they found her in a truck full of sharpened wooden spikes, it wouldn't end well for her.

Harriet hefted the stakes into the back seat, bark and splinters separating from the shafts.

"You should have let me do that." Kelsey tutted.

"It's no big deal," Harriet said. The stakes were heavy and unwieldy, but she had done it.

The drive to the school was quiet, each woman lost in their own thoughts. Harriet peered out the windows, slunk down in her seat. She was so sure they'd pass her parents on the road, a police car. When they at last pulled into the emptying school parking lot, Harriet breathed a sigh of relief. "We made it."

"We made it." Kelsey confirmed.

"There's a direct entrance to the gym," Harriet said. "Harold probably left it unlocked for us."

"This Harold guy…" Kelsey began.

"Yeah?" Harriet asked.

"He doesn't seem like a pervert."

Harriet pushed her hair out of her face. "I don't know. He's a good person, just, his jokes aren't always funny, you know? I didn't want you to think I was like that, should he say something uncouth."

Kelsey shook her head. "Harriet, I know you better than that."

"You do?" Harriet asked.

"I think so?" Kelsey said. "I mean, to me it seems like

you're risking your life to save a person you didn't even like. That's heroic, right?"

Harriet looked down at her lap. She still wore the mosquito pants. "I owe it to her. She tried to warn me. And those ladies—they can't get away with this. If we don't stop them, they'll just keep taking advantage of people, using them, sucking them dry."

"See?" Kelsey said. "Heroic."

Harriet pushed up out of her seat, opened the car door. Kelsey followed.

"Let's just bring a few stakes. One for each of us," Harriet said. "I don't want to be seen with a whole armful."

Kelsey nodded, gathered up three wooden spears. Harriet took them from her arms.

They walked across the parking lot and through some landscaping. They came to a nondescript door set into the side of the building. "Here we are," Harriet said, leaning into the door with her hip. It opened.

The sound of a basketball hitting the court echoed through the gymnasium. Harold stood dribbling beneath the basket.

"What?" shouted Kelsey. "Are we gonna outshoot them or something?"

Harold turned, smiled. "Maybe?" He tossed the ball to Kelsey. She caught it, easy, confident. She bounced the ball against the floor a few times.

"So. Where do we start?" Harriet asked. She bent, set the heavy stakes on the ground.

"Damn. Those look lethal," Harold said. The stakes were sharp, their points almost invisible.

"We worked really hard on them," Harriet said, splaying her sore fingers.

"I bought a ton of garlic. It's stinking up my car," Harold said. "We'll each have a nice necklace to wear tomorrow."

Harriet nodded. "Good. So, what were you going to show us?"

Kelsey passed the ball to Harriet who fumbled, lost the ball. It rolled to the bleachers. No one went after it.

Harold picked up one of the stakes, weighed it in his hand. "I think we need to practice with these. Striking, dodging. We can pretend the punching bag is one of those hags."

Kelsey nodded, picked up her own stake. "Can't hurt, I guess."

Harriet grabbed the last stake and followed them across the shiny gym floor. In a dim corner, a red punching bag dangled from the rafters.

"So…" she said, staring at the overstuffed bag.

Harold pushed the bag, set it to spinning and swaying. "Go ahead." he nodded.

Raising the stake, Harriet jolted forward, stabbed at the bag and missed. She couldn't stop her momentum. She stumbled toward the wall, almost fell on her face. "Fuck," she said.

"That's okay," Harold said. "Try again."

She spun around, tried to hit the bag from the side. It spun away.

"Let me try," Kelsey said.

Harold pushed the bag so it moved in a wider arc. Kelsey leaped, tapped the bag with the end of her stick. "I don't want to put a hole in your bag," she said.

Harold nodded. "Good one. Harriet, notice how she anticipated where the bag would be. That was good work. Here, Kelsey, try again." He twisted the chain the bag hung from. The bag twirled violently as it swayed.

Kelsey stepped forward, stopped its violent rocking with one hand, and pressed the tip of her stake to the bag. "Here," she said to Harold. "You try." She shoved the bag.

He spun around, slammed the blunt end of his spear into the red vinyl.

"This is stupid," Harriet said. "This isn't real."

Harold tapped his stake against his leg. "I think we learned something, though."

"What's that?" Harriet asked.

"Kelsey or I should do the killing."

"What? Why?" Harriet pouted.

"You're just a little, uh…uncoordinated." Harold smiled, attempting to lessen the blow.

Kelsey nodded. "Let us take care of her."

"No." Harriet growled. She marched to the bag, kicked it hard. It swung away and came back just as fast. It bumped into her and she stumbled. "I can do it. I need to be the one to kill her."

Kelsey and Harold looked at one another.

"Well, let us incapacitate her first, huh?" Harold said. "Then you can come in at the end."

Harriet considered this. "You make it sound so easy."

Harold tossed the stake in the air and caught it again. "She's what...120 pounds? We can take her."

Harriet looked down at her own stake. "What if she has powers?"

"Like what? You haven't seen her do anything without the tea, right?" Kelsey asked.

"I guess not," Harriet said.

"So, just don't drink anything mid murder," Harold said.

"They brought her back to life, guys," Harriet said.

Kelsey stabbed the air with her stake. "And that took, like, six of them and a sacrifice. I think we'll be okay."

Harriet's took a shuddering breath. "Okay," she said.

"Okay," Kelsey and Harold said in unison.

Chapter Sixty-Three

Harold met them at Kelsey's house. He put a string of garlic bulbs around each of their necks, anointing them with their sharp stink. "This oughta do it," he said.

Harriet fingered the papery skin. "I hope so." She'd been reading about vampires. Some corners of the internet said the only true way to kill a vampire was to cut off its head. She hoped it wouldn't come to that. She shivered.

She looked to Kelsey, who felt her own heads of garlic. "Harriet, if this makes you feel better, I'd say it's working."

Did it make her feel better? Her stomach churned and her head felt light. They were about to do something heinous, unforgivable. But they had to bring Lucy back. She nodded.

"Okay," she said.

They climbed into Kelsey's truck, Harriet in the back. Harold's head grazed the ceiling. He turned, looked her way. "You alright back there, kiddo?"

She gulped down her fear, nodded. "I'm okay." She held tight to a stake, knuckles white.

"I'll park a ways down the street," Kelsey said.

Harriet frowned, knowing that no matter where they parked on the posh street, Kelsey's beat-up work truck would raise suspicion.

They pulled into Angela's neighborhood, and Kelsey slowed. The houses here were older and more ornate than the ones elsewhere in town, but Angela's stood tall, triumphant, the only mansion on the block.

Harriet leaned toward the window, squinted to see. There were cars in the driveway, but no one on the lawn. "I think there are guests. I'm not sure. I don't know how many cars they own."

Kelsey puttered down the street before pulling up on the curb, switching off the engine. "Are you sure you want to do this?"

"Yes," Harold said.

"Yes," Harriet said.

Kelsey nodded once. "Let's go."

They spilled from the truck, and Harriet passed out the stakes, making eye contact with each of them as they accepted. Her eyes lingered on Kelsey's. "I love you," Kelsey admitted.

"Oh," Harriet said, blushing. "I love you too." Saying it made it true, she realized. She did love Kelsey. Had always loved Kelsey. Tears stung her eyes.

Harold coughed. "Um, how do we get in?"

Harriet turned. "Through the back. There's a morning room. All glass. One door, some windows. Worst case, we smash our way through."

"Christ," Kelsey said.

Harold nodded, followed Harriet as she began the walk back to Angela's.

As they approached the edge of her manicured lawn, Harriet darted behind a bush, garlic necklace swinging, and the others followed.

"Do you see anything?" Harold asked, hunkering down beside her.

"No," Harriet whispered. She leaned on her stake. "But I don't want to be seen. We need to run from bush to bush until we're behind the house. Let's go."

She didn't give them time to protest. She bolted to the nearest clump of landscaping, and they followed.

Angela's backyard boasted big, leafy trees with trunks so thick they couldn't have joined hands around them. They made hiding easy. Harriet leaned against one, felt the bark dig into her back. "There's a door on the left." She explained.

"Let's try that first." The others nodded.

They crept from behind the massive tree. Harriet stared up at the dark windows, wondered if anyone watched their approach. Her fingers tightened around the rough stake.

The door—like the walls of the morning room—was glass, with brass accents. Harriet took the ornate handle in her hand, pressed it down. To her amazement, the door swung open. "It's unlocked!" she whispered. "I thought they'd have some kind of security system."

Kelsey put a hand on her shoulder. "Bentwood's a safe place."

Or, at least, it had been.

They slid through the door. Harriet paused, listening. The morning room was empty but for the lush furniture, the gilded decor. It was a beautiful room. She admired it even now. She sighed.

"Damn," Harold said. "This is crazy."

"Wait until you see the rest," Harriet whispered.

They tiptoed across the room and into the house proper.

"Shh." Kelsey hissed, holding out a hand. They stopped. "There's a vacuum or something running. Hear it?"

Harriet strained to hear over her own pounding heart and heavy breaths, but there was a droning coming from somewhere in the house. Perhaps from above. She nodded.

"Do we follow it and see?" Harold asked.

Kelsey screwed up her face. "You think someone came back from the dead and started vacuuming?"

"Well," he said.

"It's just a maid or something," Kelsey said. "We don't want to be seen."

Harriet left the squabbling pair and snuck down the hall. Soon, she came to the dining room where their yonis had been steamed. "I've been here," she said.

She felt Harold and Kelsey behind her, a warm, vibrating mass that smelled of pungent food.

"This is where I passed out. Where they put me up on the table."

"This is a nice place, but it's kind of creepy, no?" Harold asked.

"Definite vampire vibes," Kelsey said. "Frozen in time. Where are the TVs?"

"TVs aren't fancy." She shrugged.

"Hmm," Kelsey said.

They crept on, entering a kitchen Harriet hadn't seen before. If the rest of the house was antiquated, here was where the modernity lay. Shining appliances gleamed under dramatic lighting. Harold whistled long and low.

"Where's all the food?" Kelsey asked, opening a cabinet to find nothing but crystal.

"Stop." Harriet hissed. "Stop messing around."

Kelsey let the cabinet door fall shut with a muffled

bump. The three held still, listening.

"Come on," Harriet said, and they followed her through the giant kitchen, past an island adorned with a vase of fresh flowers.

"Ms. Pendleton?" Came a voice, clear and high. "Mr. Warnike?"

Harriet whipped around, stake held high. The others did the same.

Calvin shrunk back, pressed himself against the counter.

"Oh, Calvin," Harriet said, lowering the weapon. "How are you?" Her voice shook, but she tried to maintain an even disposition.

He shrugged, looked from Kelsey to Harold. "Are you here for the meeting?"

"Yes." Harriet blurted. "We are."

"All of my mother's friends are downstairs," he said. "In the basement."

"Is your mother here?" Kelsey asked, who still held her stake at a threatening angle.

"Kelsey!" Harriet hissed.

Calvin's face crumpled. He shook his head. "My mother is dead," he said.

Kelsey let her stake arm fall to her side.

"Um, Calvin, can you take us to the basement?" Harold asked.

"I'm not allowed down there," he said. "It's danger-ous."

"That's alright," Harold said. "You can just show us how to get there."

Calvin looked at the floor. "Okay," he said. "But you're really late."

They met each other's eyes. "That's okay," Harriet said. "They're expecting us."

Calvin nodded and turned, leading them deeper into the house. "I didn't know they let boys be in Serenitea," he said as he walked.

"Oh, sure," Harriet said. "It's just very rare. But Mr. Warnike is so popular, you know that. He's been a great sales-person."

"Why do you have big sticks?" he asked, padding down a long hall.

"Uh, it's for a fence," Kelsey said. "We're going to grow some things for the farmers market next year and I wanted to show them the garden fence posts."

Calvin turned, an eyebrow raised. "I've never seen you before."

"Yeah, well," Kelsey murmured.

"We're bringing her on special for the garden project. She's a farmer." Harriet explained.

"Wow!" Calvin said. "That's awesome. Do you have cows?"

"Sure." Kelsey lied.

They came to a plain, wooden door set in a dark alcove. "They're all down there. It's gross down there, though. Spiders and stuff. It's not finished. Mother used to beg Father to finish it, but she's gone now." His voice was sad, low.

Harriet laid a hand on his shoulder. "I'm sorry, Calvin."

Kelsey's eyes were wide. Harold looked at her, curious.

It felt wrong to comfort a child whose mother they were about to murder, but Harriet did like the boy. She didn't want to see him sad.

He nodded. "Well, maybe I'll see you all after. Maybe I can come see the cows."

"Maybe." She smiled, but it was sad, not reaching the eyes.

He nodded again, slipped out from beneath Harriet's hand, and ran back down the hallway.

"Well, that was fucking weird," Kelsey said.

"He's just a little boy," Harriet said.

Kelsey grumbled something beneath her breath.

Harold grabbed the doorknob in his big hand. "What do you ladies say about attending a meeting?"

They took in deep breaths. Harold turned the knob.

Chapter Sixty-Four

Harold and Kelsey took the lead, descending the steps at a glacial pace. Harriet followed, one hand trailing along the wall, the other clutching the stake. The steps were stone, carved into the house itself, so there was no creaking to worry about, but Harriet could hear their footfalls over her own erratic breathing so she knew they weren't being quiet enough. She stopped.

"Talking." She hissed.

The others froze. Sure enough, the muffled cacophony of women talking could be heard. Harriet shook. "There's a lot of them."

Kelsey looked back at her. "It'll be okay," she whispered. "We're strong."

Harriet shut her eyes for a moment, strained to hear words in that echoing din. She couldn't make anything out.

Harold was the first to clear the steps and he held out an arm. "Stay behind me," he whispered.

The women crowded behind his back, peeked around his shoulders. The basement was large and dark and, as Calvin had promised, unfinished. Strange walls and pillars jutted out of the dirt floor. The talking was louder now, the women somewhere near.

They stepped forward as one, knelt behind a rocky wall.

"I don't see any alternative," a woman said. "She'll have to stay here."

"But it's so… dank," another said.

"Can't she come home with me? My husband wouldn't ask any questions. He knows better than that."

"I want to stay near my son," Angela said. Harriet recognized her steady tone and nudged the others, nodded.

"Why does it stink?" a woman asked.

"It's an old basement," Angela said, a hint of embarrassment in her voice.

"No, this is a new smell."

The women went quiet, sniffed the air.

"It's, like, garlic," someone said.

Harriet stood, unfurling herself tall. She bellowed a

war cry, dove out from behind the wall.

"Harriet!" Kelsey screamed.

"Damn it!" Harold shouted, barreling after the two women.

Harriet stood before the old card table. The tea ladies, as placid as ever, looked up at her. They looked amused.

She raised the stake high. "Fuck you all," Harriet shouted.

"Harriet!" Kelsey grabbed her shoulder, tried to yank her away.

"No!" Harriet yelled. "They deserve to hear this!"

"What the hell, Harriet." Harold panted. "This wasn't the plan."

"Harriet, why are you dressed like that?" Shannon asked.

Harriet ignored them. She ignored them all. "Fuck you. Fuck you and your white dresses, your poison tea. Fuck you for sacrificing my friend just so this rich bitch could live." She sneered at Angela. "And fuck your stupid fucking pyramid scheme. You're predators. Each and every one of you."

The women looked at one another. "What are you talking about?" Georgiana asked.

Eliza stood. Harriet hadn't noticed her until now and she took a step back, bumped into Harold. The other women followed suit, rising out of their mismatched chairs like a wave in slow motion. Their white dresses glowed in the dim light.

"Go on." Harriet hissed as if commanding a dog. "Get her."

But Harold and Kelsey were frozen, their stakes dangling, useless, from their sides.

"Fuck." Harriet growled. She leaped onto the card table with a dexterity that surprised her. The women gasped, drew away. She turned, looking down on each one of them, a feral animal poised to attack.

"Get down from there," Eliza said. "This is ridiculous."

Kelsey and Harold pushed each other back and forth, fighting over who would leap into the fray to save Harriet. At last, Kelsey snarled, and bashed a tea lady in the side of the head. She went down.

"That was unnecessary," Eliza said.

The women looked down at the fallen tea lady. She clutched her head in her pale hands. "Ow, what the hell?" she asked. Harriet turned in a slow circle above them.

"Kelsey," Harold said.

"What?" Kelsey said, brandishing her stake at an unperturbed Eliza.

"They're not fighting back," he said.

"Oh," Kelsey glanced up at Harriet. "What do we do?"

"This!" Harriet thundered, leaping down off the table. She landed on Angela, dragging her to the dirt floor.

At last, the ladies reacted, screamed, grabbed at Harriet with their delicate hands. Harriet straddled Angela, raised the stake high, but they snatched at her arms, threw her off balance. She writhed against them.

Kelsey beat the tea ladies off Harriet's back, smacking one after another with the side of her stake. "Do it, Harriet! Do it now!"

Eliza raised a hand, began to chant. "What the fuck!" Harold shouted, tackling the woman. They grappled together on the ground. Harold looked surprised by Eliza's strength. His eyes wide, mouth moving in silence. She was a small woman, a thin woman, but she flipped the man with ease, sat on his chest. "Help!" Harold screamed, waving his useless stake.

Harriet drove the stake down. The tip broke off when it hit Angela's sternum. Angela grunted, grabbed at the splintered wood. Harriet stabbed again, this time aiming more to the left. "Aargh!" she screamed as she stabbed. Blood bubbled up from somewhere deep in Angela's chest, staining the front of her white dress crimson.

She didn't stop stabbing.

The tea ladies crawled over one another, reaching for Harriet's swinging arms. Kelsey twirled her stake around, came at them with the sharp side. "Get back," she roared, jabbing the women in their sides, their bellies.

"Help me!" Harold screamed, but neither woman heard.

Eliza leaned forward, her long gray hair brushing his sweating face. She smelled good, like cloves and forest and fresh soil. Harold swatted at her, but his movements were slow, stunted. There was no strength behind his flailing. He cried, tears pooling in his ears.

Teeth sunk into his neck, Eliza's tongue tasting his salty flesh. "Mmm," she murmured.

"Oh god," he whimpered, feeling the burn of her teeth. He felt her tear, felt her gnash as she ate the side of his throat.

Kelsey drove her stake into any woman who dared touch Harriet. Her hands were slick with blood and she fumbled with the weapon. It fell heavy on the floor. She bent to pick it up and something slammed into the side of her head. "No!" she cried.

Georgiana swung her handbag again, this time grazing Kelsey's face.

Kelsey ducked, taking the opportunity to grab the blood-and-dirt-streaked stake from the basement floor. She batted the woman's bag away, stabbed Georgiana in the throat. Georgiana gurgled something unintelligible as she fell, blood spurting from her wound.

Turning back to Harriet, Kelsey saw her lover scream, drive the stake into the pulpy mass of organ and meat in front of her. "Fuck you!" she cried.

Kelsey tripped over a body, fell onto Harriet's back. "She's dead!" she yelled. "Harriet!"

Harriet paused, stake hovering above the splattered

remains of Angela Monroe.

Now that Harriet had stopped her screaming, the sucking sound of the stake stirring Angela's insides, Kelsey heard something softer—a whimper, a cry.

"Harold, fuck." She whirled around, ashamed to have forgotten the man. He lay near a wall, blood streaming from a wound in his neck. She rushed to his side.

"What the fuck happened?" She touched her fingertips to the ragged hole.

"Bite." He coughed. "Bit me." Blood spattered from his lips.

"Who?" Kelsey whipped around, searched the corners. Everyone was dead.

"Old bitch." He sighed, shut his eyes.

"Oh, no you don't," Kelsey said, shaking him. "You wake the hell up. Harriet!"

Harriet had resumed her stabbing.

"Harriet!" screamed Kelsey. She pushed herself up, rejoined Harriet above Angela. She yanked the bloody stake out of Harriet's grasp. Harriet looked down at her empty hands, the blood dripping from her fingers.

"Harold's hurt!" Kelsey shook her. "Get up. Harold's hurt!"

It was like waking up, the slow return to reality. The smell of blood and shit and piss and dirt. The colors of their gore, their dresses, their matted hair. "Harold?" she asked.

"Over here, look."

Harriet turned, saw Kelsey squatting by the man, her hand covering a gaping wound in the side of his neck. Harriet crawled over Angela, over all the crumpled forms between them, and joined Kelsey at Harold's side.

"What do we do?" she asked.

"We have to get him out of here. Get to a hospital." Kelsey slapped the man's face. "Harold!" she bellowed.

The man's eyelids fluttered.

"We're going to walk up the stairs now. We can't carry you. We need your help. If you want to live, you'll walk god damn it." She yanked Harold's arms.

"Mmph," Harold said.

Harriet's phone vibrated at her waist. "I'll call 911."

"And what? Tell them we just murdered every socialite in town? Fuck that!"

"We can't get him up the stairs alone!" Harriet cried.

"We have to," Kelsey said.

The women stood, each taking one of Harold's arms. Their progress was slow, but they were able to drag him through the blood-mucked dirt. They collapsed at the bottom of the stairs, winded.

"We'll never get him up the stairs." She glanced down at Harold. He was the wrong color, translucent almost. "He's bleeding out."

Kelsey put her hands under Harold's armpits, hefted

him up. "Get his legs."

Harriet grabbed the man's feet.

Groaning, Kelsey started up the stairs backward. Harold's bottom bumped against the steps. "Hold his feet, I said!"

"I am!" Harriet said, trying to hoist them higher.

Kelsey yanked Harold upward and Harriet, hands slick with Angela's blood, lost her hold. But it was okay. Kelsey, through her own goddamn determination and adrenaline and strength, dragged that man up the stairs.

"Fuck." She gasped, letting go at the landing. "We did it."

"You did it," Harriet said. She grabbed Harold's arm. "Come on. To the truck."

They dragged him through the house, smearing blood and dirt across Angela's white tile, plush white carpet, marble foyer. They dragged Harold out the front door.

"Calvin," Harriet said, as they kicked their way through the entryway.

"What about him?" Kelsey asked.

"He'll see."

Kelsey shook her head. "There's nothing we can do."

It was a miracle no cars went by as they dragged Harold through the grass, across the road. They joined hands behind Harold's back, locked eyes, and threw him in the bed of the truck.

"Fuck," they said, slamming the tailgate. "Fuck."

Chapter Sixty-Five

Kelsey drove, erratic and fast, through the streets of Bentwood. "Nearest hospital is twenty-five miles away," she said through gritted teeth.

Harriet twisted herself around, looked at Harold through the back window. A pool of blood had formed in the rivulets of the truck bed. "He won't make it."

"Then where do we go?"

"My cabin," Harriet said. "My parents—they should still be there. My mom's a nurse."

"Why the hell didn't you mention that earlier?" Kelsey asked, whipping the truck around.

"I don't know," Harriet said. "I'm all messed up." She began to cry, covered her face with her red hands.

Kelsey reached for her as she drove, placed a hand on

her knee. The bug pants were ruined, the bright mosquitos now a rusted mottle.

They tore down Main Street, passing cars and speeding around pedestrians. People stood and cursed them, but Kelsey didn't care. She turned into Harriet's drive with a squeal. Stones flew from beneath their tires.

"They're here!" Harriet cried, seeing her parents' SUV in the drive. But there was another car too, black, nondescript, surely an unmarked police car. She was shaking so much she struggled with the truck door. She tumbled out onto the grass.

Kelsey was already at the rear of the vehicle, dragging Harold's limp form onto the ground. "Go get your mom," she said.

"Let's bring him in," Harriet said. Kelsey shrugged and they reprised their positions at his arms, dragged him across the stones and root-humped yard to the door. Kelsey kicked it in.

Boxes of tea went flying, shooting across the room, hitting her mom and dad in their faces. "What the hell?" Her dad grunted.

The girls waded into the knee-high tea boxes, dragging Harold in their wake. Underwear snagged at their feet, tripping them in elastic snares. Harriet tried not to think about that—the boxes, the panties. There were more important things. "Mom." Harriet gasped. "He's hurt."

Harriet's mom's face drained of color and she kicked

346

her way through the boxes. She knelt at Harold's side, pushing boxes and panties out of the way. "Oh, Jesus," she said.

"Can you fix it?" Harriet asked, though she thought she knew the answer.

Her mother's hands shook as she stuffed panty after panty into the hole in Harold's neck. "We have to stop the bleeding. Oh god. I don't think I can do this. Call 911. Mick, call 911."

Harriet's dad fumbled with his phone, dropped it into the tea boxes. "Oh, shit," he said, diving after it.

Harriet and Kelsey looked at one another, fear distorting their faces.

"Everyone out of my way," a craggy voice said. An old man came kicking out of the bathroom, tea boxes flying before him. "Out of my way." He huffed.

"Mr. Morrison?" Harriet asked.

Her landlord looked her up and down, disgusted. "You, ma'am, are in trouble." He gestured at the windows, now uncovered. The blankets she'd tacked there lay crumpled on top of the boxes. "You didn't let the outside in."

"Oh no, oh no," Harriet's mother said, patting Harold's wound with a garish pair of panties.

"Mother is very unhappy," Mr. Morrison said.

Harriet opened her mouth, but nothing came out.

"And look at all this mess! Boxes, undergarments everywhere. No. This is not the way to treat my mother's home."

"What the hell is your problem?" Kelsey yelled. "A man's here dying and you're scolding Harriet about her housekeeping?"

Mr. Morrison rolled his eyes toward Kelsey, grimaced at what he saw there. "And you, getting blood all over mother's floor. Ungrateful!" he roared. "Out of my way. Out of my way." He pushed his way to Harold's side.

Harriet's mother's face was streaked with blood and tears. She held two fingers to the opposite side of Harold's throat. "I think—I think—"

"No!" Harriet covered her ears.

"I said out of my way, woman. Move." Mr. Morrison kicked her mother in the thigh. She yelped, crawled out of the old man's way.

The landlord stooped, bones creaking and joints popping, and threw the bloody panties that has been stuffed in Harold's wound away. "Pah!" he shouted.

"What are you doing?" Kelsey asked.

Blood oozed out of Harold's throat.

The old man shoved a gnarled finger into the hole, wiggled it around. "No," he said. "This won't do."

"What the fuck are you doing?" Kelsey repeated.

"I found my phone!" Harriet's dad yelled, surfacing. "I found it!"

Harriet sobbed.

Mr. Morrison kicked his way through the room, made

his way to the pantry. He wrenched the door open and disappeared inside. He re-emerged holding a jar of preserves, mushy and swirling in the glass.

He cleared his throat. "Silence! Everyone!"

The room fell quiet.

The old man knelt, lifted Harold's head up onto his lap. "What a mess." He sighed. "My pants. My floor."

He pried the lid off the jar and poured the slop over Harold's throat. Chunks of something slid over his skin, mingling with blood. The air smelled acidic, like vinegar. Mr. Morrison covered the entirety of Harold's wound with his wrinkled hand. He shut his eyes.

"What are you doing?" Harriet asked. "It'll get infected!"

"Fixing your problem, you ungrateful little girl."

When the old man removed his hand, Harold's skin was smooth, unbroken. It was a strange, purplish hue, but there was no wound, no blood.

"There." Mr. Morrison spat. "It's done. Now help me up."

Harriet's mom rushed to the old man's side, helped pull him to standing.

Harriet and Kelsey sat speechless, staring at the undisturbed plane of Harold's neck.

"What did you do?" Kelsey asked. "How did you do it?"

349

"Harold?" Harriet hovered over the man. "Harold? Wake up!"

The old man frowned. "He's fine. Let him sleep."

"Harold!" Harriet screamed. His eyelids fluttered.

"Hmm?" he murmured.

"Yes!" Harriet and Kelsey jumped up and embraced, trampling boxes of Serenitea. Tears poured down Harriet's face. Kelsey kissed them as they fell. Their lips met, blood and spit mingling. They cried.

"Uhh," Harriet's mother said.

"Should I call the police?" her father asked.

"It's not illegal, Mick." Her mother hissed.

Harold stirred on the floor, boxes tumbling around him. He sat up. "Woah," he said.

"I'll send an eviction notice in the morning," said Mr. Morrison, brushing off his pants as best he could. "Good day," he said.

He shuffled past them, stepping on toes and fingers as he went. He slammed the front door behind him.

"What the hell?" Harold asked.

They all stared at the place the old man had been.

"He never did like me," Harriet said.

Chapter Sixty-Six

Harriet sat on the porch at Kelsey's feet, resting her head against her knee. Kelsey ran her fingers through Harriet's hair. It'd been three weeks since the slaughter and they'd spent a lot of time that way, just touching, quiet. The sun was dipping below the horizon, setting the world ablaze in golden light. A bird cried and a rabbit sat nibbling long blades of grass by the driveway.

Harriet yawned. "I should go," she said.

"Are you sure?" Kelsey asked. She always asked that, always begged Harriet to stay.

"I gotta grade some stuff," Harriet said. "I'll see you tomorrow?"

She'd found a small garden apartment to rent in town, a simple, quiet place. A place to which she liked to return.

"I don't understand why you just don't move in with me." Kelsey pouted. She always said that.

351

Harriet smiled. "I've told you a million times, silly."

Kelsey shook her head. She didn't understand Harriet's sudden need to take things slow—something about independence, about finding herself. "I just miss you, is all."

"I miss you too," Harriet said.

Kelsey sighed, stood, and stretched her arms. "Tell Harold I said 'hey,'" she said. "Remind him about dinner."

Harriet rose to meet her. They hugged. "I will," Harriet said.

Kelsey caught her by the wrist. "I'm sorry," Kelsey said. That was something she said a lot, too.

Harriet flashed a sad smile. "It's okay," she said. "It's not your fault."

"Calvin…" Kelsey began. "Has he said anything?"

Harriet shook her head. The little boy never mentioned anyone finding slain bodies in the basement, never looked at Harriet any differently. He was studious, polite, never late for class. She knew Eliza was involved, but she wasn't sure how. When Harold was lucid enough to speak, he recounted the way the old woman had smelled as her teeth ground into his skin, the lightness of her body on top of his, but neither Harriet nor Kelsey could remember running a stake through the strange lady. "They're still looking for them. For all of them. I saw it on the news," Harriet said.

Kelsey wrapped her arms around her own body, a protective gesture. She didn't say anything.

They parted, waving to each other as Harriet backed out of the drive.

It was dark by the time Harriet made it back into town, but her headlights caught her old mailbox, the mangled tree trunks, the white posters stapled to each one. She slowed. She'd seen it a million times, but it always stopped her in her tracks. She pulled over, stared at Lucy's face staring back at her from the missing poster.

"It didn't work," she whispered. "I'm sorry."

Lucy smiled.

A thousand Lucys smiled.

Acknowledgments

I am indebted, as always, to Pete for believing in me and my weird stories (I love you). David-Jack and Leeroy gave this tale great care and a good home, and for that I'm thankful. Thank you, Ben, for fanning the flames of creative insanity when we should have been working on shitty software—I tried to channel our muse here. Chelsea and Justin, I appreciate you so much. Thanks for reading these things; you make me feel like I'm doing something right. My mom and dad encouraged me to read every day and work hard and I am so thankful for that foundation. My Grandma Gum is the only person I know who scaled the Avon pyramid and came out on top—thank you for letting us raid your basement for prizes! Thank you to all the members of the "MLM Lies Exposed" Facebook group for sharing your stories.

About the Author

Stephanie's first novel, *Singing All the Way Up*, debuted in July with No Bad Books Press and her short fiction has been featured by Books of Horror, Hearth & Coffin, Mixer, Mosaic, and Ether Arts. She received her Bachelor of Arts degree in English with a specialization in Creative Writing from the Ohio State University.

Milton Keynes UK
Ingram Content Group UK Ltd.
UKHW040912070224
437358UK00001B/55

9 780645 763874